Believe in Me

Proofreading and editing by English Major Editing
Cover design by Kelly Pennington

ISBN: 978-0-578-91357-5

Dedication

All my life I've been surrounded by people who have believed in me. Parents, spouse, family, friends, teachers, bosses, colleagues – all with the same message – "You can."

This book is dedicated to those who haven't been blessed with such a circle of people around them. Who haven't heard the words or felt the support often enough or maybe, never at all.

This is for you....

You can do it.
I believe in you.
You can.

Chapter 1

Meg

I watched in disbelief as Aaron's taillights disappeared around the corner. Had he really just driven away and left me standing here in a cocktail dress and four-inch heels outside the private club where his work event was still going full swing inside?

Seriously?!

I turned to the valet still standing nearby.

"Did he really just do that?"

The kid shrugged, obviously not wanting to get involved. "Looks like it."

I felt my irritation rise even more at his lack of concern. "What it looks like to me is that you turned over a car to a man who clearly shouldn't be driving."

The kid shrugged again. "Not my problem. He didn't even tip me." He eyed me expectantly.

I met his eyes and very deliberately shrugged my shoulders. "Not my problem."

He shot me a glare, then slunk away, back toward the valet stand on the other side of the drive.

I stood for another minute, hands on my hips, still staring in the direction Aaron had gone. Finally, I gave up and made my way back inside. Looking around, I found an out-of-the-way place to sit at one end of the lobby. This night that had started out so promising had soured quickly. Aaron and I had been having a good time, including

5

drinking a lot of top shelf liquor from the open bar. When he suggested heading to my place I'd been completely on board with that.

We'd walked out of the event, Aaron's arm around my shoulders, him calling goodbye to several of his colleagues nearby on his way out. We'd laughed as we weaved our way across the lobby, neither of us completely steady on our feet. Aaron had driven us to the event, but he was obviously in no shape to drive home. I figured we'd call a rideshare and be on our way home in a few minutes. That was until Aaron continued on outside and walked up to the valet stand.

I couldn't believe he was planning to drive and I told him so. He insisted he was fine; I insisted he wasn't. The argument turned ugly quickly. It didn't help that appearances were very important to Aaron. The fact that I was questioning him in front of the valets made matters even worse. When the valet pulled his car up, Aaron had practically fallen into the driver's seat. I'd told him I wouldn't ride with him and pleaded with him one more time to call a rideshare. His response?

"Get your fat ass in the car. I'm leaving."

I'd stared at him, completely shocked by his words. When I didn't move and didn't respond, he'd leaned across the passenger seat, said "Fine, suit yourself," and slammed the passenger door as he accelerated away.

I was still in shock that he'd said that to me. I knew he had high expectations – like I said, appearances were important to him – but he knew how hard I worked to eat healthy and maintain a good weight. I'd thought he liked how I looked. Did he really think my ass was fat? If not, why would he say that to me? Why would he leave me standing there and drive away? How could he do that?

I could feel myself starting to spiral and knew I had to calm down. I closed my eyes, dropped my head into my hands, and tried to focus on just breathing. The room started to spin and I opened my eyes abruptly. Woah, I was more drunk than I'd realized. I'd hurried to finish my last drink right before we'd left, downing it much too quickly, and it was catching up with me now. I lifted a hand to my forehead, trying to remember how many drinks I'd had, but couldn't recall. Well, it was too late to do anything about it now. Now I had to focus on getting myself home. I'd just call for a ride and…

Dammit!

I realized I wouldn't be calling for anything. My phone, and the key to my condo, were currently in the inside pocket of Aaron's suit jacket, where they'd been since he'd picked me up tonight. I hadn't wanted to worry about a purse, thinking I wouldn't need anything other than my phone and key since I'd be with Aaron all night. What the hell was I going to do now? I had no phone, no money, and I didn't know a soul at this event. I'd met several of Aaron's colleagues tonight for the first time, but I would be lucky if I could even remember their names.

"You're a smart girl, Meg. Just slow down and think." Great, I was talking to myself out loud now.

I tried to think, but my brain was slow and fuzzy. I could call my best friend, Mia - she'd come get me - but I didn't have her phone number memorized. I didn't have anyone's phone number memorized, so used to just tapping on their contact in my phone. I could go back into Aaron's work event, try to find someone I recognized, and ask them if they could please pay for a ride home. Or borrow their phone and call Mia *if* I knew her number. But Aaron would kill me. He'd be furious if I made him look bad in front of his colleagues.

I sighed, wracking my brain for options. How far was I from home? It was only about 15 minutes by car. It couldn't be that far, right? Could I possibly walk? I looked down at my shoes and sighed again. I loved these shoes, but they weren't made for walking. And a few minutes by car meant home was miles away. There was no way I could do it. Why oh why hadn't I memorized Mia's phone number? I swore I would do that first thing in the morning, but I needed to get out of this mess now. Wait…thinking of Mia, maybe…maybe I could walk to her apartment? I thought hard about where the club was located. Mia's wasn't super close, but it was maybe…two miles away? I could walk that, couldn't I? Did I have any other options? No, I didn't think I did.

Okay, I could do this. Pushing to my feet, I swayed in place, my head swimming. All I wanted to do was lay down on the padded bench I'd just been sitting on and rest for a while. But I knew I needed to move.

"Come on, Meg. You can do this."

I repeated that to myself as I left the club, putting one foot in front of the other, making my way through the dark streets in the direction of Mia's apartment. Well, I was pretty sure it was the right direction. Of course it was. I hoped. Traffic was light but constant and I was glad I wasn't completely alone. I was a little chilled in my short, strapless cocktail dress and I rubbed my hands up and down my arms as I walked. At one point I heard someone humming a song I liked. I paused and looked around, then giggled as I realized I was the one who was humming.

I wasn't giggling awhile later as I limped to a stop on a street corner. My feet were killing me. I looked up and down the street, and realized

I was completely lost. Shouldn't I have reached Mia's by now? Had I gone the wrong way? Directions weren't my best thing and with my head swimming the way it was...

I tried to stay calm as I looked around for landmarks. I'd lived in this stupid town for years! How could I not know where I was? Spinning around, I slipped and almost fell, catching myself on the light post at the last minute. I looked up and about two blocks away saw the sign for the coffee shop that was right by Mia's apartment. Oh thank God. I closed my eyes and breathed in relief. I was almost there. I opened my eyes and reached down and pulled off my shoes. I didn't care that I was walking down the street barefoot, I couldn't wear them for one more second. I started toward the coffee shop sign and soon Mia's apartment building came into view. Relief flooded through me again. Just a little farther...

It took the last of my energy to pull myself up the three flights of stairs to Mia's door. Reaching it, I rested my head against it and slapped it with my hand. It was too much effort to form a fist and knock.

"Meems, let me in." I didn't hear movement inside so I tried again. Slap, slap. "Mia, it's Meg. Open up."

Still no answer. I turned around, braced my back on the door and slid to the ground. Where was she? I couldn't sit here all night. I could already feel the cold from the concrete through my dress and...wait. I patted the ground underneath me, realizing something was wrong. Mia had a welcome mat outside her door, a silly one with crazy looking birds on it. She'd bought it right after she moved in and it had been in front of her door ever since. Confused, I looked at the door across the landing and saw the doormat sitting there. Why was it over there? I stared at it, puzzled, then squeaked as Mia's door opened suddenly behind me. I fell backwards into her entry and landed at someone's feet. Looking up - way up - I saw the last person I expected to see.

Chapter 2

Jamey

I paused as I walked up the hallway of my new apartment toward the kitchen. This was only my second night staying here and I knew each apartment and house came with its own quirks and noises, but... I could have sworn I heard something...like something sliding across the surface of the door? What the hell could that have been? I tossed the towel I'd been rubbing over my hair on the kitchen counter. I'd just gotten home from work at the pub, taken a shower, and thrown on some jeans. I'd been headed to the kitchen for something to drink but now I headed to the door, head bent, listening. I didn't hear anything else, but I could feel it. I was 100% sure there was someone on the other side of the door. I checked the peephole but saw no one. Irritated at whoever it was and whatever game they were playing, I pulled the door open.

Then stepped back quickly as Mia's friend, Meg, fell backwards into the apartment at my feet.

What the...?

She lay there, looking up at me, blinking like a little owl. Given that she'd fallen backwards into the apartment, I was upside down to her, and she looked like she was having a hard time processing that in her head.

"Jamey?" She reached her hand out slowly and touched my lower leg, like she was checking to make sure I was real.

I didn't know Meg all that well. I'd been around her a few times since her best friend, Mia, and one of my best friends, Dante, were together. They'd met as neighbors and were now living together right across the landing from me. The first time Meg and I met we'd immediately butted heads, but we'd called a truce and managed to coexist peacefully since then. She was gorgeous and feisty, but she was also dating someone, so any interest I might have had in her was a moot point.

Meg was still laying on her back on the floor, not making any attempt to sit up. A little worried, I moved around to her side and crouched down. I lifted her by her shoulders into a sitting position, ignoring the feel of her smooth, bare skin under my hands. She swayed a little as I sat her up and I realized she'd been drinking. She had that boneless quality most people get when they're drunk. She wasn't trashed, but she was beyond tipsy. As they met mine, her blue eyes were a little glazed and a lot puzzled.

"Jamey, why are you in Mia's apartment?" She said each word carefully, slowly, like it was an effort to form each one.

"It's my apartment now. I just moved in, remember? Mia moved in with Dante."

"Hmm. Did I know that?" She tilted her head and frowned, like she was working hard to put the pieces together. My fingers itched to smooth out the little wrinkle between her eyebrows, but I kept my hands to myself.

"I'm sure you did, but you were out of town for work when we moved all the stuff so you might not remember right now."

"I was? Oh."

Her little puzzled look was so fucking adorable, then her eyes widened and her frown cleared.

"I do remember! It was this week while I was in Virginia! That's right. Whew." She blew out a breath in relief. I imagined she was happy to know she wasn't losing her mind or that her best friend since third grade hadn't moved without telling her.

Meg looked through my still-open door across the landing at Dante and Mia's.

"That explains the doormat," she told me as she nodded solemnly.

I looked over at their door. The doormat? What?

Meg's finger poking me in the arm brought my attention back to her.

"Could you maybe help me up so I can go knock on their door? I don't think I can get up by myself."

I got to my feet, then reached down and easily lifted her to hers. I kept my hands on her arms since she still seemed a little off balance.

"It won't do any good to knock. They're not home. They're in Tennessee getting ready for that youth competition this weekend. And yes, you knew that."

Dante was part-owner and trainer at a local boxing gym. He mostly worked with the gym's youth programs and traveling to competitions with the young fighters was a big part of that.

"They're gone?"

Meg had been staring at their door as I talked, but now she swung her ahead around to look at me. The distress in her voice and the tears I could see welling up in her eyes caught me off guard. Like most guys I was completely helpless when a woman cried. I didn't know what was wrong, but I needed to make it better fast.

I slid my hands from Meg's shoulders down her arms trying to soothe her. Her skin was cold under my hands and I frowned a little as I realized how chilled she must have been sitting on the concrete outside. How long had she been there before I'd heard her? That thought bothered me, but I kept my voice low and calm as I tried to console her.

"Hey, it's okay. Whatever it is, we'll handle it, okay?" I bent my knees a little so I could get eye-level with her. "It's alright, I promise."

Mia nodded, still seeming shaky, but the tears in her eyes receded, thank God.

"Okay, but…I was gonna crash on Mia's couch. But now her couch is over there. And she's not. I don't know what to do."

Meg swayed again, looking up at me. Speaking of crashing, she was going to do it soon. Her buzz was gone and she was well on her way to passing out. I had a key to Mia and Dante's apartment. I could easily let her in, say goodnight, and leave her on her own. But my conscience wouldn't let me do it. I didn't know what had happened with Meg tonight, but she wasn't her usual sassy self. I'd seen her drink at my friends' pub where I ran the kitchen, but had never seen her get anything more than tipsy. Whatever was going on, I felt the need to keep an eye on her.

My mind made up, I turned Meg away from the door. Closing it behind us, I steered her toward the living room area.

"Well, if you want to crash on Mia's couch, you can do it right here. She left it for me when she moved in with Dante."

I'd moved from a studio apartment above the pub, so I hadn't had much furniture. Mia had been happy to leave me her couch, end tables, and stools for the breakfast bar that separated the kitchen from the living room. Along with my king-size bed, dresser, and a big armchair I'd moved from my old place, that was all the furniture I needed.

"But…" Meg looked up at me in confusion, still trying to process what I'd said. "This is *your* apartment."

I shrugged. "It's cool with me if it's cool with you. Not the first time someone's crashed on my couch." It was the first time a *woman* had, but I figured I'd leave that part out.

"Well….okay." I steered Meg over to the couch and she sat down abruptly. "If it's okay with you, I'll stay." She leaned forward and put her face in her hands. "I'm too tired to think anymore."

The urge to run my hand over her pretty blonde curls, mussed a little now from the evening, hit me hard, but again I forced myself not to touch her. She was drunk and almost out on her feet. I had no business touching her any more than necessary.

"Alright, we have a plan then. Hang out for a minute and I'll get some sheets and stuff for the couch."

There was no response from Meg as I headed to the hall closet for sheets, a blanket, and my one extra pillow. Thinking about the dress she had on – the very hot, but undoubtedly uncomfortable dress – I ducked into my bedroom and grabbed a clean t-shirt out of a drawer.

When I got back to the living room Meg was still in the same position I'd left her in, sitting on the couch, head in her hands.

"I brought you a t-shirt in case you want to change."

Meg started a little at my voice, but nodded and reached out for the shirt. She got unsteadily to her feet.

"I'll get the couch set up for you while you change. There are extra toothbrushes under the sink if you want one."

Meg said a quiet "thanks" as she started down the hall to the bathroom. It was so unlike her usual energy that I turned to watch her as she walked away. I frowned when I noticed she was limping, then frowned harder when I realized she was barefoot. Had she had shoes on earlier? I hadn't really noticed but now that I thought about it, she'd been barefoot when I'd helped her to her feet. Where the hell were her shoes?

I looked quickly around the living area and entry, then opened the door to look out. Sure enough, there was a pair of sexy high heels – what I'd heard Mia call "fuck me" heels – laying outside near my door. I picked them up and set them inside my door, then went back to the living room and tucked the sheets and blanket on the couch. I went into the kitchen to get a large glass of water and stepped back in the living room as Mia limped her way back down the hall.

Her make-up was gone, her blond curls laying across her shoulders.

And she was wearing my t- shirt. When I'd given it to her, I hadn't thought about the impact of seeing her in it. It was long and loose on her – it covered her more than her dress had. But I could tell by how soft her breasts looked that she didn't have a bra on. Thinking about my t-shirt touching her bare breasts and seeing her curvy, toned legs underneath, I almost groaned out loud. She looked soft and feminine and absolutely, utterly fuckable. My dick stirred with interest. Damn, what kind of asshole was I, getting hard from one look at a drunk girl who'd obviously had a shitty night and just needed a place to crash?

Telling myself to get over it, I said the first thing I thought of.

"Are you okay, Meg? You're limping."

Meg walked carefully to the couch as if she was balancing, then sat down with a soft sigh. "What? Oh." She looked down at her feet. "Yeah, I'm okay. I just have some blisters, I think." She frowned down at her feet like they'd betrayed her by getting blisters.

I crossed to her, handing her the glass of water.

"Drink this. The whole thing." I knelt on the floor and picked up one of her feet, ignoring her small squeak of surprise as I did so. Her toes, heels, and side of her foot were an angry red, with a couple places rubbed raw. I switched to the other foot and found the same thing.

"Damn, girl, what did you do tonight? Go hiking in those sexy-ass heels?"

Shaking my head, I looked up at her. She met my eyes briefly, then slid her gaze away. She'd leaned back against the couch, making my shirt ride up high on her thighs. She'd finished the water and I rescued the glass just as it was about to tumble out of her hand.

Still avoiding my eyes, she mumbled something, but I didn't catch it.

"What was that?" I was still kneeling close to her, still holding her small foot in my hand, and I found I had no desire to move away.

She cleared her throat and finally looked at me.

"I just walked in them a little too much."

I squeezed her foot lightly, careful to avoid the raw spots, then released it and rose to my feet.

"That, sweetheart, is a huge understatement. I'll be right back with some band-aids."

I set the glass from Mia's water in the kitchen then retrieved the first aid kit from the bathroom cabinet. I walked back into the living room and paused.

Meg was asleep on the couch, curled up on her side with her hands tucked under the pillow. In that position, the t-shirt she was wearing had bunched up a little. It covered her to the waist, but left her perfect,

13

round hips and ass uncovered except for a tiny scrap of black bikini panties. I stood for a minute just appreciating the view. Meg was truly beautiful and she was in great shape. I knew from experience that she could be a little rigid about what she ate, and from what Mia said, about her workout routine, as well, but there was no doubt that she was hot as hell. Combine that great body with those blond curls, blue eyes, and upbeat personality, and I was sure she turned heads wherever she went.

And I needed to stop staring at her like a perv and take care of those raw spots on her feet. I did what I could without waking her up, only a couple spots needing a bandage. Meg had fallen asleep on top of the blanket. After I finished patching her up, I lifted her as gently as I could, moved the blanket aside, then pulled it back over her after I laid her down. I stood looking down at her, wondering what had brought her to my door tonight. Whatever it was, I couldn't find it in me to regret that she had ended up here with me. I was going to dig more in the morning – if she woke up before I left for the farmers market, anyway – but for tonight I was just glad she was here sharing my space.

⌒

I was in the kitchen making coffee the next morning when I heard Meg moving around. I heard the bathroom door close, then a few minutes later I heard water running. I was glad she was feeling good enough to be on her feet and apparently wasn't suffering from a killer hang-over.

That was confirmed when she walked back into the living area. She looked soft and sleepy and gorgeous as ever. I imagined waking up next to her, seeing her looking just like that, minus the t-shirt. And given that I was wearing sweatpants and nothing else, I needed to quit thinking about Meg with no shirt on before I embarrassed myself.

"Morning, party girl. How ya feeling?"

Meg sat down at the breakfast bar with a sigh.

"I'm alright. My feet are sore, but I'm okay. Thanks for letting me crash. I don't know what I would have done if you weren't here."

"Then I'm glad I was." I lifted the mug of coffee I'd just poured in Meg's direction, silently asking if she wanted some. She nodded and made a grabby hands motion, making me smile.

I set it down in front of her and she picked it up, taking a sip immediately. I knew it had to be hot, but she didn't seem to care. She took another sip and closed her eyes.

"Thank God. I may live."

"Glad to hear it. I was going to ask if you needed milk or sugar, but obviously the answer is no."

Meg opened her eyes to look at me, still cradling the coffee cup between her hands.

"I drink my coffee black as sin and as strong as I can get it. Do you always walk around at home without a shirt on?"

That was one of the first things I'd noticed about Meg other than her smoking hot looks – hey, I was a guy, right? Her quick brain and straightforward style kept you on your toes. She wasn't mean or rude, she just seemed to say what she thought. It hadn't even occurred to me that I hadn't had a shirt on last night either.

"Well, first I agree on the coffee." I lifted my own mug, toasting her, then took a sip. "And second, I wear a shirt when I feel like it, and don't when I don't. Simple as that. And before you ask, no, I never wear shoes at home. It's strictly bare feet only."

"That's kind of how you live your life, isn't it? Do it if you feel like it, don't do it if you don't?"

I turned and reached for the loaf of honey wheat bread I had sitting on the counter. I'd picked it up the day before from my favorite bakery when I'd picked up a special bread order for the pub. I cut several slices, feeling Meg's eyes on my back as I worked.

I glanced over my shoulder at Meg as I put the bread in the toaster, then moved to the fridge for butter and preserves.

"No, not exactly. Everybody has to do stuff they don't want to. But I only answer to myself. That much is true."

Meg gave no response, just stared down into her cup of coffee like it held the secrets to the universe. Surprised at her lack of comment I turned the conversation to something I was curious about.

"Speaking of bare feet, why were you walking around without your shoes on last night?"

Meg looked up at me and frowned.

"How do you know that?"

I grabbed the toast as it popped up, put both pieces on a plate and set it in front of Meg. She looked down at it.

"I usually just have coffee for breakfast."

I picked up her cup and topped it off, but nudged the toast closer to her as I set the coffee down next to it.

"Coffee's not breakfast, it's…coffee. Necessary, but not sufficient. Eat the toast, the carbs will help you process the alcohol that's still in your system."

Meg considered the toast for a minute, then picked up a piece and took a tiny bite.

I nudged the butter and preserves her way, saying nothing. She rolled her eyes, but picked up the butter knife I'd set down and spread a thin layer on her toast. She took a decent bite, then chewing, nudged the preserves back in my direction. Just glad I'd gotten her to eat something, I conceded defeat on the preserves.

Back to my question...

"I know you were walking around barefoot because you didn't have your shoes on when you literally fell into my apartment."

Mia glanced up at me, then went back to studying her toast.

"I walked farther than I should have and the shoes were hurting me so I took them off."

Her answer only made me more curious. I had no idea why. Usually I was a "live and let live" kind of guy. I was sure she had her reasons for traipsing around in sky-high heels, then walking around barefoot. But for some reason I couldn't let it go. There was an undercurrent there that I couldn't stop myself from digging at.

I slid two slices of bread in the toaster for my own breakfast, then turned back to Meg.

"Where the hell did you walk from? Obviously you made the smart choice not to drive since you were drunker than shit, but there's this thing called a rideshare, you know? You've heard of that?"

Meg stopped messing with her toast. She set it down and dropped her head into her hands, elbows braced on the breakfast bar.

"Yes, I'm familiar. It wasn't that simple."

"Of course, it's simple. It couldn't be easier."

Why the fuck was I pushing this? Meg must have wondered the same thing because she sat up suddenly, eyes flashing.

"Geez, Jamey! What the hell is up with you? Not that it's any of your business but I was at an event, okay? I was at an event with Aaron, we had a fight, he left, I walked here. There, done, end of story."

She was right that this was none of my business, but I could feel my anger start to rise. Had she said that Aaron *left* her?

I heard my toast pop up behind me, but ignored it. I crossed my arms over my chest and focused on Meg.

"Let me get this straight. Aaron, this guy you've been dating for months now, gets mad and just leaves you somewhere. Not to mention the fact that he had to know you'd had too much to drink. He knows you're drunk and just leaves you on your own to find your own way home. Do I have that right?"

I knew she could hear in my tone how pissed I was getting just thinking about the situation Aaron had left her in.

Meg sighed, avoiding my eyes. "It sounds so bad when you say it that way."

I shook my head in disbelief. How else did she possibly think it could sound?

"Aaron was drunk, too. He wasn't thinking clearly. He was just so mad that I wouldn't get in the car with him..."

"Wait." I uncrossed my arms and stepped forward, leaning my hands on the counter in front of the breakfast bar where Meg sat. "The fucker *drove*? And expected you to get in the car with him? Are you kidding me?"

I was furious thinking of the idiot putting Meg in danger that way.

"Jamey, stop. I know he shouldn't have driven. That's what we fought about. I tried to stop him, but he wouldn't listen."

"Well, thank God you didn't get in the car with him. But why didn't you just call a rideshare to take you home?"

"I..." Meg swallowed and reached out to fiddle with her coffee cup. Finally, she looked up at me.

"I didn't have my phone. It was in Aaron's pocket. I had no way to contact anybody and no money, so I walked here."

I closed my eyes and clenched my hands into fists, barely able to contain the rage that swept through me at the thought of this beautiful woman stranded and drunk, walking what had to be a fair distance, at night, alone. I couldn't even let myself think about all the things that could have happened, all the ways that the night could have gone horribly wrong, or I would completely lose my shit. I was barely holding it together as it was. I didn't even stop to question why.

My eyes still closed, fists still clenched tight, I ground out, "Please tell me you're kicking this fucker to the curb."

"I appreciate your concern, but that's none of your business."

Meg's tone said that I had pushed her too far. I opened my eyes and looked at her. The tilt of her chin and look in her eyes all but screamed "back off."

Still, I couldn't help myself from pushing more. "You can't seriously be thinking about staying with this guy. After he left you like that? Sweetheart, if you were mine, taking care of you would be my top priority. I would never leave you somewhere, no matter how fucking mad I was. No decent man would ever do that. And getting drunk when you were getting in the car with me? I'd never do that under any circumstances, but no fucking way. This guy doesn't deserve you, sweetheart."

Meg sat looking at me, arms crossed.

"I'm not your sweetheart." The frost in her tone left no doubt how she felt about that. The fact that that was all she had to say in response to my statement said even more.

The physical jolt I felt as her words hit surprised me. I took a step back, hands on my hips and let my head drop forward. No matter how much the reminder stung, she was right. Just because I felt drawn to her, felt an attraction I hadn't felt for a woman in a long time, didn't make her mine. She belonged to someone else.

I huffed out a laugh without an ounce of humor in it and raised my head. "Right." Avoiding Meg's eyes, I headed out of the kitchen.

"I need to get to the farmers market. Help yourself to anything you need. The key to Mia and Dante's apartment is on the hook next to the door, right next to my extra key. Just lock the place up when you go and leave my extra key under their doormat."

There was no response from Meg as I walked down the hall into my bedroom and shut the door. I got dressed quickly and was searching for shoes to put on when I heard the shower turn on. Grateful that I wouldn't have to interact with Meg on my way out, I grabbed my phone and keys and headed for the door, forcing my mind away from Meg to the rest of my day.

Chapter 3

Meg

I pressed my ear up against the bathroom door, feeling like an idiot, but also listening closely for any sign that Jamey was still in the apartment. Call me a coward but my sole reason for closing myself in the bathroom and turning on the shower had been to avoid any further conversation with him. I hadn't actually gotten in the shower, I just knew there was no way Jamey would walk in while it was running.

I wanted to avoid Jamey for one reason - because I knew he was right. I could admit that to myself, even if I couldn't - or wouldn't - admit it to him. I *should* kick Aaron to the curb, that is if he hadn't already effectively done that to me by literally leaving me standing on the curb the night before. Either way, I knew that if Mia was in the same situation, I'd be furious if she even considered giving the guy in question a second chance. As for why I was considering it? That was a question I'd have to leave for later. Right now I just wanted to get out of Jamey's apartment and home to my condo. My plan was to use the key Jamey had for Mia and Dante's apartment to borrow some of Mia's clothes and her car. Mia and I had been best friends forever. I'd borrowed clothes from her and driven her car plenty of times and I knew she wouldn't mind.

Hearing no noise in the apartment, I cautiously opened the bathroom door. From the stillness I could tell that Jamey wasn't waiting somewhere in the apartment to surprise me. As Jamey had told me I would, I found Mia & Dante's key on the hook by the door along with his extra key. Once I found those, I looked around for my dress and shoes from the night before. I found my dress folded and sitting on the couch with my shoes sitting on the floor nearby. Laying on top of my dress was a note.

Call me when you're ready and I'll call a rideshare to take you home.

Underneath was a number that I assumed was for Jamey's cell phone.

I picked up the note and stood looking at it for a moment. While I'd been hiding in the bathroom avoiding him, Jamey had been thoughtful enough to fold up my dress, which I knew I'd left just laying somewhere, found my shoes, and stripped the sheets and blanket off the couch where I'd slept, which any halfway decent guest should have done herself. And even after I'd been incredibly rude to him and he'd clearly been pissed at me, he'd thought ahead and realized that I still needed a way to get home. In my head I heard his words from earlier…

"If you were mine, taking care of you would be my top priority."

The contrast between his behavior and Aaron's the night before was stark and obvious. I didn't know whether Jamey was making a point or just being a really good guy after the way I'd responded to his concern earlier. But the fact was that a guy who had met me a handful of times, who I had no real connection to other than through mutual friends, was showing more consideration for me than the guy I'd been dating for months had. I believed Jamey when he said there was no way he would either leave a woman stranded or drive while intoxicated, let alone expect someone to get in the car with him.

I sat down on the couch, resting my head in my hands. My mind swirled, a confused mess of thoughts about Jamey, Aaron, and what I should do next. I wasn't sure how long I sat there but I finally decided to just focus on the practical next steps of getting some clothes to wear, getting home, and figuring out how to get my phone back from Aaron. The rest could wait for now.

I pushed up from the couch. With my dress, shoes, the keys and Jamey's note in hand, I walked over to Jamey's door, unlocked it, and peeked out. Considering I was going to have to cross the wide landing to Mia and Dante's door wearing nothing but a t-shirt and panties, I was never so glad that I was on the top floor of the building and that Mia, Dante and Jamey had the only apartments on this floor. Seeing no sign of anyone, I stepped out, quickly locked Jamey's door behind me, then hurried over to Mia and Dante's door and let myself inside.

Ten minutes later, I was standing in Mia and Dante's living room, ready to go. I'd borrowed a t-shirt, tank top, shorts, and flip flops from

Mia. I wouldn't win any fashion contests, but I looked okay and at least I was completely clothed without having to do the walk of shame and wear my dress and heels home. The tank top made it less obvious that I didn't have a bra on and flip flops were about the only shoes I really wanted to put on my still-sore feet. My dress, heels, and the t-shirt Jamey had lent me sat on the floor next to me in a borrowed tote bag.

The only thing I had to do now was to decide whether to stick with my original plan and borrow Mia's car, or to call Jamey and let him call me a rideshare. I wanted to take the easy way out, borrow Mia's car, and avoid having to talk to Jamey. But then I'd have to figure out how to get Mia's car back to her and probably end up inconveniencing her in the process, though I knew she wouldn't mind. I also realized that I would have to contact Jamey one way or another to let him know that I'd gotten home. If I didn't, I was 100% certain he'd worry. Ignoring him, especially after everything he'd done for me, would be a bitch move. I'd owe Jamey money if he paid for my ride home, but logistically that was easier to solve than figuring out the return of Mia's car. And I'd have to get his t-shirt back to him, anyway.

Realizing I'd made my decision, I walked into the kitchen and picked up the phone handset. I'd never thought I'd have a reason to be grateful that the apartments still had landlines, yet here I was. Squaring my shoulders and taking a deep breath, I dialed Jamey's number.

"I assume this is Meg since my phone says 'Dante – home' and I know he's not there."

I was a little taken back both by Jamey's greeting and by the little rush I felt just hearing his voice.

I managed to get out, "Yes, it's Meg."

"I'll need to get your home address. Hang on, let me find a pen."

I could hear voices in the background and something that sounded like pots hitting each other. I realized that Jamey must be in the kitchen at the pub.

"Got it. Go ahead."

I gave Jamey my address, then rushed on in case he started to hang up.

"Jamey, I appreciate this, really. I'll pay you right back, I promise."

"No problem. I'll request your ride right now."

The background noise cut off and I realized that Jamey had hung up. Either he was still pissed or the kitchen was extremely busy already. Considering that the pub wasn't even open yet, my money was on the first option. I was going to have to find a way to get back on even ground with him and soon. It was just one more item on the long list of things I had to figure out.

I hung up and headed for the door, grabbing the tote bag on the way. I stepped outside, locked the door and considered what to do with the keys. Jamey had said to leave them under the doormat, but that made me nervous. That was home security 101, right? Never hide a key somewhere obvious? I knew I needed to get downstairs or I'd risk missing my ride, so I made a quick decision to keep the keys and return them to Jamey along with his t-shirt and the money I owed him. Decision made, I started down the stairs to catch my ride.

⌒

Twenty-five minutes later I was walking toward my condo holding a master key borrowed from the condo management office. Luckily, the staff there recognized me and had no issues with giving me the key. Realizing again how dumb I'd been to go out with no money and no ID and to hand my phone and key over to someone else, I swore that I would never, ever be that careless again. I'd figured my way through it, but I'd been very lucky along the way. I hadn't let myself think about it, but the number of things that could have gone wrong was almost endless. I remembered Jamey's anger from that morning and knew that it was justified. I'd gotten away with it, but I promised myself I wouldn't tempt fate that way again.

As I approached my door I saw a bag hanging on the doorknob. Looking inside, I saw my phone and my key. I was grateful that Aaron had dropped them off, though leaving my key hanging on my door wasn't exactly safe.

I let myself in, closed and locked the door behind me, and flopped down on my couch. If we hadn't had so much to drink or if Aaron had called a rideshare, he and I would probably be sitting in my kitchen right now, drinking coffee after having slept in. Aaron was strictly a night-time sex guy, but he'd usually let me get away with snuggling up against him for a while before we got up. Not wanting to think about Aaron right then, I got up and made my way upstairs to my bedroom, grabbing my phone on the way.

I did a quick check on my phone for messages before I got in the shower and saw that I had a text from Aaron.

Aaron: Call me when you get home.

Really? That was it? No "sorry I was such a dick last night" or "I can't believe I left you stranded without your phone or your key" or some other acknowledgement that he'd messed up? Just "call me when you get home"? Whatever. I was in no mood to talk to him right then, so he could just wait. He wouldn't like it, but I couldn't bring myself to care at the moment.

I stripped off my borrowed clothes, sending another silent thank you to Mia. I walked into the large attached bathroom and flipped on the shower. This bathroom was my favorite place in the condo. It had beautiful granite countertops, nice fixtures, and a double sink. But my favorite things were the big shower with several shower heads and the separate, deep whirlpool tub. The rest of the condo was fine, nothing special really, and a little big for just one person, but the master bath and the huge walk-in closet in the master bedroom had sold me on it. I'd always heard that bathrooms and kitchens sell houses and, in my case, at least the bathroom part of that saying was true. The kitchen was nice, I supposed, but I didn't do much cooking so it didn't figure heavily on my list.

I wanted to linger in the shower, but I had unfinished business with both Aaron and Jamey and I knew I wouldn't be able to settle until I figured out what to do about each one. Aaron was easy for now. I was going to ignore his instructions to call him and send him a simple text instead letting him know I was home. Beyond that, I didn't know yet. A lot depended on how he responded.

As for Jamey, for some reason that felt a lot more complicated. True, I needed to return his shirt and keys and pay him back for the ride home. That was the easy stuff. But I also needed to apologize for responding so rudely to his concern earlier. It was true that I wasn't his sweetheart, but I shouldn't have responded like that. At the very least, I could have just thanked him for his concern and told him I wasn't sure yet what I was going to do. That was the truth, too. As angry as he'd been, it may not have satisfied him, but if he'd pushed then I'd have been more justified in telling him to back off.

I stepped out of the shower and dried off, then wrapped my hair up in the towel. Once in my bedroom, I slipped on clean panties and a bra, then headed back to the bathroom. As I dried my hair, my thoughts drifted back to Jamey and the first time I'd met him.

We hadn't gotten the best start. It was also the first time Aaron had met Mia and Dante and I'd been nervous, wanting them to like him. We'd all met at the pub near Mia and Dante's apartment. Aptly named Brothers Pub, it was owned by two of Dante's closest friends, twin brothers Kendrick and Callahan, and Jamey ran the kitchen. The four of them grew up together and considered each other family, like Mia and I did with each other. Jamey had stepped out of the kitchen just as

Mia and Dante had arrived, and Mia had introduced him to us. We'd started discussing getting something to eat, and unfortunately, right in front of Jamey, I'd been a little hypercritical about the food. Having only had drinks at the pub before that night, never food, I'd expected it to be typical bar food. When everything Jamey had sent out to us turned out to be amazing, I'd made it my priority to catch him before we left that night to acknowledge how wrong I'd been.

While the others had chatted, I'd kept my eye out for Jamey in case he stepped out of the kitchen again. When I'd finally seen him, I'd headed his way immediately.

As I moved into my bedroom to get dressed, I remembered my conversation with Jamey that night.

Keeping my eye on Jamey, I made my way across the pub as quickly as possible. I needed to catch him before he went back in the kitchen. As he turned to go I called his name to get his attention, afraid he wouldn't hear me over the noise. Thankfully he must have because he looked in my direction and stopped, then stood, hands in his front pockets, waiting for me to get to him. The position called attention to his muscular biceps and forearms and the ink swirling over both. I forced myself not to stare as I made my way closer.

"Hey, Jamey," I said when I finally stood in front of him. Standing this close to him I realized how tall he was, easily over 6 feet tall. How had I not noticed that before? I was 5'5 in my bare feet, but even in my 4-inch heels I had to look up at him.

"Meg." Jamey dipped his chin in acknowledgement, then just stood there, looking at me. Okay, he wasn't going to make this easy. I might as well get on with it.

"I apologize about before. I know I sounded like I was criticizing your cooking. I'm sorry it came out that way."

He continued to look at me, not saying a word. I clamped down on the urge to say more just to keep talking, to fill the void, and looked at him in return. Finally, he spoke.

"I don't mind criticism." Jamey shrugged. "You don't like my food, you don't like my food. Not everybody does. If something is off and needs to be fixed, I want to know about it. I don't mind fair criticism at all."

He shifted a little and the look he was giving me changed, his blue-grey eyes growing a little stormy.

"What I do mind is being condescended to. I mind people assuming things about me, about my food, before they've even tried it. Before

they've even so much as looked at a damn menu. That's what I mind."

I felt about three inches tall. He was right.

"I'm sorry. I didn't mean to be condescending but Mia and the guys told me that's how it came across. The food is amazing, Jamey, everything you sent out to us. I'm sorry that I sounded like I didn't think it would be. Can we please start over?"

I extended my hand. "Hi, I'm Meg. I'm a friend of Mia's. It's a pleasure to meet you."

Jamey continued to look at me for a second, then reached out to take my hand in his. He didn't shake it, just held it wrapped in his. His palm was slightly rough, his hand huge and warm as it wrapped around mine.

"Jamey. The pleasure is all mine."

He held my hand for a second more, then released it and stepped back. He tilted his head in the direction of the kitchen door.

"I need to get back. Enjoy your evening."

Before I could respond he was pushing through the kitchen door. I stood there, still feeling his hand on mine. The thought rose up inside my head that I hoped it wasn't the only time I ever got to touch him.

And now I needed to go find him and apologize again. For some reason the two of us just seemed to rub each other the wrong way. It was strange, really. I knew that part of the issue on my side was that I was more aware of him than I should be given that I was dating someone else. Well, I *had* been dating someone else. Whether or not I still was was an open question at the moment. But still, objectively Aaron was a very attractive man. Women openly stared at him when we were out together. He had classic good looks, dark hair, and deep blue eyes. He worked out regularly and stayed in great shape. He drove an expensive car and lived in a beautiful condo downtown. He was very confident and a little arrogant. People envied him and he knew it and liked it.

Jamey, though. Jamey was just as confident, but in a whole different way. I hadn't spent a lot of time with him, but it was clear that he was 100% sure of himself and comfortable in his own skin. It radiated off him in waves and it was sexy as hell. He commanded your attention without saying a word. Add to that his dark blondish hair, his blue-grey eyes, his hot body, and those gorgeous tattoos, and it was hard to look away. I thought of how he'd looked that morning standing in his kitchen, sweatpants hanging low on his hips, his beautiful upper body on display and hair still mussed from sleep. Heaven have mercy. It was enough to make a girl drool.

My phone pinged with a new text message, snapping me out of my daydreams about Jamey's hotness.

Grabbing my phone off the dresser, I saw that the message was from Mia.

Mia: Hey girl. I'm hoping the fact that you didn't text me to check-in last night or this morning means you had a great time and slept in.

Ha. Well, the sleeping in part was partially true, but as for the rest...

Me: Um, no. Looong story. I'll fill you in when you get home.

Mia: What?! Oh no! Short version...?

Me: We got drunk, Aaron ditched me, Jamey saved me, here I am. The end.

I watched the three little dots appear, then disappear, then appear again.

Mia: You're right. I need the long version. Call me later?

Me: Yes. Love u.

Mia: Love u too.

I figured while I was texting I might as well text Aaron and get that over with. I sent a short message simply saying I was home and thanking him for dropping off my phone and my key. That was it. The next step was up to him.

I couldn't decide what to do about Jamey, so I decided to set it aside for the moment. I didn't want to have any more missteps with him. If I let it settle a little, and maybe asked Mia what she thought, hopefully I'd figure out how to interact with him without embarrassing myself again. At this point, he had to be wondering why the hell a smart, sensible girl like Mia kept me around.

Putting Jamey out of my mind, I grabbed a load of laundry and headed downstairs. That was another favorite feature of my condo – the stackable washer/dryer in the little laundry closet right off my kitchen. After many years of apartment living and communal laundry rooms, I was grateful every time I was able to do my laundry without leaving my condo.

I pulled up a playlist on my phone and set to checking off my list of chores. The hours passed as I cleaned, did more laundry, ironed, and paid a couple of bills. Finally, the growling in my stomach made me stop and check the time. I was surprised to find that it was already after 7pm. Heading to the kitchen, I grabbed a frozen premade meal – a healthy version of vegetarian lasagna – out of the freezer. I stopped by a café near my office a couple of times a week to grab coffee or lunch and always picked up at least one of their "grab & go" meals for my freezer. They were the perfect solution for having a decent meal while also requiring the bare minimum in terms of cooking.

After I ate dinner, I decided to call Mia. She'd be home the next day, but I figured I'd fill her in and get it over with. I knew what she was going to say – I needed to break things off with Aaron. But she also might be able to help me figure out what to do about Jamey, and that was uppermost in my mind right then.

Mia answered on the first ring. We chatted about nothing for a minute before she cut right to the chase and asked what had happened the night before. I filled her in on the details, including my disagreement with Jamey that morning.

"So that's it." I waited for a response from Mia, but heard only silence. Had she fallen asleep on me?

"Meems, you there? Did you finally decide you need to go find a normal best friend?"

"No, what fun would that be?" Mia sounded like she was considering something. "I'm just wondering why part of the story didn't include the details of your sarcastically-worded breakup text to Aaron. I mean, you've obviously broken things off with him, right?"

I sighed and rested my head on the back of the couch.

"Not yet. I just…" I just what? Wasn't ready to admit that my "perfect" boyfriend was nowhere near perfect?

"Meg." Mia said everything in just that one word.

"I know, alright? I know. But in so many ways, he's the man I always pictured being with. Handsome, successful, confident – he ticks all the boxes, you know?"

"Except for the ones where he loves you and cares about what you want and treats you well."

Ouch. I knew this was Mia's form of tough love, but it still stung a bit.

"You're right." I knew she was, I might as well admit it. "He hasn't texted me back, so it's probably over anyway."

"Let's hope." Mia's voice softened. "I'm sorry, sweetie. Are you okay? I know you didn't love him, but.."

"No, I didn't. I'm okay. It just sucks that things ended that way. If they did end. I don't even know at this point." I reached up and rubbed my temple, trying the fend off the headache I could feel coming my way. "Now I just need to figure out how to apologize to Jamey."

"Just call him tomorrow. Or stop by the pub. You're more likely to find him there than the apartment. It doesn't need to be complicated."

It sounded so straightforward, so matter of fact when Mia said it. But I knew that the simplest conversation between Jamey and me could suddenly become tangled up and end up with me looking bad.

I said as much to Mia and heard a little humming sound like she was thinking.

"You and Jamey do seem to strike sparks off each other. You're always a little prickly, so no surprise there, but Jamey is usually so easy-going."

Once again, she was right. I definitely could be prickly.

"He just gets under my skin. Like this morning. I was rude. I know it. And I need to apologize. But he needs to quit calling me sweet-heart."

I cringed a little even as I heard myself say that. I sounded like a petty bitch.

"Have you asked him to?"

Mia's question made me pause for a second. Had I? He'd only called me that a few times. Had I ever directly asked him not to?

"Not in so many words, but I think I've made it clear that I don't appreciate it."

"If you really want him to stop, just tell him. I'm sure he'll respect your wishes."

For some reason Mia's calm answer irritated me a little.

"I shouldn't have to, though. It's demeaning to use endearments for women just because they're women."

Even as I said it, I knew that wasn't Jamey's intention. It just didn't ring true with the rest of his character. It was obvious from even a small bit of experience with him that he neither saw women as inferior in any way nor would he act in a demeaning way to anyone.

As if she'd read my mind, Mia's response was gently chastising.

"Coming from some men, maybe, but not Jamey. I think you know that. Why does it really bother you?"

"Because…" I realized that I didn't have a good answer. Why did it bother me? Because I felt like it *should* bother me? I turned the question back on Mia. Jamey called her "honey" all the time.

"Doesn't it bother you?"

"No, not a bit," Mia responded.

Honestly, Mia's answer didn't surprise me. She was much nicer than me and much less prone to get annoyed with the people around her. That was a very good thing for me considering I could be a pain in the ass at times.

Mia went on.

"Let me ask you something, Meg. Have you noticed that Jamey

doesn't use endearments for all women?"

I frowned, thinking that through. What difference did that make?

"No, I haven't noticed that. I haven't spent as much time with him as you have."

I could hear Mia's hum of agreement.

"That's true, you haven't. But he doesn't. He only uses them with women he has a personal connection to. Not co-workers or the women who hit on him at the pub, only women in his circle. And he uses a different one for each of us. Did you ever notice that he always calls you sweetheart?"

I sighed. It appeared that there was a lot I hadn't noticed.

"No," I admitted. "It never occurred to me."

"It's true. I noticed it awhile ago. He always calls me honey, never anything else. Dante's sister is princess, which all the guys call her actually. You're sweetheart. My point is it's like it's his name for each of us, not some generic throwaway like a guy who calls every woman 'babe' because he can't be bothered to learn their names."

"So I'm supposed to see it as some kind of compliment? Is that what you're saying?"

"Well, it certainly isn't an insult. And it isn't meant to diminish you in any way. But if it bothers you for whatever reason, just ask him to stop."

Mia and I talked for a couple more minutes, then hung up after making plans to have lunch in a few days. As I was hanging up with her, my phone pinged with a text from work saying that I was needed to fill in for a sick colleague on an important client site visit and I had a flight to catch at 6am the next morning. The rest of the consulting team would be leaving tomorrow, as well. I'd worked with this client in the past, so I was a natural choice to fill in. I just wished that I'd been *asked* if I could fill in, rather than being told I needed to be on a plane in less than 10 hours and be gone for several days. What if I had kids? What if I had a pet? Hell, what if I had any kind of life whatsoever outside of work? My job as a management consultant with a well-known firm required long hours and a lot of travel. I should have been used to it by now, but for some reason lately it had been bothering me more and more.

Grumbling to myself, I pushed off the couch and headed to my bedroom to pack. Once there, I spotted the t-shirt Jamey had lent me, freshly washed and folded, sitting on the corner of my bed. Seeing it reminded me that I hadn't contacted him yet. I needed to do that tonight. I couldn't just leave town and not at least let him know that it would be a few days before I could return his keys and shirt.

I decided to text Jamey rather than calling. Saturdays were busy at the pub and a text would be less of an interruption than a call. I backtracked to the kitchen and grabbed the note he'd left me that morning from where it sat on my counter along with his keys. I put his number in my phone, then tapped out a message.

Me: Jamey, this is Meg. I just found out I have to go out of town for work for a few days. Is it okay if I return your keys and t-shirt and give you the money I owe you as soon as I get back?

It took a few minutes for Jamey to text back. I hoped I wasn't being too much of a pain texting him at work. It didn't sound like it from Jamey's response when it popped up.

Jamey: Sure, no problem.

Me: Thank you. Sorry to bug you while you're busy.

Jamey: It's fine. I stepped outside for a minute.

For some reason, that made me feel good. Like it was a big deal that even though he was busy, he wasn't too busy to take a few minutes for me. I shook my head at my overthinking.

Me: Ok. I also need to apologize for being rude this morning.

It was probably poor etiquette to apologize via text, but I didn't want to wait on that until I got back. It needed to be said now.

Jamey: Don't worry about it.

Well, I was worried about it, and I told him so.

Jamey: Well don't.

See? This was why he made me crazy. Why couldn't he just respond the way he was supposed to?

Me: Just say apology accepted and then I won't worry about it anymore.

Jamey: Apology accepted and then I won't worry about it anymore.

I rolled my eyes, but also had to hold back a laugh. Smartass.

Me: <eyeroll emoji> What are you, 10 years old?

Jamey: 32 actually but don't make the mistake of thinking that means I'm mature.

Me: Thanks for the warning, but I would never make that mistake. I've heard the stories from Mia about how dumb you and the guys act when you're all together.

Jamey: Can't deny it. All true.

Me: It's okay, you can't help that you're a guy.

Jamey: Uh, thanks? Or wait, am I supposed to apologize? Is this one of those trick questions where I'm in trouble either way?

Me: Probably option C, but I'll overlook it because I owe you.

Jamey: Do not.

Me: Do, too.

Jamey: Do not.

Now I did laugh out loud, glad that Jamey couldn't hear me. This guy was something else.

Me: Are we seriously doing this?

Jamey: Looks like it.

Me: Next you'll be telling on me for supposedly touching you. Mom, she's touching me!

Jamey: If you were touching me, I promise I wouldn't be complaining.
Wow.

I had absolutely no comeback for that. The thought of running my hands over Jamey filled my mind. I shook my head to clear the image. How the hell could I respond to that? I decided to just change the subject completely.

Me: I'd better go, I have to be up at 4:30am to get to the airport.

Jamey: Safe travels.

Good, he'd dropped it. That was what I'd wanted. Right. Good.

Me: Thanks, I'll let you know when I get back, hopefully no later than Wed.

Jamey: Ok, works for me.

Me: Goodnight Jamey.

Jamey: Goodnight Meg.

Jamey: Eat breakfast. Every day.

Me: No.

Jamey: Yes.

I was not having this conversation. He was not telling me what to do even if it was good for me.

Okay, that sounded dumb even to me.

Me: Fine.

Jamey: Good girl.

Me: I'm not even going to respond to that.

Jamey: How is responding to say that you're not going to respond not responding?

Me: Why are you still texting me? I said I'm going to bed.

Jamey: Okay, last one. Good night.

Me: I bet if I text you you'll still text me back. You can't stand not to.

Jamey: Bet you're right.

I laughed out loud. I could almost hear him say that.

Me: I hate to admit it but that made me laugh.

Jamey: Good. That's a good way to end the night. Sweet dreams.

I decided to let him have the last word. I smiled again, the ridiculous exchange filling my mind as I started to pack. I was in a much better mood than I'd been just a few minutes ago and I knew I had Jamey to thank for that. Just one more thing I owed him for.

Chapter 4

Jamey

*M*eg wasn't even here and she was driving me crazy. Good crazy – if there is such a thing – but still crazy. I couldn't stop thinking about her. I'd told my brain 100 times to cut that shit out and think about something else, but my brain wasn't on board with that plan. It kept circling right back to Meg. A hot-as-hell woman had been hitting on me hard at the pub the night before, jet black hair spilling down her back, killer curves on display, and a blatant invitation in her eyes. Everything that should have had me hard in seconds. But nothing. My dick didn't so much as twitch. Hell, I'd stood there thinking about Meg for most of the time the woman was talking to me. When I'd excused myself politely, the disbelief in her eyes had been clear. I couldn't blame her. I could hardly believe it myself. But I wasn't going to waste her time – or mine – when the only woman I seemed to be able to focus on was Meg.

Every time I thought about that stupid-ass text conversation we'd had a few days before, I couldn't stop the grin that covered my face. It had been dumb, no doubt, but it had also been fun. I loved that Meg always came right back at me and gave as good as she got. She made me think and demanded my attention when I was with her, either in person, texting or on the phone. She kept me on my toes and I liked that.

I also liked that my comment about not complaining if she touched me had stopped her in her tracks. I'd meant it 100% but I think part of me just wanted to see how she'd respond. From the pause in the conversation and then the complete change in topic, I'd say that I'd flustered the hell out of her. I'd have loved to have seen her expression. Of course the pause could have meant that I'd made her uncomfortable, maybe shocked or disgusted her, but I didn't think that was the case. The fact that she'd continued the conversation made me even more sure of that. If I'd offended her, she'd have told me to fuck off and that would have been it. Considering the way that she'd run her eyes all over my body on Saturday morning, I was pretty sure she'd been anything but pissed off at my comment that night.

And now, here I was, actually nervous because I knew that Meg was going to stop in the pub sometime that day to return my keys and t-shirt. I hadn't been nervous to see a girl since high school. Meg had been out of town for work for several days and had finally gotten home early that morning. She had the day off due to having just gotten home, so she was planning to stop by the pub before we got too busy.

I knew Meg was out of my league but something about her had grabbed my attention and wouldn't let go. I'd actually thought about texting her a couple of times while she was out of town, but one thing held me back. I had no idea where her relationship with the dickhead stood. I hoped like hell she wasn't still seeing him after the way he'd treated her, but I'd already gotten bitten once for expressing that opinion. I was smart enough not to make that mistake again. I'd seen Mia earlier in the week and had thought about asking her, but I didn't want it to get back to Meg. Mia had thanked me for helping Meg out and shared that she'd told Meg that the dumbass needed to go. Hopefully Meg had listened to her best friend, but until I knew for sure I needed to hold back.

I made myself stay in the kitchen, prepping things for later, until one of the servers stuck her head through the door to let me know someone was asking for me. I needed to do a check on several items behind the bar, so I grabbed the list for that and pushed through the kitchen door into the pub.

Meg was standing near the bar, looking at the taps, head cocked like she was trying to read them. I said her name and when she turned to look at me, her face lit up like she was glad to see me. There was no denying I was glad to see her, too. Her blond curls were pulled up in a ponytail and her jeans and black sweater showed off her curves. She looked a little tired, like the past few days had taken a bit of a toll, but she was still beautiful as always. I wanted to just stand there and take her in. Of course, she'd wonder what the hell was wrong with me if I did that, so I just said hello to her like a normal person.

"Hey, Jamey. Thanks for saying it was okay to drop by."

She held out a bag to me.

"Here's your shirt and keys. How much do I owe you for the ride?"

I set the list I was holding on top of the bar and reached out for the bag. I turned to set the bag behind the bar, then turned back to face Meg and crossed my arms over my chest. I knew Meg was going to push back on what I was about to say.

"I'm not trying to start an argument with you, but you really don't need to pay me back for that. It was only a few bucks and I was glad to be able to do it for you since I couldn't stick around and take you home myself. "

I left out the fact that we'd been pissed at each other when I'd left the apartment that morning. It seemed like we'd gotten past that and I wasn't about to stir it back up.

Meg stood and considered me for a second. I could tell from her expression that she was weighing her response. Finally, she nodded like she'd made a decision.

"Okay, fine. I'll let it go. I don't want to be one of those people who can't be gracious when someone does something nice for them."

I nodded back at her. We'd really said all that needed to be said, but I didn't want to let Meg go yet. I grabbed onto the first topic I thought of.

"How was the trip?"

Meg's shoulders slumped a little, but then she straightened them again.

"It went well. We'll need to go back, but we got a lot of good work done. It was…it seemed long." Her quick smile was a little less vibrant than usual, her eyes tired. "I'm glad to be home."

"No place like it, right?" Then because she looked like she could use one I asked, "Hey, can I grab you a drink?"

Meg looked over at the bar, then back at me.

"I should probably get out of your way."

I heard her words, but her tone was saying something different. I tilted my head toward the bar stool Meg was standing next to.

"Nah, you can keep me company while I do my bar checklist."

Meg considered for a second, then agreed and hopped up on the bar stool. I moved down the bar to fix her the soda water and lime she'd asked for. I set it down in front of her as she studied the checklist I'd left sitting on bar. I had no idea what could be interesting about it. It was just a list of bar items I kept stocked, with my initials scrawled next to a few that I'd already checked earlier.

Meg gave me a small smile as I set her drink down, then picked it up for a sip. She tapped her nail on one of the spots where I'd initialed the list.

"JSM, what does that stand for?"

Ah, that's what had caught her eye.

"It's just my initials," I responded, glancing down at the list, then back up at her.

"No, really? I thought it was a secret password."

"Smartass," I said under my breath as I turned to grab the list of drink specials for the week, making sure I said it just loud enough for her to hear it.

"You know it."

I turned back around and looked at Meg. She had her full gorgeous smile on her face now. Between that and those beautiful blue eyes focused on me, it was hard to concentrate.

"What's your full name, Jamey?"

I set the list of drink specials down and looked at Meg. I had work to do before the place got busy, but I couldn't resist her pull.

"Tell you what…if I can guess yours, you can take a shot at guessing mine."

"Deal." Meg smoothed her hair back like she was ready to go. "Shoot."

I stood across the bar from her and braced my hands on the top.

"I need your initials first." In reality I didn't need her initials at all because I already knew her full name. Mia had told me when I had asked once about the nickname – 'Mik' – that she sometimes called Meg. But Meg didn't need to know that. Yeah, I was cheating a little – okay, a lot – but we were just playing.

Meg titled her head, considering. "I guess that's fair. My initials are MIK."

I crossed my arms and stared at her for a few seconds like I was thinking hard.

"Megan Isabella Kennedy."

Meg's mouth dropped open in shock.

"What?!" she shrieked, causing a couple of guys sitting farther down the bar to turn and look at her. Noticing their look, she lowered her voice, but still pinned me with a suspicious glare.

"How could you possibly know that? I mean, Megan for Meg is pretty easy, although it could be Margaret or Marguerite, and there aren't that many 'I' names, I suppose, but Kennedy? There are like a million K names out there."

I wasn't about to give up how I knew her name, so I just shrugged and picked up the inventory list again.

"Just lucky, I guess. Your turn…if you're still up for it."

She responded to the challenge in my voice, sitting up straighter and tossing her ponytail over her shoulder.

"If I'm still up for it..ha," she scoffed. "Be quiet and let me think. JSM..JSM.. hmm.."

Meg tapped her pretty pink lips with her finger, drawing my attention there. I wondered for a second what she would do if I stepped closer and sucked on that full lower lip of hers.

"James Steven Murphy."

I shook my head and started checking the stock of fruit behind the bar.

"Not even close."

"Okay, how about…James Seth Miller."

"Nope."

"Darn it. James..Simon..um, um..Matthews!"

"No, again."

"Was any part of that even close?"

Meg was starting to pout a little bit and it was adorable. I laughed, seeing the fire light up in her eyes as I did. This girl loved a challenge.

"No, it wasn't."

"So your first name isn't even James?" She sounded offended, like I'd tricked her somehow. It made me laugh again, but I didn't say anything else.

"Not James…not James…" she muttered under her breath, her head cocked a little to the side, fingers tapping on the bar."

"Okay, it's…" Meg squinted her eyes and narrowed her gaze on my face as if she'd be able to read my name written on my forehead if she just concentrated hard enough.

"Jamal..Sterling..Murgatroyd!"

I couldn't stop my grin as I shook my head at her. "Jamal Sterling? Do you think my parents hated me?"

Granted, my dad wasn't my biggest fan and I was pretty sure my mom had named me, anyway, but over his dead body would any son of his have a name like Sterling.

"And who the hell actually has the last name Murgatroyd?"

"Fine, then, I give up. Just tell me." Meg's shoulders slumped as she leaned one elbow on the bar and rested her chin in her hand. She looked so despondent. Goddamn this girl was cute.

I turned to look at her, eyebrows raised. I'd tell her in a minute, but I had to give her some grief first.

"You give up? After what, four guesses? I'm not sure that level of effort deserves a response."

"Ja-mey!" she wailed, like I was an older brother who was teasing her. She sat up straight and leaned forward a bit, giving me a nice glimpse of some beautiful cleavage. Her eyes narrowed again. "If you don't tell me, I'll text you at all hours with guesses. Don't test me, Mr. whatever the hell your name is. I'll do it, I promise."

Laughing again, I gave in. "I don't doubt that for a second. My full name is Jameson Scot – one 't' – MacGregor. Happy?"

"Jameson Scot MacGregor," she repeated. "Wow, a bit of Scottish ancestry there, huh?"

"Yeah, just a bit. And my dad - named Angus by the way, I kid you not - is quite proud of it."

And that was about the only thing I could ever remember him being proud of. Certainly not me or anything I'd managed to accomplish in life.

"I can tell. And your mom – is she Scottish, too?"

Meg rested her chin in her hand again, but this time she looked like she was settling in for a chat.

I leaned my hip against the bar and thought about my mom for a minute. My memories of her were hazy, most of the details lost to time. I remembered her smile and the way that she'd sit on the floor with me to play or read to me. I remembered that her favorite scent was cherry blossoms. Most of all, I remembered how utterly lost and alone and scared I'd felt when she'd died. Shaking away those thoughts, I responded to Meg's question.

"She used to say that she was a mutt, a bit of this and a bit of that, not enough of any one thing to matter more than the other."

"She 'used to say'? It sounds like she's passed on." Meg's voice was quiet with concern. For some reason, the warmth of that concern surrounded me like an embrace.

"Yeah, a long time ago when I was little."

Meg shook her head, her expression serious.

"I can't imagine growing up without my mom. Or without either of my parents, really. We don't always agree on everything, but they've always been there for me. I'm sorry, Jamey. That must have been tough."

She had no idea. The moment my mom died it was as if the sun had switched off, all the warmth and light in my life suddenly gone. My dad had made a point each and every day to let me know that I was an unwanted burden, that he only fed and clothed me and saw that I went to school because he had to. He hadn't been a great father even before my mom died; after that, he barely tolerated my presence in his house.

Realizing I hadn't responded, I forced myself to smile at Meg.

"I made it through okay."

I knew she could see my tension and hear it in my voice. I could tell by her look that she didn't want to let it go that easily, but thankfully she did. Tilting her head, she squinted like she was assessing me.

"Yeah, I guess you turned out alright." Her teasing tone was gentle, much softer than her usual straightforward style. She shrugged. "I mean, you can cook okay and all."

I huffed out a laugh.

"At least I have that going for me."

"Well..." Meg climbed down from the bar stool and picked up her purse before turning back to me. She looked at me for several seconds like she was weighing her words, then surprised the hell out of me by saying, "I think you have a lot going for you." Taking a look at the stools along the bar, nearly full now with customers, she took a step back. "It's getting busy, I should get out of your way and let you work. Thanks again, Jamey. See ya."

Before I could recover from my shock, she was walking away from me and out the door.

Chapter 5

Jamey

On my way to the farmers market on Saturday morning I decided to detour to a coffee shop I wanted to check out. I wanted to hit the farmers market right when it opened at 7am, but it was still early – a few minutes shy of 6:30am – so I had time for a quick stop.

I pulled into a parking spot along the curb in front of the coffee shop. I could see a couple of people moving around inside, but the 'open' sign in the window was still dark. The business hours listed on the door told me that they opened at 6:30am on Saturdays, so I only had a few minutes to wait. I rolled my car windows down, pulled up the notes app on my phone, and made a few notes about produce to keep an eye out for at the farmers market. I regularly hit the market on Saturday mornings to see what I could pick up, but this morning I was on a mission for something specific. We'd gotten in a big batch of blackberries from one of our local suppliers. Michael, the cook who was making most of our desserts these days, would use most of them, but I had an idea in my head for a salad with field greens and blackberries that I wanted to try. If I could pick up the fresh greens I wanted at the market this morning, I'd put the salad on the specials menu for the day and see what happened.

I glanced up from my phone as I closed my notes app and noticed two things – the now-glowing 'open' sign in the coffee shop window and a flash of yellow from the building next door. A smile spread across my face as I realized the flash of color was Meg exiting the glass-fronted building, her vibrant yellow dress glowing in the morning sun. She had paired nude heels with the sleeveless dress that skimmed her body and ended an inch or so above her knee. She had her sunglasses on, a huge leather bag over her shoulder, and a mango-colored drink in her hand. With her golden blond hair, yellow dress, and orange drink, she shone like a ray of sunshine.

She hadn't noticed me. I could have just let her go on with her day and gone on with mine, but I hadn't seen her in more than a week and I couldn't resist grabbing a few minutes with her. I stepped out of my car and headed for the sidewalk, calling out to Meg as I walked.

"Hey there, early bird."

Meg had turned to walk in the opposite direction but when she heard my voice she stopped and turned back. She returned my smile and headed in my direction.

"Hey there, yourself. Looks like I'm not the only early bird."

She stopped in front of me and pushed her sunglasses up on top of her head. Her beautiful blue eyes made me lose my thoughts for a second like they always did.

"Whatcha doing in this part of town so early on a Saturday?"

I shook off my Meg-induced haze and answered her question.

"I'm checking out the coffee at this place." I tilted my head in the direction of the coffee shop behind me. "I want to find a new supplier for the pub. The stuff we get from our current supplier is just some generic brand. It's always been okay but the quality has been going down recently. We're expanding the dessert menu and maybe thinking about adding Sunday brunch, so we need to upgrade the coffee. I've looked into a couple of other places but nothing has really wowed me yet. A couple of regulars at the pub told me this place was good, so.."

Meg stood listening to me, head cocked, and I realized that I was rambling.

"And that's way more than you probably wanted to know." I hoped the smile I gave her didn't look as embarrassed as I felt at my run-on mouth.

"No, it's interesting." Meg shifted, pulling her bag up on her shoulder. "It seems like you're always trying out something new for the menu."

A breeze blew a few strands of hair across Meg's face. I jammed my hands in my back pockets to keep myself from reaching for it and smoothing it back into place.

"Guilty as charged. I like to play."

Amusement sparked in Meg's eyes but I went on before she could make a sassy comment about all of the ways I probably liked to play.

"So you know why I'm here. What brings you out so early on a Saturday looking like you're ready to take on the world?"

"My gym's in this building." She waved her hand toward the building I'd seen her come out of. "They open at 5am every day except Sunday. I come get my workout in and then head to the office. My office is just a couple blocks away, so I park there, walk here, work out, and walk back. And" – she lifted the mango-colored concoction she held in her hand – "have breakfast on the way."

She brought the straw to her lips and took a sip. My dick, which was already interested in the fact that I was standing close enough to Meg to smell her light scent, stirred again imagining her pink lips wrapped around something other than a straw. Needing a distraction before I embarrassed myself even more, I dug deeper into Meg's explanation.

"So let me get this straight. You've already walked here from your office, worked out, gotten dolled up, sort of gotten breakfast, and are headed to work at" – I checked the time on my phone – "6:37 am. You're aware it's Saturday, right?"

Meg rolled her eyes at me.

"Yes, Captain Obvious, I'm aware. I work all the time on Saturday and I do this almost every morning. And I'm not all dolled up. It's just a simple dress and heels."

I shook my head as I allowed myself a few seconds to really look at her.

"That might be, but you look like a million bucks."

The way that "simple dress" hugged her ass and those heels accentuated her toned legs made my hands itch to touch her.

"Whatever, Jamey. Quit staring at my ass. I know it's big. You think I'm in the gym every morning because it's fun?"

Meg shook her blond curls and rolled her eyes at me again, giving me that sass I liked a little too much. But along with the sass I heard the tightness in her voice. I knew Meg was her own worst critic when it came to her body. God knew why when she was fucking perfect. I was treading a thin line here, but I couldn't let her comment stand.

"Say what you will, I'm the one looking and your ass looks mighty fine to me."

I kept talking as Meg's mouth dropped open and she stared at me. Changing the subject to distract her, I nodded at the cup in her hand.

"What's for breakfast?"

Meg continued to stare at me for a few seconds like she was trying to process my question.

"What's for...oh." She looked down at the cup. "It's a mango smoothie. It's made with almond milk, a protein blend, an electrolyte mix, and an immune booster."

For some reason, the way she recited all that made me chuckle. I couldn't resist the urge to tease her just a little.

"Of course it is. I wouldn't expect anything else."

Meg shifted her stance, her free hand landing on her hip. I loved the way her eyes sparked when we went back and forth like this.

"You're the one who told me to have breakfast every day. I can't even think about food this early and there's a juice bar in the gym, so a smoothie it is." She toasted me with the cup and took a sip.

I held my hands up in surrender. "Whatever works for you." It was better than starting her day with just black coffee.

"This works." Meg straightened up and I could tell she was ready to go. "And speaking of working, I need to go do that. But first I have a tip for you. If you want great coffee, try the coffee shop right by your apartment. The place called The Coffee Spot. They roast their own beans and the coffee is incredible. Seriously, best coffee ever."

"Huh, I've never stopped in there. I'll give it a shot."

"Good, I promise you'll be glad you did. There, that's my good deed for the day." Meg settled her bag on her shoulder again. "I'm sorry I've got to run."

I hated to let her go, but I knew she was right. We both needed to get moving.

"If you want to wait while I grab coffee, I'll return the good deed and give you a lift."

Meg smiled but shook her head as she took several steps backwards. "Thanks, but I'm good. See ya, Jamey."

Meg turned and I forgot to respond as I watched her walk away, taking in the view.

Shaking myself out of a daze for the second time that morning, I headed into the coffee shop. It was time to get on with the rest of my day.

Chapter 6

Meg

I was running late to pick up Mia for a rare girls' day out when I heard my phone ping with a text just as I was heading out of my condo. I dug in my bag to find my phone. If it was from work I was going to tell them I had a family obligation and couldn't deal with whatever the crisis of the day was. Mia *was* practically family, after all, and I'd promised to spend the day with her. It was a beautiful Sunday and there was no way I was going to cancel on my friend again because of work.

I looked at my phone and was surprised to see that the text was from Jamey.

Jamey: Thanks for the tip about The Coffee Spot yesterday. I stopped in this morning for coffee and you were right. It's great stuff.

I didn't have much time, but I couldn't resist a quick response to Jamey.

Me: Ah, the three little words I love best.

Jamey: What..it's great stuff?

Me: No, silly, "you were right". I never get tired of hearing that.

Jamey: It's nice that you're so humble. But go ahead and gloat on this one if you want, because you called it. I don't know what they do to their coffee, but I could get addicted fast.

Me: I hear you. I've actually bribed Mia numerous times to get her to bring me some.

Jamey: Luckily I'll have easy access. I talked with the couple that owns the shop this morning. We have to work out the details, but they'll soon be the official coffee supplier of Brothers Pub.

Me: That's great news, Jamey, really. And yet one more reason to hang out at the pub.

Jamey: Can't have enough of those. Thanks, again, for the tip. Funny how sometimes you're looking everywhere for something and all along the perfect answer is right in front of you.

Me: Yeah, funny how that happens…

Chapter 7

Jamey/Meg

Jamey: If you were buying a woman a gift for a made-up anniversary, what would you get her? Asking for a friend.

Meg: Really? I had no idea you were seeing someone.

Jamey: I'm not.

Meg: Then why are you buying a woman an anniversary gift?

Jamey: I'm not. I told you I was asking for a friend.

Meg: You know that saying that pretty much means you're *not* asking for a friend, right?

Jamey: In this case, it doesn't. I really am.

Jamey: Or wait, I'm really not.

Jamey: Dammit, whatever. What would you get?

...

...

Meg: You're a little testy today.

Jamey: Meg, I'm begging you. Please focus. The sooner you tell me, the sooner I can tell Dante and escape this hell.

Meg: This is for Mia? Dante is the friend?

Jamey: Well, shit. I wasn't supposed to say anything. Don't tell Mia, it's a surprise. Dante's driving us all crazy trying to figure out what to get her for the six month anniversary of the day they met.

Meg: You mean the day he scared her to death and she ran away and slammed the door in his face?

Jamey: That's the one.

Meg: That's sweet, I guess.

Jamey: Not the word I'd use, but whatever. So...what? Jewelry, choco-

late, lingerie, what?

Meg: Lingerie is a gift for the man. It's like me buying something I want, then saying it's a gift for you. No lingerie.

Jamey: Fine, good, off the list. So jewelry and chocolate? That good?

Meg: Sure, if he wants to be completely generic and boring.

Jamey: Are you trying to make me cry? Is that why you're doing this?

Meg: I'm trying to help. You're the one who asked me.

Jamey: Yes, help. I need that. Pleeeease tell me what Dante should get Mia.

Meg: Well, since you said please.

…

…

Jamey: Um..hello?

Meg: Be quiet, I'm thinking.

…

…

Jamey: So sorry to disturb you, but could you think faster? I need an answer sometime before we hit the next anniversary, whatever the hell that's gonna be.

Meg: Time.

Jamey: What? Time? What the hell does that mean?

Meg: Dante should give her time.

Jamey: Time to do what? Speak slowly and use simple words, Meg. My brain is on the fritz from listening to Dante dither back and forth and change his mind a million f-ing times about this.

Meg: Did you really just use the word dither?

Jamey: Meg. HELP. ME.

Meg: Dante should plan something so they can spend time together.

Jamey: Uh, you're aware they live together? They spend time together every day.

Meg: Nope, not the same thing. They see each other every day, although Dante's been so busy with the renovations to the gym I'm not even sure that's true right now, but this is setting aside time just for them. He should plan a day when they can have fun and just be together.

Jamey: You really think that would work?

Meg: Of course. They could go to one of the festivals or fairs that pop up all over this time of year. They can eat deep-fried God-knows-what and play impossible games and hold hands and kiss on the Ferris wheel. Mia will love it.

Jamey: That's too easy. It does sound like Mia, though. You're sure he won't get in trouble for not buying her a present? He'll kick my ass if I tell him this and then he gets in trouble.

Meg: He won't get in trouble. Promise.

Jamey: You are one brilliant lady. I told Dante to ask you a week ago but instead he decided to pester the shit out of the three of us and probably Dev,

too. Not gonna lie, you saved my life. Or at least my sanity.
Meg: Well, then, my work here is done. <dusts off hands>

Chapter 8

Meg/Jamey

Meg: I need a male opinion.
Jamey: No, those jeans don't make your ass look big.

…

Jamey: What, wrong answer?
Meg: Will you be serious for 2 minutes?
Jamey: I can probably make it for 3. What's up?
Meg: Okay. Like I said, I need a male perspective on something.
Jamey: I have one of those. Whatcha got?
Meg: My colleague, Anne, and I are having a difference of opinion about something. She and I have a meeting with a client tomorrow. He's the new CEO of a big tech company we've worked with before. This is our first meeting with him.
Jamey: Got it so far.
Meg: The thing is, well,….he's short. Like my height, 5'5"-ish. So short compared to an average guy.
Jamey: That's a problem? You lost me.
Meg: Sort of. The problem is Anne and I disagree about what shoes we should wear to the meeting. And I heard you just say WTF, but it really is a thing, so just shut up and listen.

…

Meg: Jamey?
Jamey: You told me to shut up and listen. This is me listening. I can't wait to find out where this shoe-related drama goes next.
Meg: You are such a smartass. The drama is that Anne thinks we should wear flats so we're not taller than him. I say I'm going to wear heels like I

*always do and she can do whatever she wants. With heels I'm maybe 5'9"
but who cares? Anne thinks he'll feel threatened or like we're trying to in-
timidate him if we're taller. So here's male perspective time. Is that true?*

Jamey: *What, that he'll feel threatened or something?*

Meg: *Yes, exactly.*

Jamey: *Wear the heels. Men don't care about that shit.*

Meg: *Are you being serious?*

Jamey: *Of course I'm being serious. When am I not serious?*

Meg: *Uh, should we look back to the beginning of this conversation?*

Jamey: *Good one. Yes, I'm being serious. The height thing is all you ladies.
Men don't care.*

Meg: *Oh, really. Have you ever dated a woman who's taller than you?*

Jamey: *Um, Meg, I'm like 6'1"-6'2". I don't come across many women
who are taller than me.*

Meg: *Valid point. So you think it's fine to wear heels.*

Jamey: *Absolutely. I have no doubt he'll be blown away by your experience and knowledge because by all accounts you kick ass at what you do.
And if he sneaks a quick look at your smokin' hot legs along the way, who
can blame him?*

Meg: *That's sexist.*

Jamey: *You asked for a male perspective, right?*

Meg: *Sigh. Yes. Yes, I did. Thanks. That helps. I think.*

Jamey: *You're welcome. Do you ever quit working? It's almost 10pm.*

Meg: *I'm in CA. It's not even 8 here.*

Jamey: *What time did you start this morning?*

Meg: *No comment.*

Jamey: *Have you eaten yet?*

Meg: *You're obsessed with feeding me.*

Jamey: *I'm obsessed with feeding everyone. It's kinda what I do.*

Meg: *Another valid point. I'm meeting Anne to go grab dinner in about
10 minutes.*

Jamey: *Good. Be safe. Eat some great fresh seafood for me.*

Meg: *Yuck! No can do. No seafood for me unless it's fried, so…no seafood
for me.*

Jamey: *Fine, picky girl. Then have a glass of CA wine for me.*

Meg: *Consider it done.*

Chapter 9

Jamey/Meg

Jamey: How'd the meeting with the new CEO go?

Meg: Don't ask.

Jamey: Shit, what happened?

Meg: Didn't I just say don't ask?

Jamey: Crap, did you not wear the heels? Did it mess with your mojo?

Meg: Why do I even respond to your ridiculous comments?

Jamey: It's one of the mysteries of the universe. Tell me what happened, Meg.

Meg: Will that get you to leave me alone?

Jamey: If that's what you want.

Meg: Fine, then. He wants to "think outside the box", do something "cutting edge", "architect a visionary course for the tech company of the future" blah blah blah.

Jamey: I have no idea what you just said.

Meg: That's the problem – he doesn't either! He says our approach is tired and stale and he's had it with "old school" consultants. I'm 25, Anne's 27, and our firm regularly wins awards for innovation. Instead of working with us, he's bringing in some guy he met playing racquetball two weeks ago. The guy may be a genius, I don't know, but from what I heard of his sales pitch it sounds like he cut words out of a marketing textbook and pasted them together. It's fine if he's giving us the boot. That's his call, right? But why waste our time, make us do all the prep work, have us fly out to California, and then not even glance at the materials we put together? What the hell is that? A power play?

Jamey: Probably. I'm sorry, Meg. That sucks. I know how hard you work.

Meg: Exactly! And this was a complete waste of time that I could have used for one of the million other clients I'm supposed to be working for right now!

Jamey: It was. That's frustrating. Would it help if I sing to you?

Meg: If you sing to me? What…???

Jamey: Usually in this kind of situation I'd make you comfort food. Homemade mac & cheese, loaded baked potato soup, white cheddar grits – that stuff can cure almost anything. But you won't eat any of that. So maybe I could sing instead.

Meg: Can you sing well?

Jamey: Not at all.

Meg: So why…?

Jamey: I'm thinking it'll be so bad it'll take your mind off Mr. "Big Words That Mean Nothing" CEO. Like when your head hurts, then you hit your elbow on something and you forget all about your headache?

Meg: You are so strange.

Jamey: Not the first time I've heard that. So no go on the singing, huh?

Meg: No, but I appreciate the thought. I actually feel a lot better. Thanks for not leaving me alone like I told you to.

Jamey: No problem. You take a lot of pride in your work. It's hard when someone disrespects that.

Meg: Sometimes you say something and it's exactly what I was thinking. How do you do that?

Jamey: It can be a burden to be so wise and awesome, but I manage somehow.

Meg: Well, thanks for sharing your wisdom and awesomeness with me tonight.

Meg: And I might just take you up on that homemade mac & cheese at some point.

Jamey: Say the word and its yours.

Chapter 10

Meg

I sat, drink in hand, and looked around the small group gathered on the open-air landing between Dante & Mia's apartment on one side and Jamey's on the other. Now that the weather was warmer, we'd all taken to hanging out here whenever a few of us were free. It was a great space, kind of like a covered terrace. It was on the top floor of the building, so we weren't bothering anyone else, and it was the perfect size for our group. At the moment the group included Dante, Mia, Jamey, me, and Dev. Dev, like Dante, was a former champion boxer, and he and Dante co-owned the boxing gym where they were both trainers. It was the same gym where Mia would be working the front desk once their planned expansion was complete. She currently worked as a front desk supervisor at one of the nice hotels downtown. As inseparable as she and Dante were, she had jumped at the chance to work at the gym.

I laughed to myself as I thought about how life had changed in the months since Mia had gotten together with Dante. The fact that I had a "group" at all was a huge change. Mia and I had been best friends since third grade, and there were a few co-workers I'd sometimes eat lunch or hit a happy hour with, but that was it. I loved to go out and be social, but I'd never been one to have a big circle of friends. My circle still wasn't big, but there was no denying I had one. Dante, Jamey, Cal and Kendrick were as close as brothers. They had basically adopted me along with Mia when she and Dante started going out. Dev and Dante had known each other for years. Dev had formed an even stronger bond with Dante, Mia, and Jamey when he and Jamey had together helped Dante to apprehend a former acquaintance who had attacked Mia. She hadn't been hurt, at least not seriously, but it had scared all of us and brought us closer.

Missing from our gathering today were Cal, Kendrick, and Dante's younger sister, Ellie, who all the guys except Dev called "princess", her childhood nickname. I'd only met her once or twice but she was in the process of moving to town, so I figured we'd see much more of her after that. Cal was usually pretty scarce, too, since he traveled so much for his job as a tour manager. And Kendrick…we saw Kendrick when he was able to tear himself away from the pub.

Mia caught my attention as she sat down in the chair next to me.

"What's going on, Mik? You ready for school?"

Before I could answer, Dev spoke up from where he sat on the other side of Mia.

"I didn't know you were in school, Meg. What are you studying?"

I leaned forward a little so I could see Dev better. I heard Dante and Jamey step out of Jamey's apartment behind me as I answered.

"Well, I haven't started just yet, but I'll be doing an online MBA program."

"Yeah? Good for you." Dev held his fist out and I reached over to bump it with my own. "That's impressive, Meg."

I smiled at Dev, but shook my head. "I don't know about that, but thanks. I applied really late so I was just glad I got accepted."

"Why an MBA? Is this for your job?"

I was momentarily distracted when I saw Jamey – shirtless and barefoot again, damn him – out of the corner of my eye. He didn't sit down along with Dante, but stayed standing at the edge of the group, hands in the front pockets of his shorts, looking down at the ground like he was thinking. I dragged my attention back to Dev's question, wondering what Jamey could be thinking about.

"Yes…well, sort of." Dev's quirked eyebrow at my vague response made me smile.

"I don't *need* it for my job, but my company will pay the tuition, and it will definitely help me get a promotion later."

"You see, she doesn't spend enough time working now," Mia said from next to me. "She wants to get promoted so she can work even more. Apparently the two bachelors degrees she already has aren't enough."

I reached over and poked Mia in her side, making her laugh.

"I don't actually have two degrees, I just had a double major in college. It's not a big deal."

Dante jumped in from where he sat on the other side of our little circle.

"Well, if an MBA and promotion are what you want, I think it's great that you're going for it."

Mia reached over and squeezed my arm.

"You know I think it's great, too. Even if it *is* Aaron's idea."

Mia winked at me as I rolled my eyes at her mention of Aaron, who she knew I hadn't been in contact with since the incident at his work event. But I had to give credit where it was due.

"Yes, it is. And he's right. It's something I should do."

"I guess, but I just worry about you working so much."

That made me smile. Mia was such a mother hen. Everybody should have a best friend like her.

"And you worry too much. You know I like to work hard and be busy. I'll figure it out."

Out of the corner of my eye I saw Jamey shift abruptly and realized he hadn't said a word since he and Dante had come out of his apartment. It wasn't like Jamey to have nothing to say. As I looked over at him, he pulled his phone out of his pocket, frowned at it for a second, then shoved it back in his pocket. He looked up and gave the group a quick smile that looked forced.

"Sorry, guys, I've gotta run. The new cook at the pub needs a hand."

Before anyone could get a word out, Jamey disappeared into his apartment, then reappeared almost as quickly, wearing a shirt and shoes this time, keys in hand. Raising his hand in a wave to us, he jogged down the stairs and out of sight.

Chapter 11

Jamey

She was getting an MBA.

When the fuck had that happened? She'd said she was just getting started so it had to be recent. How the hell had I missed it? I was practically obsessed with Meg at this point, but somehow I'd missed this news until now.

Hearing her say it had been like a kick to the stomach. And hearing her brush off her double major in college had made it worse. Thank God Dante and I had just stepped out of my apartment and nobody had been paying any attention to me. I was sure the look on my face would have given me away in those first few seconds.

I knew I should be proud of Meg and happy for her but all my selfish ass could think about was how much farther out of reach it put her. There was no way a highly educated ambitious rising star like Meg would settle for someone like me.

The secret I'd kept buried for years burned in my brain. It was something not even my closest friends, the men I considered my brothers, knew about me. Only one other person in the world knew that I was a high school dropout. Even then, it was only because she'd come across me in a moment of weakness, right after I'd realized that life had screwed me over yet again and, with one mis-step, had ensured that there was no way I was going to be able to graduate. She'd promised to keep my secret for me and I knew she had and would. I hated it, hated the way it would make people think of me if they knew. I'd worked for years to put it behind me, to overcome it and not let it dictate who and what I could be. But suddenly I felt the weight of shame and regret in a way I hadn't in a long time.

If I'd thought Meg was out of my league before, she was practically on a different planet now. I'd managed to ignore that fact for awhile, but it was as clear as a punch to the face now and equally as painful. And from what Mia had said it sounded like Meg was back with that dickhead Aaron again. I'd thought that she'd shown him the door after he'd driven off, drunk as shit, and left her, but I guess I'd gotten it wrong. It pissed me off that she'd let a guy treat her like that, but I had no right to tell her different.

Like a coward, I'd faked an urgent text from the pub to give me an excuse to leave. I couldn't believe I'd stooped to that, but I'd had to get out of there. I couldn't stand to hear her talk about it anymore. Any thoughts I may have let slip in about getting together with Meg were just a great example of me fooling myself. Guys like me didn't get women like Meg – that was the cold, hard reality.

I needed to get my head straight and leave Meg alone. I'd spent too many years fighting the voice in my head – the one that sounded a lot like my father – that told me I'd never be anything, never be good enough. After years, I'd finally gotten to a good place and had been doing fine for a long time. Then Meg had come along and all of the shit was floating right back to the surface. It wasn't her fault and she hadn't done it on purpose, but there was no denying that she'd knocked me off my hard-won center. I had to get back on my feet and find my balance again.

I couldn't avoid Meg completely, but I'd do what I could. She wasn't part of my world – not really. It had been a stupid dream to think she ever could be. No more fooling myself. As of today, that was done.

Chapter 12

Meg

Jamey was avoiding me.

At first I'd thought I was imagining it, but after last night I was sure. I'd gone to happy hour at the pub with some co-workers. Usually if Jamey saw me he make a point to come over and say hi. But not last night. Oh, he'd seen me. We'd locked eyes the second I walked in the door, almost like he'd known I'd be there and was watching for me. And had he come over? Had he even smiled at me from across the room?

No.

No, he had not.

He'd nodded at me. Nodded. Like I was an acquaintance or a friend of a friend of a friend he'd met once months ago. Then he'd looked away, said something to the bartender he'd been talking to, and turned and walked into the kitchen without looking back.

I hated to admit it, but it had hurt. Jamey and I had initially had a rocky start, but we'd gotten past that. In the past few weeks, we'd been friendly and even a little flirty. His comments about how smart and hot I was still made my head spin. So to have him all of a sudden start treating me like someone he barely knew and apparently didn't want to be around had me confused. I didn't know what was going on with him, but I was going to find out.

And I was going to use Mia as bait.

There was no way Jamey would ignore Mia if she was at the pub.

Other than Dante's mom and Cal and Kendrick's mom – both of whom had practically helped raise Jamey, according to Dante – Mia was Jamey's favorite person. Mia had that effect on a lot of people. She was one of the sweetest people on earth and somehow made you feel good just by being around her. So I got why she was a favorite of Jamey's, even if it did make me just the teeniest, tiniest bit jealous.

Normally I just tried to take Jamey's affection for Mia in stride, but today I was going to use it to my advantage. I'd asked Mia to meet me at the pub for a late lunch to get her read on how Jamey was acting around me. When I'd talked to her about it she'd said that she hadn't noticed a difference, other than the fact that Jamey hadn't been around much in the past week or so. She'd just chalked it up to him being busy at the pub, which was probably at least partly true, but it still didn't explain his behavior the night before. So she'd agreed to meet me and see what she thought. I was on a tight deadline at work and really didn't have time to leave for lunch, but I didn't care. I'd just work late – well, even later than my usual late nights – to make up for it. Whatever the hell was going on with Jamey, it needed to end today.

I'd asked Mia to wait for me in the parking lot of the pub so we could go in together. I knew she thought I was going overboard, and maybe I was, but I was on a mission. Mia got out of her car when she saw me pull in and met me by the front door with a quick hug.

She pushed her sunglasses to the top of her head as she turned to open the door.

"I still think you're reading too much into whatever's going on with Jamey, but we'll see what happens."

I didn't comment, just followed Mia into the pub and over to the bar. For once, Kendrick was absent and one of the other bartenders, Amy, was wiping down the bar. Amy was short and curvy, with bright green eyes and jet-black hair cut into a blunt bob. Amy was in her early forties and had worked at the pub since day one. She was loud and funny and, as Kendrick would tell you, one hell of a good bartender. We sat down at the bar and she headed our way.

"Good afternoon, ladies. What can I get you?" Amy took a last swipe at the bar, then tossed the bar rag on the sink.

Mia responded for both of us.

"Hey, Amy. A diet for each of us, please. And would mind telling Jamey I'd love to say hi if he has a minute?"

Amy gave Mia a wry smile as she filled two glasses for us.

"I'm pretty sure he always has a minute for you, doll."

We thanked Amy as she set our drinks up on the bar, then crossed to the kitchen door and stuck her head through to pass Mia's message along. I felt my stomach jump at the thought of Jamey walking through the door and seeing me sitting there along with Mia. I knew he wouldn't be expecting me and I was a little afraid what his reaction would be. But this was why I was here – to get to the bottom of whatever the hell Jamey's problem was – and I wasn't going to run away now just because he might not be happy to see me.

Just as I finished that thought, Jamey stepped through the door. He hesitated for half a second when he saw me and the smile he'd had on his face slipped a bit, then he seemed to catch himself. He continued our way, but instead of coming around and giving Mia a hug as he normally would, he stepped behind the bar. He would have had to walk past me to get to Mia and I felt a twinge in my heart at the thought that he hadn't hugged her because he'd wanted to avoid being even that close to me.

Coming even with Mia, Jamey folded his arms across his chest and looked at her. I looked over at him, but he kept his eyes focused on Mia.

"I was surprised when Amy told me you were here. You know I'm always happy to see you, honey, but I don't remember ever seeing you in here this time of day."

Jamey was right. It was different for both me and Mia to be there in the middle of a weekday. Though it was hard to tell if he was referring to both of us or just Mia since he still hadn't so much as looked at me.

Mia nodded and looked over at me.

"You're right, it's different, but Meg and I wanted to grab a late lunch."

Jamey finally glanced my way and acknowledged my presence with a quick "Hey, Meg."

His tone was flat and his eyes barely touched me before bouncing back to Mia. He went on before I could even return the greeting.

"What can I get you both?"

Mia asked for a burger and baked sweet potato fries – her favorite – and I asked for a house salad with no cheese and no dressing.

Mia bumped me with her shoulder.

"That's it? That's your whole lunch?"

I glanced at Jamey, not really wanting to discuss this is front of him. He stood, hands in his back pockets now, frowning down at the ground, but not moving toward the kitchen. He was obviously waiting for my answer, too.

"I've gained a couple pounds, so I need to dial back. A burger and sweet potato fries sounds great, but I can't afford the calories. I don't have your great metabolism."

I tried to keep my tone light and casual as I said it. Mia just rolled her eyes at me. I heard Jamey mumble something under his breath, then he raised his head and looked at me. Finally, really, looked me in the eye. His eyes were the color of storm clouds and when he spoke he made it clear he wasn't any happier than Mia with my lunch order.

"I'm putting some grilled chicken breast on your salad. It's good lean protein. Just shove it to the side if it's too fattening for you."

Jamey sounded rough and angry. He wasn't even trying to be polite at this point. Without another word, he turned and walked through the door to the back.

Mia and I sat looking at the door for a few seconds, then looked at each other.

"Ok, you're right. Something's up." Mia picked up her drink and took a sip.

"Yeah, ya think?" I picked up my drink and did the same, wishing there was more than just diet coke in the glass. "What the hell was that?"

"No idea." Mia stared again in the direction Jamey had gone. Finally shaking her head, she picked up her drink again. "I really don't know. Jamey's never moody, but now…it's like he wants to take care of you, but also wants to strangle you."

"Well, I'm definitely picking up on the 'wants to strangle you' part. The 'taking care of' part…not so much."

As I finished speaking, Kendrick pushed through the door from the back, and headed over to us.

"Afternoon, ladies. I heard you were here. It's good to see you both."

I wasn't sure that *everyone* at the pub thought it was good to see us, or at least me, but it was nice to hear it from Kendrick. He was a quiet guy, but he didn't miss much. He also had a hidden smartass side that we didn't see much, but he could be funny as hell when he let it fly.

"There you are! Thank God. We were worried that the bar was going to crumble into pieces without you standing behind it for so long."

Kendrick smirked in response to my comment and amusement lit his moss green eyes. He grabbed our glasses for a refill as he responded.

"Yeah, yeah. And this is coming from the person who works how many hours a week? Can I even count that high?"

See what I meant about that smartass side? What he said was true, though. I worked insane hours.

I laughed and raised my hands in surrender. "Touché."

"I think you're both crazy for working so much. I get that you both love what you do, but you need to relax and live a little." Mia was going to make a great mother someday. She already had the mom voice down perfect.

"As long as you lovely ladies visit me, that's all I need to be happy."

I didn't know what had gotten into Kendrick today. He was being way more playful than usual. His grin and his blatantly cheesy statement sounded exactly like his much more outgoing twin, Callahan.

"Wow, did Cal just walk in?" I twisted on the bar stool, looking behind me.

Kendrick and Mia laughed.

"And that's a touché for you, Meg," Kendrick said with a smile as a guest sitting down the bar caught his attention. "I'll be right back."

As Kendrick stepped away, a server brought our food and slid it onto the bar in front of us. Neither Mia nor I mentioned the fact that Jamey hadn't brought the food out to us himself as he usually did.

I looked down at what Jamey had sent out to me. True to his word, he'd made me a small grilled chicken breast, but he'd placed it to the side rather than directly on the salad, I guess taking care of the "shoving it to the side" that he'd mentioned earlier. But what really caught my eye was how he'd prepared my salad. He'd added extra veggies that he knew I liked and chopped everything up the way I preferred. He'd even included several lemon slices, letting me know he remembered that I would often squeeze lemon juice on my salads instead of using dressing when I was really watching my weight. So he'd made his stubborn point by including the chicken, then made my salad exactly the way he knew I'd want it without me asking. All while he was clearly pissed at me.

I sighed. Maybe I understood both parts of Mia's "he wants to take care of you and wants to strangle you" comment, after all.

As if hearing my thoughts, Mia looked over and pointed at my food.

"See? What did I say?"

She held out both hands like she was weighing two objects.

"Take care of you" - she bounced her right hand up and down – "strangle you" – she bounced her left.

She put her hands down and picked up the burger that was giving me serious food envy. I eyed her burger, then my salad and chicken. Feeling less than enthusiastic about my chosen lunch, I sighed again and picked up my fork.

"Yeah, I get it. That man is going to make me crazy."

"Of course he is." Mia spoke around the bite of burger she'd just taken. "That's what they do best."

We turned our conversation to other topics as we ate. I needed to figure out the puzzle of Jamey MacGregor, but I also wanted to catch up with Mia. I hadn't had much one-on-one time with Mia lately and I missed knowing what was going on with her. Kendrick chatted with us here and there in between serving guests and talking with employees.

Too soon it was time for both Mia and me to get back to the rest of our day. I still felt like I needed to try to clear the air with Jamey, so I hugged Mia, thanked her for meeting me, and sent her on way, then tried to figure out the best way to get Jamey back out front to talk with me. I was about to ask Kendrick to go find him for me when Jamey appeared. As he had earlier, he hesitated for a second when he saw me, then continued towards me. He reached for our empty lunch dishes and I heard him grunt as he noticed that I'd eaten everything, including the chicken. He set the dishes aside on a tray and turned back to me. Apparently he wasn't feeling quite rude enough to just walk away without a word. I waited, curious to see what he would say now that Mia wasn't there as a buffer. We stood there for a few awkward seconds, neither one of us speaking. Finally Jamey shifted, shoved his hands in his back pockets and met my eyes.

"I'm glad you ate the chicken. I'd say 'I told you so' but I'm afraid you'd punch me."

Jamey's lips quirked up in a faint smile and I felt myself smile back at him in return. I appreciated his attempt to lighten things up.

"No punching, I promise. Not today, anyway."

Jamey's smile grew a bit bigger at my words. He dropped his eyes to the floor, but stayed put where he was, so I continued on.

"I *do* eat, Jamey. I'm just so close to getting back down to my goal weight. I have two big consulting engagements coming up. I really need to lose these last four pounds again so I can feel confident and be at my best."

Jamey blew out a breath and shifted on his feet again.

"I don't get you, Meg. You're the best consultant your firm has and you can't feel confident unless you lose four pounds?"

I tried to keep my rising irritation under control. I crossed my arms over my chest and reminded myself to breathe.

"Why is this a big deal to you, Jamey? Are your feelings hurt again because I only want to eat healthy food? Are we back to that?"

Jamey just looked at me, his blue eyes stormy again.

"I have goals. You know that. Goals for my life, goals for my career, goals for my health. I set them, I work toward them, I achieve them. That's what I do. So yes, it will make me feel more confident if I know I've achieved my weight goal."

"Yeah, I know you're working on all these goals. That's all we hear about is which goal you're working on. My question is are those things Aaron wants for you? Or are they things you actually want for yourself?"

What the....? That was it. I'd had enough.

My fists hit my hips and I could feel my cheeks burn with anger.

"The real question is why you're being such a jerk! What is it about me having goals for myself that irritates you so much? Yes, Aaron's really focused on being fit. And yes, he helped me set my weight and fitness goals. And they're tough, just like all my other goals. I like to challenge myself. Why is that such a problem for you? Because you don't challenge yourself at all?"

I saw Jamey flinch, as if I'd struck him with a physical blow, and I immediately wanted to take back my harsh words. They weren't true and he didn't deserve them.

Jamey ran his hands through his hair, his frustration with me obvious.

"I'm not saying you shouldn't challenge yourself or want to be healthy. I'm saying you shouldn't obsess over a few pounds." Jamey exhaled roughly. "You're beautiful, Meg. Straight up fucking gorgeous. And a few pounds more or less isn't going to change that. You just..." Jamey shook his head as he looked away from me, then he met my eyes again. "You shouldn't be with a guy who makes you feel like less when you're everything a sane man could ever want."

He turned and walked away, pushing through the door to the kitchen as I stared at his back. I stood there, staring at the door, Jamey's words ringing in my head. I was gorgeous? Everything a man could want? Then why did he act like I was the last thing *he* wanted?

Kendrick caught my eye from the far end of the bar, concern clear on his face. I knew he'd stayed where he was, refilling bar items that probably didn't really need to be refilled right now, to give Jamey and me some space. But the pub was still relatively quiet at the moment and I knew he'd probably overheard at least part of our conversation. I walked over and sat back down on the bar stool closest to me, my brain swirling, not sure what to do next. Kendrick walked toward me, drying his hands on a bar towel, assessing my expression as he got closer.

"You alright, Meg?"

"Yes? Maybe? I don't know?" I shook my head at Kendrick's quiet laugh.

"I'm just confused. Obviously. Jamey just seems so mad at me."

Kendrick tucked the towel in its holder and reached for a couple of emptys sitting on the bar near me.

"Don't worry too much about it. Just give him a couple minutes and he'll settle down and be back out here."

We heard the back door of the pub slam, and Kendrick shook his head and huffed another quiet laugh. I looked at him and shrugged my shoulders, not sure what to do.

"Or... maybe not." Kendrick tossed the emptys in the bin and turned back to me. "Do you want to go talk to him or should I?"

I looked over at the kitchen door, hesitating, as Kendrick went on.

"For the record I think it really needs to be you, but I'll do it if you don't want to."

I hesitated for another second, then pushed myself off the barstool. "No, I'm the one he's mad at. I'll do it."

"If it helps I don't think he's mad at you exactly. I think he's...just mad."

Following Kendrick's instructions, I went through the kitchen door, down the hallway, and out the door to the back. I saw Jamey right away, leaned back against the wall, one leg bent, foot resting against the brick. He was smoking, and he turned to look at me, eyes narrowed, then turned his head to exhale the smoke away from me. I paused for a second, my hand still on the door, then let it close quietly. Jamey didn't say anything, just stood looking at the ground rather than at me. But he wasn't telling me to leave, wasn't walking away himself, so I took that as a positive sign.

"I didn't know you smoke." I hadn't meant to start with that. One minute it was in my head and the next minute I was blurting it out.

"I don't. I quit." Jamey moved his hand to flick ashes to the side. He brought the cigarette to his mouth, inhaling, then turned his head away from me to blow the smoke out again. "At least I had. Just another mark against me, I guess."

The sarcasm in his tone made my stomach clench. Jamey was usually so easy going, so confident and self-assured. I hated that something

I had done was making him act like this, even though I didn't really understand what it was. Whatever it was, I wanted to fix it.

"Jamey, I'm sorry I made you mad, both today and whatever I did to make you want to avoid me. I wasn't trying to criticize you or the pub, or…well, anything really. I just…I decide how I want something to be, set a goal for myself, and when I don't reach it, I…I get frustrated. I'm sorry if I talk too much about it. And I'm sorry my frustration spilled over on to you."

Jamey turned and stubbed out the rest of his cigarette in the covered bucket of sand obviously intended for that purpose. He turned back to face me, hands tucked in his front pockets, but kept his gaze on the ground between us.

"I'm not mad. Not really. At least not at you. I was just frustrated, too." Jamey raised his head and finally met my eyes. His hair was messy from running his hands through it and the muscles in his shoulders were bunched up, his whole body tense. "You sell yourself too short, Meg. There's nothing wrong with setting goals, just like there's nothing wrong with wanting to be healthy. As long as they're *your* goals, what you want for yourself, not what someone else is telling you that you *should* want or you *should* be."

I felt my irritation rise again at his words. "So I'm just supposed to do whatever I want and to hell with what anyone else thinks? We all have expectations we strive to meet, Jamey. And unless we're hermits, some of those expectations come from other people."

Jamey tilted his head back and exhaled a deep breath.

"You're right." He looked at me again, then shook his head. "And even if you're not, it's none of my business. You can live your life however you want. It has nothing to do with me."

I felt a pang in my chest at his words and barely suppressed a wince. Whatever thoughts I'd had that Jamey might be interested in me had clearly been wrong. I didn't respond, just stood where I was as Jamey moved past me to go back inside. As he drew even with me he stopped, his arm brushing my shoulder. He stood for a second, still looking straight ahead. When he spoke, his voice sounded rough.

"Just don't settle, Meg. You're worth so much more than that. You deserve the best."

His words made me catch my breath. I wanted to press closer but I was afraid of losing the moment, scared of breaking the fragile thread that seemed to tie us together.

I let myself look over at Jamey, studying his profile as he kept his eyes focused on the door in front of him.

"And Aaron's not the best?"

Jamey's eyes flicked toward me, then refocused on the door.

"You know better than that."

I swallowed hard and forced myself to ask what I really wanted to know.

"And you?"

Jamey's jaw clenched and I felt the muscles in his arm bunch. He dropped his head for a second, then stared resolutely straight ahead again. His answer, when it came, sounded like he'd dragged his voice through gravel.

"No, sweetheart, I'm not the best for you. You know better than that, too."

I didn't move as Jamey opened the door and stepped inside, letting it close quietly behind him.

Chapter 13

Jamey

I lingered near the front door of the gym, my ass perched on the edge of the reception desk, drink in hand. I'd been nursing the same beer since I got here almost an hour before and it was much too warm to drink at this point. I'd known it would be a mistake to come to the party to celebrate the grand re-opening of the renovated space, but there was no excuse I could think of short of being seriously ill or actually dead that would be acceptable.

I was happy for Dev and Dante. They had worked hard to build the quality and reputation of the gym. The financial backing from sponsors that had allowed them to renovate and expand was evidence of that. My reasons for not wanting to be here had nothing to do with how proud I was of them and everything to do with the beautiful blonde I was doing everything in my power to avoid. I'd seen glimpses of her across the gym, but so far had managed not to run into her.

Since the day I'd told Meg I wasn't good enough for her, she'd done her part to avoid me, too. She'd stopped coming into the pub altogether, either by herself or with her colleagues, and I hadn't run into her even once coming or going from Mia and Dante's apartment. Whether she hadn't been over or had just gone out of her way to make sure I wasn't there, I didn't know. The thought of Meg purposely avoiding me, thinking of ways not to be around me, made my stomach knot up and my chest tighten. I hated it, hated not seeing her, but for now it was the only way. In time the craving I had for her would lessen, would get to the point where I could be in the same space with her without wanting to drag her against me and kiss her senseless. I wasn't going to stop being around Dante and she wasn't going to stop being around Mia. As long as they were together, which would hopefully be forever,

Meg and I would have to find a way to coexist.

But right now, I still felt that craving in every part of my body and soul. I'd gotten used to seeing her regularly either at the apartment or at the pub, of getting a hit of her smile and scent, her sassy sense of humor and quick brain, just enough to feed my growing addiction. I'd never kissed her, never held her, barely even touched her, but the loss of her regular presence in my life was a physical ache. And I was just going to have to man up, grit my teeth, and get through it. I reminded myself for the thousandth time that it was better to step away now than to wait for Meg to kick me to the curb later when she found out how much better she could do than me. Chest tightening again at that thought, I stood up from the desk, ready to ditch my warm beer and slip out while everybody was caught up in the festivities.

Looking up, I saw Dante coming toward me and almost groaned out loud. He had a look of determination on his face that didn't bode well for me slipping out without an argument. I stood and waited for him, knowing he'd just follow me if I tried to avoid him. There was no one else near the desk, so at least we'd have some privacy for whatever Dante wanted to say to me. He didn't look pissed but it also didn't look like this was going to be a casual, friendly chat.

"Hey, Dante." I greeted Dante as he got closer to me. I'd seen him, Mia, and Dev for a couple minutes when I first came in, given him and Dev a fist bump and Mia a hug, but they'd been swarmed enough that I'd been able to move away pretty quickly after that. My main concern had been putting distance between myself and Mia before Meg inevitably showed up, but I'd also been hoping to avoid a conversation with Dante. I was sure Kendrick had talked to him and told him that he'd basically banned me from showing up at the pub for a couple days. I'd practically been living there, showing up even on the days I was supposed to be off. If I hadn't moved my bed with all of my other belongings to my new place across from Mia and Dante, I'd probably have slept upstairs in my old apartment above the pub. The kitchen at the pub was the one place I still felt in control, still felt like I knew what the hell I was doing, and I was spending as much time there as I could. It was the one place I could put my thoughts of Meg aside for a few minutes at a time, though she'd pop back up before long. I'd wonder what she'd think of a new dish or hear something that would make her laugh and she'd be right back front and center in my brain. But as usual, cooking calmed me, centered me, and I at least had peace for a few minutes at a time.

Dante stopped in front of me and just looked at me in that way he had. It was like he was trying to look inside me, to pull out answers to the questions in his mind without having to ask. After knowing him for so many years I was immune, and just stood waiting impatiently for him to get on with it.

He noticed me shifting around and he eyed me, eyebrow lifted in question. "You got somewhere to be?"

"I know you have something to say to me, Dante. Just spit it out already." I sounded more impatient than I'd intended but just being there, knowing I could come face-to-face with Meg at any moment, had used up more of my patience than I'd realized.

"Alright then." Dante crossed his arms and widened his stance a little like he was settling in for a confrontation. "What the fuck is wrong with you?"

Well, that was blunt, especially for Dante, but I kept my expression bland as I raised my beer to my mouth. "What do you mean?" I kept my tone casual and took a sip of beer. And promptly grimaced as the warm, flat liquid hit my tongue.

"Cut the bullshit, J. Kendrick says you're working crazy hours for no reason" – Damn it, I knew Kendrick would tattle on me like a little girl – "you haven't stopped by the apartment in almost two weeks, and you've stayed as close as possible to the door tonight, like you're going to bolt at any second."

I started to speak, but Dante's next words stopped me cold. "Mia said Meg's acting weird, too. Mia said she refused to go to the pub the other night and she hasn't wanted to come to the apartment, either, even to pick Mia up."

Well, I had my answer on that one. Meg truly had been avoiding me.

"Did you and Meg have a fight? I'd thought maybe you two were…" Dante's voice trailed off but his question was clear.

"No, we're not getting together," I said, my stomach clenching at my words. I forced my voice to stay even, made my words sound casual. "And no, we didn't have a fight just…a disagreement, maybe. It'll be fine."

There, that sounded normal enough.

Then I met Dante's eyes and knew that he wasn't buying it for a second. That was one bad thing about being friends with someone for so long. They saw through your crap and called you on it.

"I know you're into her, Jamey. It's obvious to anyone who knows you. Or hell, to anyone who's paying attention. I know she was with that idiot, Aaron, for a while, but she's not anymore. What's the problem?"

It was news to me that she'd broken things off with Aaron. My heart jumped for a second, but I clamped down on it just as fast. It was good that Meg had moved on from that asshole but that still didn't mean that I was the right guy for her. I was still a high school dropout and she was still a rising star on her way to a master's degree and a promotion.

"I'm not the right guy for her, Dante. I'm not," I insisted as Dante started to interrupt me. "She deserves a guy who can match her accomplishments. She has clients all over the country, she's in demand as an expert for some of the biggest companies. I'm just a guy who can cook and who runs a kitchen in a little pub in Kentucky. She needs a guy who's an expert like her, someone who's educated."

"You *are* an expert at what you do. And who the fuck cares about your education? She's not hiring you for a job, Jamey. She's not asking for your resume." I just shook my head at Dante as he went on.

"Mia's more educated than me. Do you think she cares? Do you think I care? I know Meg graduated from college and she's working on her masters for her job, but what difference does that make? You're normally one of the most confident guys I know, Jamey. So what if you just have a high school diploma?" I closed my eyes, Dante's words like a knife to my heart. "Other than Kendrick, that's all any of us guys have. Do you think Meg looks down on us for that? Do you think Mia does?"

I couldn't even look at him. "You don't know what you're talking about, Dante. Go back to your party. Leave this alone."

"Fine, then tell me. Tell me so I do know. Something's wrong, Jamey. I can't leave it alone."

The frustration was clear in Dante's voice and on his face. This was hurting him, *I* was hurting him, by refusing to tell him what was going on. He knew something was wrong and couldn't understand why I wouldn't let him help me fix it.

Suddenly I felt defeated, tired. I'd kept this secret buried so deep for so long. Maybe it was time to let it out, just get it over with once and for all. I knew I was still backsliding, the old feelings of inadequacy threatening to overwhelm me. I'd started smoking again, a habit I'd kicked years ago. Those voices in my head telling me that I wasn't good enough were still lurking right around the corner. I'd come so far, fought so hard to silence those voices and get to where I was. I was proud of all I'd taught myself, proud of the work I did at the pub, but lately the doubts were sliding in more and more.

Giving in, I raised my eyes to Dante's. I let him see my worry, not even trying to hide it.

"Fine, you win." So I wasn't exactly giving in gracefully. "Where can we talk in private?" There was no one near us but I didn't want to take the chance of anyone walking up.

"Let's go to the office." Dante turned and led the way, raising his hand in acknowledgement a couple times as people we passed said their congratulations, but not stopping or slowing down to chat.

As I followed Dante, I felt my stomach start to churn. I reminded myself that Dante was my brother. I was closer to him and Cal and Kendrick than anyone on earth. We'd had each other's backs since we were kids. This wasn't going to change that. Dante and the others would be my brothers no matter what. I repeated that to myself as Dante closed the office door behind us. We could still hear the noise from the party, but it was muffled.

"You're sure you want to do this now? It can wait til after the party. You deserve this celebration."

I was delaying the inevitable, but this was Dante's big night. I felt like shit pulling him away from it, even if he was the one who had forced the conversation.

"Fuck the party. Tell me." Dante stood as he had before, arms crossed over his chest, stance wide as if he was braced to take whatever he needed to.

I sat on the edge of the desk, took a deep breath, and ripped off the bandage.

"I never graduated from high school."

There was no sound from Dante. I lifted my head to see his reaction. He shifted to stand with his hands on his hips, a frown of confusion on his face.

"What do you mean, you never graduated from high school? How is that possible? You went all the way through. I know the rest of us were a year behind you, but we saw you at school every day."

"I did go all the way through, but I failed civics class my senior year. You know I sucked at memorizing facts and spitting them back and that's all that class was. So I failed it. That class is a requirement. Without it, I couldn't graduate. I was supposed to make it up in summer school, but that would have cost money I didn't have. So I didn't take it. And I never graduated."

"Jamey..man." Dante rubbed his hand over his head and down his face. "Why didn't you say anything? We would have figured something out."

"I felt stupid enough failing the fucking class. I wasn't going to ask my friends for money for summer school. And there was no way I was going to my dad for it. You know when I moved out he made it clear I was on my own. Besides, it would have just been more ammunition for him to tell me what a fuck-up I was."

"Yeah, I know you're right." Dante crossed the room and sat on the edge of the couch that took up one wall. He leaned forward, forearms resting on his thighs and looked at me.

"By why didn't you ever tell us? Why keep it a secret?"

I shrugged, knowing I didn't really have a good reason.

"I just felt stupid. Who the fuck fails civics? And then I guess I was ashamed that I couldn't put a few hundred dollars together for summer school. Since I was eighteen and living on my own the school didn't contact my dad. It wasn't like I'd planned to go to graduation anyway. I skipped it to hang out with you guys like I would have anyway and just never said anything. Everyone just assumed I graduated and I let you. It just never came up. It's not like I was going to casually bring it up in conversation like 'Oh yeah, by the way, I'm a high school dropout. I couldn't even achieve that basic milestone.'"

"I just can't believe you never told us. I know I'm making this all about me right now and it's not, but...did anybody know?"

I paused a second, knowing this answer was going to make things worse, not better, but also knowing that I couldn't avoid it without lying to my brother's face, something I'd never do.

"Ellie knows."

Dante sat up straight and his frown intensified. "My sister knew? Why? Why her and not me?"

The betrayal in Dante's voice made me cringe. This might be worse than I thought.

"I didn't tell her on purpose. She saw me right after I found out, right after I realized that I didn't have the money for summer school. She caught me kicking the shit out of that beater car I used to drive. She got it out of me before I even knew what she was doing. You know how Ellie is."

Dante grunted and I took that for agreement. His sister could worm information out of you like no one else I'd ever known. The FBI and CIA had missed out big by not recruiting Ellie.

"She promised not to say anything until I figured out a way to tell you guys. I never did, so she never has either."

Dante rubbed his hands over his head again like he was trying to think.

"Okay, I guess I see how all of this could happen, especially with the way your life was back then."

I relaxed for a second, relieved that the betrayal and confusion were gone from Dante's voice and expression. I tensed right back up as he went on.

"But why let it get in the way of something with Meg now? She's not gonna care, Jamey. She has a ton of respect for what you do."

"You're wrong, Dante. It will get in the way whether I want it to or not. She might be impressed by the fact that I can cook because it's something she apparently sucks at. That's one thing. But in the long run, with her degrees and consulting all over the country and her big goals for herself, is she really going to want to be with some guy who didn't even graduate from high school? Even if we did get together, sooner or later she'll realize she can do better. I'm just saving us both the wasted time along the way."

Chapter 14

Jamey

I was still brooding about my conversation with Dante almost a week later. Now that Dante knew my secret, I needed to find a time to tell Kendrick and Cal. But that wasn't what had me brooding. It was the questions running in a loop in my brain. Could I really tell Meg? Was it possible that she wouldn't care? Was it worth the risk to tell her? I realized that it might be a moot point. I wasn't even sure if Meg was interested in me, or interested in anyone for that matter, since she'd just recently broken up with that ass, Aaron. She and I had flirted a little and she'd asked that one question about whether I was the best guy for her, but nothing beyond that. How much was I willing to risk to figure out if Meg wanted me at all, then to see if she still wanted me after learning that I'd never graduated high school?

Lost in my own head, I jumped when my phone rang. The sound was jarring in the quiet of my apartment. I'd spent the day running errands – forced into another day off from the pub by a concerned Kendrick – but was still full of nervous energy. Before I'd gotten tangled up in thoughts of Meg again, I'd been thinking about heading into the kitchen to find something to cook. Cooking always calmed me down. I put that thought and my thoughts of Meg on hold while I answered the phone. I settled back on the couch and hit the speaker button.

"Yeah." It wasn't the most cordial way to answer, but anyone who knew me knew what to expect.

As if I'd conjured her up with my thoughts, Meg's voice rose loud and clear through my phone. As soon as she began to talk, the panic and stress in her voice had me sitting straight up from my slouched position.

"Jamey? Oh thank God. Thank you so much for answering. I really need your help."

I didn't even hesitate. I sat forward on the couch, my whole body tensed, needing to get to Meg. I stared at my phone as if I'd be able to see her if I just stared hard enough.

"Where are you, Meg? Are you hurt?"

"No, I'm not hurt."

I relaxed just a fraction, then tensed again as her next words sounded like she was close to tears.

"I'm at home. I'm supposed to be making dinner for my dad and his new wife and I've completely ruined it! I made a huge mess of it, Jamey, and I don't know what to do. They're going to be here in an hour. I guess I can order something to be delivered, but I made a big deal over the fact that I was going to cook for them. Why did I say that? I know I can't cook! Jamey, what do I do?"

If there was one thing I could fix for Meg, this was it. The need to jump through the phone, take her in my arms, and tell her everything was going to be okay was overwhelming. Since I couldn't do that, I did the next best thing.

"Meg, just listen, okay? I'm on my way. We're going to fix it and everything is going to be fine. Don't be upset, alright? It will all be okay."

"You're coming here?" I heard Meg breath out and it sounded like a sigh of relief. "Jamey, you're the best. I'll pay you back somehow, I promise."

I carried my phone with me as I moved toward my bedroom to change out of my old sweats and find some shoes.

"Not necessary. I'm glad I can help. I'm headed out now. Don't panic, sweetheart. I'll be there soon."

I realized too late that the "sweetheart" had slipped out and I waited to see how Meg would react. Either she didn't hear it, she'd decided she didn't hate it, or she chose to ignore it.

"Okay, I'll try. I'll clean up the mess so it won't be in the way. Thank you, Jamey."

Meg hung up before I could respond. I tossed the phone on the bed, pulled on clean jeans, a t-shirt and shoes, and ran to help my girl.

⌢

I pulled into a spot near Meg's condo in record time. I had her address in my phone from when I'd called the rideshare to take her home a couple months before. She lived in a popular area on a well-known street. I'd taken every shortcut I knew to get to her as quickly as I could. As I'd driven, I'd flipped through potential entrees in my head. Not knowing what ingredients or cookware or anything Meg had in her kitchen made it difficult, but I was confident I could come up with something.

Meg must have been watching for me, because she opened her door for me as I hurried up her sidewalk. She looked gorgeous as always, blonde curls spilling across her shoulders and a pretty blue sweater molding itself to her curves. The sweater made the blue of her eyes even more vibrant than usual. Those eyes were full of gratitude as they met mine.

Meg stepped back as I stepped through the door.

"Jamey, I am so glad to see you."

Knowing that was only because she needed my help, and wishing that it meant more, I just acknowledged her statement with a quick smile and moved on.

"The cavalry has arrived. Show me what we have to work with."

Meg led the way to the kitchen while I concentrated on keeping my eyes off her perfect ass. If I was here for different reasons, maybe I'd let myself look, but as it was, I didn't feel like I should. Once I stepped into Meg's kitchen I felt some of my tension ease. It was a beautiful kitchen, well laid out, with ample room for both prep and cooking. She had several pots hanging on a rack, a decent-looking set of knives in a holder, and a crock full of various kitchen tools sitting on the counter. For someone who claimed not to cook, her kitchen looked pretty well equipped. When I mentioned that, she looked around as if seeing some of the items for the first time.

"That's all my mom. She's a really good cook, but the kitchen she has now is small. When she visits she likes to go all out. The pans and the knives and everything are mostly for her."

"Remember to thank her for me the next time you talk with her. She's set us up really well."

I rubbed my hands together, still looking around the kitchen.

"Time to get down to business. What do we have to work with in terms of food and how much time do we have?"

Meg waved her hand toward the cabinets and fridge.

"Feel free to look through everything. I have the basics – milk, eggs, some veggies, pasta, chocolate sauce – but you'd know better what you're looking for."

I couldn't resist teasing her as I moved toward her fridge to check out the contents.

"Chocolate sauce is a basic?"

Her face lit up with a smile and I could see some of the tension leave her shoulders.

"In my house it is. Chocolate sauce and wine. Pantry staples."

"Good to know. Those could come in handy."

I peered into Meg's fridge, cataloging the contents, considering and rejecting dishes in my head as I went.

"And how long do we have?"

I saw Meg fidget from the corner of my eye and prepared myself for the worst.

"A little less than half an hour."

She sounded nervous, like she thought I might yell at her for not giving me enough time. I looked over to reassure her.

"Plenty of time, as long as we stick with something simple."

Meg didn't look convinced. I turned to face her fully, making sure she met my eyes before I spoke.

"Meg, we've got this. Trust me, okay?"

She held my eyes for a second, then nodded.

"I trust you, Jamey. Just tell me how I can help."

I turned back to her fridge, scanning the contents again. I saw eggs, butter, quality parmesan cheese... and an idea started to form in my head.

I turned my head to look at Meg again.

"You said you had pasta, right? What kind?"

Meg hurried over to open a cabinet. I could see boxed foods and canned goods on the shelves.

"I have linguine and penne."

That was what I wanted to hear.

"Okay, good."

I opened her freezer and saw a box of frozen peas in among the other frozen goods. Not my favorite thing to cook with, but they'd do. I needed one more key ingredient and we'd have our entrée.

"How about bacon?" I hadn't noticed any in the fridge, but maybe I'd missed it.

Meg shook her head, and twisted a piece of hair around her finger, looking worried again. I was already thinking of alternate dishes, when she gave me much better news than I'd expected.

"No bacon, but I do have pancetta. I was going to make pancetta-wrapped asparagus for my dad. He loves asparagus."

The rest of the menu fell neatly into place in my brain.

"So you have pancetta and fresh asparagus?"

Meg nodded at me, her expression cautiously hopeful.

"I do. Is that good?"

I started pulling ingredients out of the fridge while I answered.

"No, sweetheart. It's perfect."

I was so happy that not only were we going to be able to pull this off, but also make a great meal in a pinch, that I didn't even care that I'd slipped up on the "sweetheart" again. I just needed to check one more thing before we started.

"Last question. Any food allergies we need to worry about – gluten, dairy, egg, anything?"

Meg was shaking her head even as I was speaking.

"No, nothing. Have you figured out what to make?"

I turned to face her, leaning back on the counter.

"How about linguine carbonara and oven-roasted asparagus? We'll have to steal the pancetta from the asparagus to use it for the carbonara, but we can season the asparagus with garlic, pepper, and lemon if you have those."

Meg nodded and smiled her pretty smile. She looked like upbeat, energetic Meg again. I hoped to never see the stress and panic from earlier in her eyes ever again.

"That sounds perfect, Jamey. My dad and Catherine will love that. I can't believe you looked in the fridge for all of about 30 seconds and came up with a complete meal."

I had to grin at Meg's tone. She sounded both awed and a little annoyed.

"Years of practice. Alright, let's get moving."

I set Meg to work gathering pans and utensils we'd need while I grabbed more ingredients from the fridge and cabinets. Soon Meg was working away trimming the asparagus as I cut the pancetta in strips and set some peas to thaw. Meg got a pot of water boiling for the linguine, I prepped the eggs and opened a bottle of white wine. As Meg finished one task, she asked me what to do next, then moved on to that. We worked together smoothly, never bumping into each other, never getting in each other's way. I knew better than most people how difficult it could be to get used to cooking with someone else in the same space, the amount of patience often required to integrate even an experienced new staff member into the flow and patterns of the kitchen. With Meg and me it was as if we'd cooked together a hundred times. We didn't talk much, both of us focused on doing what we needed to do, but the silence was comfortable and easy. The thought came to me that this was something I wanted to do again. Sharing this with Meg, spending time with her this way, was messing with my head a little. It felt like the pieces of my life were coming together right in front of me in an unexpected way. I looked over at Meg, a little frown of concentration on her face as she carefully placed the asparagus in the roasting pan, and felt my heart jolt at the rightness of being here with her.

She looked up and smiled when she saw me watching.

"Look okay?" She glanced down at the pan again, reaching out to move a stalk of asparagus a millimeter to the right.

"Looks perfect." I wasn't talking about the asparagus, but I knew she'd never realize it.

"Good." She set the pan of asparagus on the counter next to the stove, staging it to go in the oven when the time came, then looked around the kitchen.

"What's next?"

I looked over what we'd done and checked the time again. Just a few minutes before her dad and stepmother were set to arrive. We were right on track.

"We're good in here. You probably have time to set the table like you wanted to."

Meg had mentioned earlier that she planned to pull out the "good dishes" for dinner. It seemed a little formal to me since it was just her dad and stepmother, but what did I know? My dad and I could barely speak a civil word to each other and hadn't done even that much in years. And Meg's need to impress her parents was clear. Her near panic at almost ruining what seemed like it should be a simple dinner at home said volumes. I was glad I'd been able to help her.

I was slipping the asparagus into the oven when the doorbell rang. Perfect timing. Meg's guests could have a few minutes to settle before dinner was ready to go. I'd finish things up and get everything ready to serve, then turn things over to Meg. She'd bought cannoli from a tiny bakery downtown for dessert, so my help wouldn't be needed there. Once dinner was ready to leave the kitchen, I would head home and let Meg and her guests enjoy their night.

I heard voices in the front hallway, then they moved away from the kitchen into what I assumed was Meg's living room. I was checking the linguine when Meg rushed back into the kitchen a few minutes later.

"I'm sorry, Jamey. I didn't mean to leave you to do everything." Meg's face was flushed, her cheeks pink and her blue eyes bright. I could almost feel her nerves from across the kitchen. She crossed to the bottle of wine I'd opened earlier for the carbonara and reached for wine glasses in a nearby cabinet.

"No problem at all." Compared to what I handled almost every day at the pub, it was no trouble to have only two dishes to worry about. "We're just a few minutes away from dinner. Do you want me to plate it individually or go with family-style?"

Meg finished gathering the glasses and wine and turned, her head tilted as if she was considering the options.

"Let's do family-style. Catherine barely eats. I don't want to waste your incredible food by putting it on her plate if she's not going to eat it."

I couldn't help but grin at her assessment of the food.

"That's pretty high praise for food you haven't even tasted yet."

She rolled her eyes over her shoulder at me as she crossed the kitchen with the glasses and wine in her hands.

"Please, Jamey. *You* made it. I have no doubt it's amazing."

She nodded toward the top cabinet next to stove.

"Serving plates and bowls are in that cabinet. I'll be right back to help."

I stood for a second as Meg left the kitchen, feeling the warm buzz in my chest from the compliment she had just given me. I had no idea why this girl got to me the way she did, but I couldn't deny it was true. Shaking my head to get myself moving, I turned to open the cabinet Meg had pointed out. Reaching up to the top shelf I pulled down a serving plate and bowl. I chuckled a little wondering how Meg, who was a good eight inches or more shorter than me could possibly reach them.

"What has you so amused?" Meg asked as she walked back into the kitchen. When I told her, she smiled back at me.

"That tells you how much cooking I do and how often I use my serving pieces. My mom bought them for me, I guess hoping they would help motivate me to cook, but it hasn't worked yet."

I couldn't help but think if we were together, I'd change her mind about that. But we weren't and it wasn't my place to change her mind about anything. That was that.

I pulled my mind back to the task at hand.

"Everything is pretty much ready to go. It'll hold for a few minutes if you don't want to eat this second, but I wouldn't hold either dish beyond that. I know you haven't had much time to visit yet, but..."

"No, now is good. My dad and Catherine always eat early so they were ready as soon as they walked in the door. I already told them to go ahead and have a seat in the dining room."

I tossed the pasta with the sauce and poured it into the bowl as Meg arranged the asparagus on the serving plate. I squeezed a little fresh lemon juice on the asparagus as Meg pulled serving utensils from a drawer. As I looked at both dishes, I was satisfied with a job well done, glad that I'd been able to help Meg when she needed me.

I found myself wishing I could stay, nowhere near ready to give up the close proximity I'd shared with Meg over the past hour or so. But I knew that it was time for me to go.

"Alright, then. You're all ready to go. I can let myself out. You have a good evening, okay?"

I hadn't even taken a step when Meg stopped me, a frown on her pretty face.

"You're leaving?" Shaking her head, Meg stepped closer. "Jamey, you can't leave. You have to stay. You're the one who made all of this."

Meg looked over at the food, then back at me. As soon as I saw the plea in her eyes, I knew I was going to stay. There was no way I was going to be able to resist her. Still, I tried. I crossed my arms over my chest and widened my stance a bit, bracing myself against Meg's pull.

"You made it, too. You don't want me here, Meg. This is your family."

Meg stepped closer again and I could just pick up her light scent. Her little pink tongue slipped out to wet her full lower lip, making me want to close the small distance between us, cover her mouth with mine, and slide my tongue along hers.

"I do want you here. I set a place for you, Jamey. It never occurred to me that you would leave. I know my dad and Catherine would love to meet you. Please, Jamey?" Looking in her beautiful blue eyes, I could tell she was sincere. She really did want me to stay. I knew it was a mistake to do it, to let myself have the illusion of belonging with Meg, even for the evening. But I also knew it would take a stronger man than me to walk away and disappoint her.

"Okay, I'll stay."

Joy flared in Meg's eyes and it was all I could do not to grab her and pull her into me. Instead I dropped my arms, and stepped back, reaching for the food. I was going to stay, but I was also going to remind myself that this wasn't a big deal. I was staying for dinner because I happened to be here. This evening meant nothing beyond that.

~

I followed Meg into the dining room. Seated at the table were a man who appeared to be in his early fifties with touches of gray in his light brown hair and a woman who looked significantly younger. Her dark brown hair showed no signs of gray and, unlike the man, there were no wrinkles evident on her face. Either Meg's father had married a much younger woman or she put a significant amount of time and money into making it look that way. They were both dressed somewhat conservatively and looked "country club fit" like they each golfed or played tennis or swam at the club regularly.

As we walked toward the table, I saw Meg's stepmother take notice of the tattoos covering both of my arms and the backs of my hands. Considering I had a short-sleeve t-shirt on, they were honestly kind of hard to miss. Bracing myself to see judgement fill her eyes, I was surprised when she merely seemed to take note of them, then turned her attention to Meg as we set the food down and Meg introduced me.

"Dad, Catherine, this is Jamey. Jamey, this is my dad, Ron, and his wife, Catherine."

We all exchanged "hellos" and "nice to meet yous" as I held Meg's chair for her, then seated myself. Everyone served themselves as Meg poured glasses of water from the carafe she'd set on the table.

"Jamey runs the kitchen at that pub I was telling you about, Brothers Pub, near where Mia lives?"

Ron & Catherine responded that they remembered as Meg turned to me with a smile.

"I have to confess that Jamey's responsible for the fact that we have an edible dinner tonight. I was determined to get it right this time but" – Meg shrugged – "I ran into a little trouble and Jamey came to the rescue."

I was a little surprised she'd admitted that after her panic about making a bad impression. I smiled back at her but shook my head.

"We both made dinner. You would have figured it out on your own, but I was glad to help."

Ron and Catherine laughed as Meg shook her head at me in return. Ron smiled as he looked at his daughter.

"If you were talking about anything other than cooking, I'd agree with you that Meg could figure it out on her own. I'd put my money on

Meg to do anything else she set her mind to. Cooking, though…" The smile on his face widened. "We've been witness to enough culinary mishaps by Meg to know that's just not one of her many talents."

"Gee, thanks, Dad." Meg rolled her eyes as her cheeks turned a faint shade of pink. "Please embarrass me more in front of the best cook I've ever met. And I will deny it to the death if you tell Mom I said that."

We all promised never to mention it and I was surprised to find myself enjoying the company. As stressed as Meg was over living up to her parents' expectations, I'd expected her dad to be stiff and domineering. I'd had no idea what to expect of her stepmother, particularly given Meg's "Catherine barely eats" comment earlier. Granted, it had only been a few minutes, but neither Ron nor Catherine seemed like the type to force Meg's life in one direction or another.

We began eating and the conversation turned to the condo Ron and Catherine were trying to buy. Everything that could go wrong, had, in a "you can't make this stuff up" kind of way. Ron and Catherine recounted one setback after another, laughing and groaning, the strength of their connection shining through it all. It was clear that no matter what the circumstance, they were in it together.

Wondering what it would be like to have that kind of connection, I almost missed Catherine's compliment on the food.

"This really is wonderful, Jamey. I'd love to have the recipes if you don't mind sharing them."

A little surprised, I reached up and rubbed the back of my neck. I was glad everyone was enjoying the food, but they were acting like I'd created something special when in reality we'd just thrown together something quick.

"I don't really cook from recipes, but yeah, I'll try to write down what we did."

Catherine thanked me as Meg looked at me curiously.

"So you never use recipes? How do you learn to make something new?"

"If something seems a little complicated or I'm making it for the first time, yeah, I'll check out a recipe to get a general idea. And we follow recipes at the pub for consistency. Other than that, I just wing it."

I had to laugh at the pouty face Meg gave me. She looked truly offended that I didn't follow recipes and it was cute as hell.

Catherine smiled at Meg, as well.

"It looks like Meg's as jealous of your cooking abilities as I am. Did you go to culinary school?"

I had to fight to keep a straight face. My "school" had been the many years working long hours in the kitchens of little dive bars and family diners, before eventually moving on to larger kitchens once I'd gained more experience.

"No, no culinary school for me, just on the job training. I guess my teachers were all the experienced cooks along the way who took the time to show me how to do things. Add that to time trying things out on my own, and" – I spread my arms wide for a second – "here I am."

"We're lucky you are. And that you choose to share your gift with us."

Meg reached over and lightly squeezed my arm, her words and her action shocking the hell out of me. I wasn't too humble to admit I was a good cook, but what was this about a "gift"?

"Hear, hear." Ron raised his wine glass in a toast to me, with Meg and Catherine joining in.

I managed to say thanks while hopefully hiding how my head was buzzing. All the attention and praise directed at something that was such a core part of me had me a little off balance. And the way Meg was looking at me, admiration shining in her eyes, was really doing a number on me.

Thankfully, Meg mentioned dessert. She and Catherine stood and started gathering dishes from the table. I rose to help but was waved back into my chair by Meg.

Needing to get myself back on a more even keel, as Meg and Catherine headed toward the kitchen to make coffee and get the cannoli, I volunteered, "You'll be glad I had nothing to do with making dessert. I can't bake to save my life."

"Oh, thank God, he's human after all," Meg responded as she and Catherine disappeared into the kitchen.

That was the sassy Meg I knew. She was much less confusing than the sweet sincere version who had been sitting next to me a few minutes before.

Ron drank the last of his wine, then set his glass down. I could feel the questions ready to start in 3..2..

"How did you and Meg meet?"

And here we went.

Ron seemed like a good guy and we'd been having a nice time, but I was sure I was about to get warned away from Meg. It would be done subtly and politely, but the message would be the same. Meg deserved a man who was more like her.

I forced myself to relax and answer Ron's question. No need to get all tensed up about it. We both knew where this was going.

"We have mutual friends. Her friend, Mia, is with my friend, Dante."

At the mention of Mia, Ron nodded.

"Mia is a sweet girl. Incredibly shy growing up. At times it was funny to see her and Meg together. They were such an odd pair – bold, outspoken Meg and shy, quiet Mia."

He chuckled softly as he shook his head.

"The things those two would get into. And God only knows what Meg would have dreamed up if Mia hadn't been there to balance her. In some ways, that's still true now. If you know Meg at all, you know how driven she is."

He glanced at me for a moment as I nodded in confirmation. Yeah, I was well aware of a lot of things about Meg and one of those was definitely her drive to achieve.

Ron went on.

"She's always been that way to some extent. Her mother and I encouraged it, maybe too much, when she was younger. We talked to her a lot about striving to be the best at everything she did. We wanted her to set high expectations for herself. Doesn't every parent want that?"

When Ron looked at me this time, I could only respond with a shrug. My mom had died long before I was old enough to achieve much of anything and the only expectations my dad had set were to get a damn job to help pay the damn bills and to get the hell out when I turned 18. Oh, and the expectation that I was too stupid to amount to much in life. He wasn't exactly "parent of the year" material.

Ron took in my shrug and went on.

"Well, anyway, we only intended to cheer her on, so to speak, but I'm not sure we did her any favors. She's always been really hard on herself. It became even more obvious in her late teens when her mother and I divorced. Suddenly she had a personal goal statement and checklists and life milestones all mapped out."

Ron huffed out a laugh.

"I'll tell you…I ran a successful business for 31 years without every writing a personal goal statement. There's nothing wrong with having checklists and a plan – of course there's not – but sometimes I wonder…"

He looked down at the empty wine glass he still held loosely between his hands, then back up at me, the love and concern he felt for Meg filling his eyes.

"I wonder if any of it makes her happy."

I shifted in my chair, not sure I should share this but…

"Funny you should say that. Meg and I had a similar conversation a couple of weeks ago."

Ron nodded at my comment.

"Good. I'm glad she has you in her life to try to help her balance, like Mia does. Achievements are to be celebrated, no question. But at the end of the day, what I want most is for my girl to be happy."

Ron met my eyes directly as he said that and I knew he was saying much more than his words. He was telling me that Meg's happiness was the priority and ultimately asking my intentions. I knew that I should tell him that Meg and I were barely even friends – more like acquaintances, really – and that she hadn't given me a place in her life to even try to make her happy. But even if I should respond that way, I knew I wouldn't. If I was being honest – with both Ron and myself – I wanted that place in Meg's life. I wanted to be the one to try to make sure she was happy. I hadn't been acting like it, and I sure as hell didn't deserve it, but I wanted it, anyway.

Hearing Meg and Catherine's voices as they started back to the dining room from the kitchen, I met Ron's eyes and gave him the answer he was looking for, the one I knew was the truth.

"Yes, sir. That's what I want most, too."

Chapter 15

Meg

I waved at my dad and Catherine as they pulled out of my driveway, then shut the door and leaned back on it. We'd had a great evening and they'd both mentioned that they hoped to see more of Jamey in the future. I'd realized pretty quickly that my dad and Catherine had assumed Jamey and I were together. Jamey had to have realized it, too – it was obvious based on the comments they'd made and the looks they'd given us – but for some reason both Jamey and I had just let it go without clarifying that under normal circumstances Jamey barely spoke to me anymore. He'd been different tonight, though, so maybe he was over whatever had made him go from friendly flirting with me to acting like he wanted to be anywhere else when I was around.

I stepped into the kitchen and saw Jamey loading the dishwasher. The man obviously didn't listen at all.

"Jamey, I told you to leave the dishes and I'd get them later."

Jamey shot me a quick grin as he leaned over to put the last dish in, then straightened up and closed the dishwasher. He leaned back against the counter and crossed his arms over his chest, highlighting those damn spectacular biceps of his. Thank God he at least had a shirt on this time. It was hard enough to focus on his words as it was.

"You have to be the only woman who's ever complained that a

man *did* load the dishwasher."

That wicked grin of his should be illegal, too. And he had a point, but…

"And you have to be one of the most stubborn men I've ever met."

Still grinning, he tilted his head like he was considering that.

"Eh, maybe, when it comes to some stuff. Probably guilty as charged."

Jamey remained where he was, leaning back against the counter like he was settled in. I was honestly surprised that he hadn't headed for the door the second we were done with dinner. I'd thought he was likely just being polite to my dad and Catherine, but now they were gone and he was still here, talking with me like he had all night.

Hoping that meant that the recent freeze-out I'd experienced from him was over, I settled back, too, against the counter behind me.

"Well, stubborn or not, you're an amazing person, Jamey. I really, *really* appreciate your help tonight."

For a second I was worried that I'd said the wrong thing. Jamey shifted like he was suddenly restless and dropped his eyes from mine. I was sure he was about to make an excuse to head for the door. But then he settled back against the counter and shrugged. He met my eyes again, but his smile looked forced this time.

"It wasn't anything special. I was glad to help. Anyone else would have done the same."

"Come on, Jamey." I wasn't going to let him get away with brushing this off. As cocky and confident as he always seemed on the surface, I'd noticed that he always downplayed compliments and brushed off praise, almost like it embarrassed him. He'd gone out of his way to help me and we both knew it.

"Maybe if I was your best friend or…" *Crap! I'd almost said girl-friend..* "or someone you were close to, then it wouldn't be as big a thing, although I kind of still think it would be. But you don't even like me and you dropped everything without question, rushed over here, and spent your whole evening helping me. In my book, that makes you pretty special. So there."

I'd hoped that my smartass "so there" would make Jamey smile, for real this time, and maybe just acknowledge the compliment with a smartass comment of his own. Instead he frowned at me, lowering his hands to grip the counter on either side of his hips.

"What makes you think I don't like you?"

Jamey's voice was rougher than it had been a minute ago, his tone serious. I couldn't believe his question, though. Was he really going to make me say this out loud? He looked at me as if he was really waiting for an answer. Okay, I guess he *was* going to make me say it.

"Really, Jamey? What makes me think that?"

Both my tone and my look told Jamey to cut the bullshit. We both knew how he'd acted around me for the past few weeks. I wasn't trying to start a fight, especially after he'd been so great to me over the past few hours, but I also wasn't going to act like he'd been warm and friendly to me recently. The abrupt change in his behavior toward me had hurt. I knew he'd be able to hear that in my voice, but I couldn't hold it back now that I'd gotten started.

"Hmm, let's see. Maybe it's the fact that you suddenly seem to never be around when I am and barely look at me or talk to me when you can't avoid being in the same space with me. Or the fact that you never come out of the kitchen at the pub anymore when I'm there and duck right into the back if you're out behind the bar when I walk in. I don't know what I did, Jamey, but whatever it was, you've made it obvious you don't want to be around me."

As I talked, Jamey's eyes grew darker and his grip on the countertop tightened. I realized that this conversation had gone somewhere I hadn't intended it to go. I hadn't meant to get so serious. I'd just wanted to thank Jamey and get him to acknowledge he'd done something nice for me. And here I was dumping all my confusion and hurt from the past few weeks on him. That was no way to say thank you.

Taking a deep breath, I started again, forcing myself to sound more upbeat.

"Anyway, it doesn't matter. You really helped me out tonight and I appreciate it. Thank you."

I expected Jamey to say "no problem" or something similar and head straight for the door to get away from the crazy girl who couldn't even say thank you nicely without essentially accusing him of being a jerk. Even though he kind of had been. Realizing I'd likely made things worse with my little tirade rather than better, I couldn't hold back a sigh. I just couldn't win when it came to trying to behave like a normal human being around Jamey.

That was what I expected to happen.

The very *last* thing I expected was for Jamey to straighten away from the counter as if hearing me sigh had forced him to move, and to walk toward me slowly. I stayed where I was, not knowing what to do and not capable of moving even if I'd needed to. I was frozen, caught in Jamey's eyes, mesmerized by his intense stare as he drew closer. He stopped directly in front of me, not quite touching me but close enough that his body just barely brushed mine as he took a deep breath.

"I owe you an apology."

Jamey's voice was soft and tense. I could see that same tension in his eyes and almost feel it radiating off his body. Still locked in place, I stiffened even more as Jamey's hands came to rest on the counter on either side of my hips. He still wasn't touching me directly, but he was so close that with his height and broad shoulders he was all I could see. His scent and the heat of his body wrapped around me. We stood staring at each other, neither of us saying a thing, then Jamey jerked his eyes away from mine and swallowed.

He dropped his head slightly, avoiding my gaze. He was obviously struggling with something. I wanted to reach out and touch him, to run my hands down his arms or through his hair and soothe him, but I forced myself to stay still and give him time.

"I'm sorry I made you think that you did something wrong or that I don't want to be around you."

Jamey raised his head again and looked at me. I saw heat in his eyes and felt my stomach jump in response. But there was something else there, too, something that puzzled me. I could swear I saw resignation in his eyes, as well. Where could that be coming from?

"I do want to be around you, Meg. More than I should." If I thought my stomach had jumped before, it was doing cartwheels now.

"I've tried to stay away, but I don't think I can. I don't think I can do it anymore."

I couldn't stand it. I had to touch him. Jamey stiffened when I placed my hands on his sides, but then stepped closer until he was pressed against me lightly, stomach to hip. He looked down at me and I could feel my cheeks flush at his closeness. I reached one hand up, winding my fingers in the soft hair at the back of his neck. I felt his slight shudder at my action and was glad for the sign that I was affecting him as much as he was affecting me.

I thought about the last thing he'd said.

"Why do you think you should stay away from me? Did I make you think that?"

Jamey finally, *finally* touched me, running his hand over my hair as he shook his head.

"No, it's me. I'm not the right guy for you. I know that, but I can't make myself care anymore. I can't stop thinking about you. You're always there, Meg, always in my head, no matter what I do."

I'd never been the focus of so much intensity in my life. I was surprised I didn't burst into flames from the heat in Jamey's eyes. It gave me the courage to say what I was thinking.

"Good, I'm glad you can't stop. I want you thinking about me. I want to make you as crazy as you've made me."

I tilted my chin up, looking at Jamey, our lips mere inches apart. I wanted his mouth on mine more than I could ever remember wanting anything. Before I could let myself think about it, I raised up on my toes, pulled his head down to mine, and pressed my lips to his. Jamey didn't pull back, didn't hesitate, fusing our mouths together and stepping closer to press his body more fully against mine. He lifted me up to sit on the counter and my legs went around his waist. He slid his tongue along the seam of my lips, then slipped it inside my mouth with a groan as I opened up for him. Jamey skimmed his hand up my back and under my hair, gripping the back of my head as he tilted his to deepen the kiss. He groaned again as I dragged my nails down his back. He put his hand on my lower back and pulled me forward, pressing my core against the bulge in his crotch and rocking against me slowly.

The friction was so perfect, so exactly what I needed, it was almost overwhelming. I leaned my head back, pulling my lips away from Jamey's and closing my eyes.

"Oh God, Jamey, that's so good." I felt Jamey's lips skim up my neck and across my exposed collarbone and shuddered. If we kept up like this, I knew I'd be coming apart in no time.

Just as I had that thought, Jamey's kisses became softer, less urgent. He kissed me lightly right under my ear, making me shiver. He placed one more soft kiss on my cheek, then pulled back just enough to look at me. His usually blue-gray eyes were so dark they looked almost black and I could feel his heart race under my hand that rested on his chest. One of his hands gripped my thigh, with the other he ran one finger lightly over my cheek as he looked at me intently.

"What's wrong, Jamey?" I had no idea why he had pulled back or what might be going on in his head.

Jamey continued to study me for a second, then slid his hand from my face to the back of my head. He wound his fingers in my hair again, holding me is his firm grip, and I found that I liked it. A lot.

"I want to make you come, but not like this. Not this time."

Jamey's cheeks were flushed and his voice was rough. He sounded like 100% turned on, sexy man. He tightened his grip on my thigh as he continued.

"I don't want the first time you come for me to be from a quickie on the kitchen counter, with your panties pushed aside and my fingers inside you. I want you completely naked, laid out in front of me so I can do all the things I've thought about nonstop since the first time I met you."

At Jamey's words, I felt my breathing pick up and my nipples draw even tighter inside the cups of my bra.

"I want to make you come a dozen different ways, make you feel so good you're drowning in it. Until your voice is hoarse from screaming my name and you forget that the rest of the world even exists. I want to watch your beautiful blue eyes darken as I touch you, see your body move, feel the bite of your nails as you hold on to me and ride out your pleasure."

Heaven have mercy. I was going to pass out just from Jamey talking like this soon.

"I want it all from you, Meg, want to know that you're with me 100%. I don't just want to get you off. I want to give you more than you've ever had before."

Jamey unwound his hand from my hair and stepped back a fraction, his eyes still pinned on mine.

"If that's too much for you right now, if it's all too quick, I understand."

Jamey took a deep breath, like he was trying to calm himself down a bit.

"I don't want to push you into anything you don't want or aren't ready for. But I'm not going to pretend I just want a quick fuck from you either."

My heart was racing and I was so turned on I couldn't even form words. I slipped down off the counter, sliding my body against Jamey's as I did, then took his hand and led him out of the kitchen. Jamey followed without a word, hand in mine, up the stairs and into my bedroom. I stopped next to my bed and turned to face him. I reached up to pull him to me for a kiss, but he held me in place with his hands on my waist.

"I need to know what's in your head, Meg. I need the words."

I slid my hand down to Jamey's chest and fisted my hand in his shirt, giving me an anchor to hold on to, something solid in the tidal wave of desire that was sweeping me away.

"It's not too much and it's not too quick. I want you, Jamey. I want everything you said."

Jamey's eyes flared at my words. He dipped his head, his lips covering mine. For a moment, he kissed me like he was drowning and I was his last chance at oxygen, his tongue slipping over mine and his hand gripping the back of my head. Then he pulled back just slightly, our lips still touching, so that I felt his next words as much as heard them.

"If we do this, Meg, it can't be a one and done. I need more than that from you. I can't..."

Jamey's words ground to a halt. He swallowed and I felt him begin to draw back slightly. No way was I letting him pull away from me now.

I went up on my tiptoes again as I had in the kitchen and stopped Jamey's retreat with my lips on his. I slid my hand up to his face and felt his stubble tickle my palm. I looked directly in his eyes and let him see how much I wanted to be with him. He seemed to need reassurance that I was with him, so I wanted to leave him with no doubts that I was.

"No one and done, Jamey. I promise. I want more from you, too."

Jamey's eyes cleared. In the next second he scooped me up and laid me on my back on my bed with his big body stretched out over me. He balanced his weight on one forearm, cupped my face with his other hand, and kissed me like his life and mine depended on it. He pushed one knee between my thighs, giving me a little more of his weight. I circled one hand around his side to rest on his back and ran my other hand up his arm, slipping under the sleeve of his t-shirt to grip his bicep.

Jamey pulled his mouth away from mine and ran his lips across my jaw and down my neck, while I tilted my head to give him better access. He brushed his hand over my stomach as if he was feeling the softness of my sweater.

"As pretty as this sweater is on you, it needs to come off."

I pushed Jamey back slightly so I could sit up and pull the sweater off over my head, then settled back into Jamey's arms. He ran his fingers lightly along the edge of my bra and my breath caught in my throat at the barely-there touch. Looking down at the bra that seemed to have captivated Jamey, I almost groaned out loud when I realized what I was wearing. When I'd dressed for the evening, I'd planned on dinner with my dad and Catherine, then an evening on my couch with a book or movie or both. I certainly hadn't planned on ending up in bed with anyone – especially Jamey – or anyone other than me seeing what I was wearing underneath my sweater and jeans. The bra and panties I had on were as basic as they got – just a plain white bra and bikini bottoms. Yet Jamey was staring at me like I was the sexiest woman he'd ever seen.

"Well, if you need any proof that I wasn't out to seduce you tonight, you have it." I knew Jamey could hear my amusement in my voice. "I'd have at least thrown on something with a little lace if I'd known you were going to see it."

"You don't need lace, sweetheart." Jamey leaned down and pressed a kiss to the center of my cleavage. "I'm just wondering how the hell I got to be the one lucky enough to see you like this."

Jamey's mouth met mine again as his arms came around me. The world stood still as we kissed, on and on, our bodies pressed tight against each other, legs tangled together. At some point, I felt my bra loosen, then Jamey pulled the straps down my arms and tossed it away. He lay me back on the bed, all of his attention riveted on my bare breasts. My already hard nipples tightened almost painfully under his gaze and in that moment I wanted his mouth on me so badly I ached. After what seemed like forever, but in reality was probably seconds, Jamey met my eyes. I'd never been the focus of such blatant, raging want before. At that moment, I felt like the most desirable woman on earth.

Jamey leaned forward, placed on gentle kiss on the swell of each of my breasts, then raised his eyes to mine again.

"Megan Isabella Kennedy, you are stunning."

Jamey's voice was quiet and rough, the intensity making me shiver. He leaned forward once again and ran the tip of his tongue around the edge of one nipple. Sensation shot through me and I couldn't help the soft whimper that escaped me.

At the sound, something seemed to break loose in Jamey. Leaning into me he sealed his lips around my nipple and sucked hard, his hand coming up to fondle and pluck at the other. I felt my back bow up off the bed as a lightning bolt of lust shot straight to my center. I wrapped my arms around Jamey's head and held on. He switched his attention to my other nipple, flicking his tongue back and forth across it, then sucking hard on it as he had with the other. Jamey kissed and sucked and fondled my breasts and I felt myself grow wetter between my legs. I moved my legs restlessly, trying but failing to get the friction I wanted. In response, Jamey wedged his thigh higher between mine and pressed exactly where I wanted him. I felt his hand slip down my side and across my stomach. He rolled off me slightly, transferring his attention to press kisses along my neck and bite lightly on my earlobe as his hand played with the button on my jeans.

"Is this okay, sweetheart? Can I touch you here?" Jamey ran his fingers down the seam of my jeans, pressing lightly against me, leaving no doubt about what he wanted. His touch felt so good, even through the denim. I was almost desperate to let him know I wanted the same thing.

"Yes. Please Jamey." I was close to begging and I didn't even care.

Jamey sat up a bit, his hands working on the button and zipper of my jeans, and I noticed that he was still fully clothed. I reached out and ran my hand along his side underneath his shirt. His muscles jumped under my hand and he looked up at me.

"You, too, Jamey. I want to see that sexy body of yours."

Jamey grinned at my words, but shook his head.

"Not yet, sweetheart. I'll let you take my shirt off, but it's best I keep my jeans on for now."

Jamey slid my jeans down my legs, leaving my panties in place for the moment, then raised up on his knees next to me so I could reach his shirt. I slid my hands up under it, running them slowly across his stomach and chest, taking my time while I lifted his shirt off. Jamey stayed still under my touch, his eyes letting me know that he knew exactly what I was doing. When I finally lifted his shirt off and tossed it away, I returned his words from earlier and meant every single one.

"Talk about stunning. Jameson Scot MacGregor, you define the word."

Jamey's mouth crashed on to mine again and I wrapped my arms around him as he lowered his body against mine. He rolled to my side and slid his hand down my body and into my panties. I opened my legs, welcoming Jamey's touch. He ran his fingers across my folds, stroking me from my entrance to my clit several times, then plunged two fingers inside me. I tore my mouth from Jamey's and arched my hips up toward his hand.

"God, Jamey. That's so good."

I felt Jamey's fingers withdraw, then nearly came off the bed when they pressed and circled and rubbed firmly on my clit. My heart raced and I could feel myself panting. Jamey lowered his head, captured my nipple in his mouth again, and I knew that I was seconds from coming. I felt my hips begin to rock along with Jamey's touch, then he plunged two fingers back inside me and the whole world detonated around me. The explosions rolled through me, wave after wave, and I knew I was saying Jamey's name over and over as I came. I held tightly to him, vaguely aware that I was probably leaving nail prints in his shoulder but unable to make myself loosen my grip. Finally, the waves subsided and I floated back to earth. I opened my eyes, unaware until then that I'd even closed them, and was met by Jamey's very hot, very satisfied stare. He looked like a man who was both very turned on and very pleased with himself.

Closing my eyes again, I turned and burrowed into Jamey's chest. I felt his arm curve across my back and his legs tangle with mine.

"I'd give you shit for how cocky you look right now, but you deserve it after that."

My words had to be muffled, crushed up against Jamey's chest as I was, but as I felt and heard the rumble of Jamey's chuckle, I knew he'd understood me.

"If you think I look cocky now, just wait. I've barely even gotten started."

Jamey rolled me to my back and captured my mouth in a long, slow, deep kiss. His mouth left mine and, eyes still closed, I sighed as I felt his lips skim across my collarbone. I lay, almost in a trance, as he kissed my breasts and nipples, then softly ran his hands and lips over what seemed like every inch of my torso. I was so relaxed that it wasn't until he pressed a kiss directly over my mound that I realized his intentions. At any other time, I would have loved to have Jamey's mouth on me, to feel his tongue on my clit and pushing inside me, but that wasn't what I wanted now. Right now, I wanted Jamey inside me and I didn't want to wait anymore.

Reaching down, I wound my hand in Jamey's hair and tugged gently but firmly. He pressed one last kiss on my stomach, then rested his chin there and looked up my body at me, a question in his eyes.

"I want you inside me, Jamey."

The fire flared in Jamey's eyes and he levered himself up the length of my body to lay beside me. He rested his weight on one forearm and smoothed his other hand over my hair.

"I want that, too, sweetheart. You know I do. And you'll have me, I promise. But I want to taste you first. I've thought about it so many times, you coming on my tongue, tasting your sweetness. I want to make you feel so good."

At Jamey's words, I could feel myself begin to grow wet again, the picture painted by his words clear in my mind. I almost gave in, but then I thought of how Jamey would feel inside me, and felt an overwhelming need that obliterated everything else.

I ran my hand over Jamey's chest, in awe that I was able to touch him the way I'd wanted to forever, even as I spoke to deny him what he was asking for.

"I want to make you feel good, too, Jamey. I want you inside me. I promise next time, okay?"

Even though I knew Jamey wouldn't be mad about being told no or pout like some men would, I was still a little nervous telling him what I wanted. I knew Jamey had heard the nerves in my voice when he responded.

"Sweetheart, I always, *always*, want to know what you want. And I guarantee you that it will never make me mad, especially when the answer to what you want most is to have me inside you." Jamey smiled that sexy smile of his and dipped his head down to mine for a quick kiss. "That will always bring a smile to my face. Okay?"

I nodded at Jamey and reached up to pull his head back down to me. I said "okay" just as Jamey's lips met mine. I opened my mouth for him and Jamey's tongue slipped inside. The kiss quickly became heated as we pressed our bodies together and ran our hands over each other. Finally desperate for air, I pulled my mouth away from Jamey's and kissed along his shoulder, biting down lightly where his shoulder met his neck. Jamey groaned and grabbing my ass in both of his hands, ground his hips into mine.

"Feel what you do to me, sweetheart? How hard you make me?" Jamey kept my hips pinned to his with one hand, while he ran the other up to grip the back of my head, holding me in place for a hard, deep kiss. "Are you ready, sweetheart? Ready to feel me inside you?"

"I'm ready. I want that, want to feel you."

At my words, Jamey gave me another hard kiss then rolled off the bed to stand beside it. Eyes on me, he unbuttoned and unzipped his jeans and pushed them down his legs, taking his briefs along with them. He'd kicked off his shoes earlier, so he stepped out of his jeans and stood in front of me on full display in all of his naked glory. I propped myself up on my elbows to enjoy the view while he stood and let me take him in. His body was impressive, his tattoos beautiful, and my hands itched to touch as I ran my eyes over his muscled arms, torso and legs. My eyes caught on his erection, impressive in its own right, long and so hard, and already tipped with moisture in anticipation.

"Sweetheart, you keep looking at my dick like you want to eat it up and I'm going to come right here where I'm standing."

My cheeks flushed a little at Jamey's comment, but I could tell from the heat in his voice how much he liked having my eyes on him. Meeting his eyes with my own, I lay back on the bed in invitation.

"Well, come on then. Show me what you got."

Leaning down, Jamey grabbed his wallet out of the pocket of his jeans, pulled out a single condom, tossed it on the bedside table, then joined me in the bed.

"If I'd had any clue we might end up here, I'd have grabbed a few more. I'll make it count, though."

"I'm sure you will, but just so you know, there are some in the bedside table, too."

"Thank God for a woman who plans ahead."

The world faded away as Jamey and I explored each other's bodies, learning with every kiss and lick and touch how to give each other pleasure. Jamey's hands on me felt incredible and I couldn't get enough of running my hands over him, his skin hot and smooth under my hands. At some point, Jamey reached down and slipped my panties off my body. He cupped my center with his big hand, then slowly slid one finger inside me and stroked my inner walls. I gasped at the sensation and he leaned over to capture my mouth with his. I ran my hand down his side and over his nice firm ass, then slipped my hand between his legs to gently cup his balls. Jamey's breath stuttered and he rested his forehead on my shoulder as I fondled and stroked him. It felt like every muscle in his body had frozen as he held himself rigid, completely in my control.

"Fuck, Meg." His voice was low and rough in my ear. "Fuck."

Pulling away from my touch, Jamey rose to kneel between my bent legs. He reached for the condom, tore it open, and rolled it on with quick, efficient motions. Hooking his arms under my legs, he pulled me toward him. A second later I felt his hardness against me, slipping through my folds and grazing my clit with every pass. Jamey's eyes were pinned where we were almost joined, watching himself as he slid back and forth and drove me slowly toward the edge. Jamey's cheeks were flushed, his whole body was taut, and I could tell his movements against me were making him as crazy as they were me. Finally, just as I was about to tell him I couldn't wait another second, he paused and I felt him position himself right against my entrance, nudging me, but not yet slipping inside. He looked up at me, eyes dark and jaw clenched, and I nodded, giving him the reassurance I knew he was looking for. Eyes still on mine, he pushed inside me, slow but steady. My eyes dropped closed as I absorbed the sensation of having Jamey inside me for the first time. Partway in, he withdrew, then pushed back in, deeper this time until he was fully inside me.

"Meg, sweetheart, open your eyes. I need to see you."

I forced my eyelids open and looked at Jamey, running my hands up his arms and gripping his biceps.

"You feel incredible, Jamey."

"And you feel the same. So hot and tight."

Jamey stretched out over me, holding his weight on his forearms.

He began to move, sliding in and out of me and kissing my neck and shoulder while I ran my hands over his back. He slid his hand under me, tilting my pelvis up. With the change in our position before I knew it I felt myself starting to spiral toward the peak. Jamey's rhythm was perfect, edging me closer and closer with every stroke. I rocked my hips to meet Jamey's and gripped his body at the intense pleasure. Then just as I was seconds away from catapulting off the edge of the world, Jamey paused and pushed back up to his knees. He kept stroking in and out of me, but slowed to a gentle, leisurely pace. Frustrated, I frowned at him, but he merely grinned back at me. When I rocked my hips against him, he planted his big hands firmly on my hips and held me still.

"I was so close, Jamey. Why did you slow down?" I could hear the whine in my voice, but couldn't have stopped it even if I'd tried.

"Because you were so close. It would have been good for you, sweetheart, but I want it to be way better than good. I want you to fly higher than you ever have."

"I don't know. It was feeling pretty damn spectacular before you shifted into low gear." Again, pouty, but I couldn't help it. And that cocky grin on Jamey's face wasn't helping any.

"And it will feel even more spectacular making yourself wait." With that, Jamey picked up his pace a little, still keeping my hips pinned to the bed so he was completely in control. "Trust me, sweetheart, I'll get you there."

After a few seconds Jamey shifted again, looping his arm under my leg, opening me up so that he was able to stroke deeper. He pistoned in and out of me and within seconds I was back teetering on the edge. I arched into Jamey's body, reaching for just that tiny bit more, and felt myself start to come apart.

"Jamey. I'm.." was all I got out before the tidal wave hit me full force. The pleasure was so intense I could barely breathe. My heart slammed against my chest and colors swirled behind my eyelids. I felt Jamey shift to lean over me again. He slammed his hips into mine over and over, his breath ragged and harsh in my ear. Finally, just as I started to come down, I felt Jamey stiffen. He pressed into me hard, then stilled, and I felt his big body shake with the force of his orgasm. I ran my hands over his back, reveling in the freedom to touch him as he slowly relaxed and his breathing slowed down.

"You are so fucking perfect." Jamey's lips brushed my cheek and his breath tickled my ear. I felt my heart swell and reminded myself not to read too much into anything Jamey said right then. Words spoken in the wake of an earth-shattering orgasm shouldn't be taken too serious-ly. Trying to keep it light I responded in kind.

"And you're pretty damn perfect, too."

Jamey pressed a kiss to my temple, then pulled away, sliding out of my body and heading to the bathroom to deal with the condom. As he walked back into the bedroom I wondered for a second if he would get dressed and leave, but I barely had time to think it before he was sliding back into bed and pulling me close. Neither of us said a word, but the quiet felt intimate and warm, like both of us were content just to be together. Before long I felt Jamey's breathing slow and even out and I knew he was falling asleep. Snuggling closer, I drifted off.

⌒

I woke the next morning right into the middle of a fantasy I'd had forever. I was laying on my back with Jamey pressing soft kisses along my inner thighs. My legs were splayed open and Jamey's hands rested along my side and on my stomach. Just as I surfaced enough to be aware what was happening, I felt Jamey's tongue slide along my folds and begin to gently circle my clit. At my quick breath, Jamey dragged his tongue over my clit once more and then kissed it. He rested his head on my thigh, wrapped his arms around my legs and looked up at me. His hair was going in all directions and his blue-grey eyes shone with desire and something that looked like happiness.

"Morning, beautiful."

I returned Jamey's good morning and he gave my legs an affection-ate squeeze. His eyes slipped back down to where his mouth had just been, then back up to mine.

"I couldn't wait anymore. I was dreaming about tasting you and I woke up and…" Jamey broke off and kissed the top of my mound again as if he couldn't help himself.

Like I had the night before, I reached down and wove my fingers in his hair. But I wasn't pulling him away this time.

"I'm glad. I can't wait anymore either."

At my words, Jamey gave a soft groan and turned his face into my thigh.

"Thank you, God."

I felt his words against my skin. Not knowing if he even realized he'd spoken out loud, I stayed quiet, stroking my hand over his soft hair. Seconds later, Jamey's tongue touched my clit again and the world around me ceased to exist. Jamey licked and sucked and stroked, his lips and tongue and hands my only reality. Before I knew it I could feel myself getting close to the peak. I rocked my hips against Jamey's face without thought, chasing what I needed. Jamey shifted just a bit, bringing his hands to my hips and holding me firmly in place. The complaint I was ready to voice died in my throat as Jamey sealed his lips around my clit and sucked hard, shooting my heart into overdrive and catapulting me right up to the edge. I felt my legs tense and start to quiver as I teetered, close, so close to flying. Jamey shifted again, laying one arm across my hips. Suddenly, he flattened his tongue against my clit and drove two fingers inside me, hitting the perfect spot. I strained against his hold, my hips arching hard against the bed, and flew into a million pieces. Jamey continued to flick his tongue across my clit and pump his fingers in and out of me, prolonging the waves of sensation that swept through me. As they finally subsided, I fell limp against the bed. Jamey swept his tongue through my folds one last time, making me jolt, then trailed kisses across my skin as he worked his way up my body.

As he drew even with me, he turned me on my side facing away from him, looping his arm across my body and pulling me back against him. He nuzzled my neck and kissed my shoulder, all while I could feel his rock-hard erection nudging against my back. His hand slid up my body and fondled my breast, while he rocked his hips against me. I pushed back against him, loving the feel of him against me, his big body pressing into mine. Jamey rolled away, then I heard the sound of a drawer opening and the crinkle of a condom wrapper. A few seconds later, Jamey's arm came around me again. He slipped his hand underneath my thigh, lifting my top leg and pulling it back toward him. I felt his erection nudge at my entrance and arched back against him slightly so that he slipped inside. Jamey rocked his hips, pushing more fully inside me, then stopped. He brought his hand up to my face, tipping it up to his for a long kiss. He began to move inside me, his hand constantly moving across my body, caressing my skin as he rocked. I reached behind me and gripped the back on his neck, needing something to hold on to as the incredible feeling of having Jamey inside me threatened to sweep me away again. Soon Jamey's arm clamped around me and his pace quickened, his body slamming into mine with each thrust. Before I knew it, I was coming again, pulsing around Jamey's erection again and again. His strokes became erratic, then he buried his face in my neck as I felt him swell inside me. He shuddered against me as he came, his strokes slowing until finally he rested against me.

"That is definitely the way to start the day."

Jamey's breath brushed my ear as he spoke. I turned my head to give him a kiss and was met with a look filled with lazy satisfaction.

"I'll second that."

That got me the grin I was looking for. Jamey gave me my kiss, then gently pulled away to deal with the condom.

As he had the night before, when he came back in the bedroom he slipped back into bed and pulled me close.

Playing with a lock of my hair that was laying over my shoulder, he asked, "What does your day look like today?"

I mentally flipped through my schedule for the day. It was still early. I'd have to skip the gym, but if I got moving I could probably wrap up my workday by 7 o'clock or so. I told Jamey that as his fingers continued to drift through my hair.

"I can be done at the pub by about 8." Jamey shifted a little so that he could look down at me. "Is that too late? Can I see you tonight?"

Jamey's words sent a thrill running through me. I was still a bit off balance by the abrupt change in his behavior toward me. Hearing him say that he wanted to see me again that night soothed some lingering apprehension that I hadn't even realized I was feeling until that moment. I still needed to get to the bottom of whatever had caused him to be so cold toward me, but right then I was just happy that he seemed to want to spend time with me as much as I did with him.

We agreed that I would meet Jamey at his apartment that night. He asked me almost shyly if I'd stay the night and I agreed to that, as well. While I rushed through getting ready for work, Jamey managed to find enough ingredients in my kitchen to make me a breakfast smoothie to make up for the one I would have gotten at my gym. He joked that it didn't have an immune booster, which earned him a sharp poke in the ribs from me, but I readily admitted that it was way better than anything I'd ever gotten at the juice bar. When he kissed me sweetly before we parted ways in my driveway, I wondered for a second whether this was really my life. Spending an incredible night with a hot-as-hell man who not only woke me up in the nicest way possible, but also wanted to do it all again tonight. And on top of all that, he made sure I had breakfast. Shaking my head, I climbed in my car and headed to work. I had a lot to do and a great incentive to make sure I got it all done on time.

Chapter 16

Jamey

*I*t wasn't the norm for me to leave the pub before closing on the nights I worked, which, if I was being honest, was most nights. Unless I had plans to meet up with the guys, I usually stayed and helped close things down. It was either that or go sit in my apartment alone. I was happiest when I was in the kitchen, so I might as well be at the pub as anywhere else.

But tonight? Tonight I watched the clock like my life depended on it. And felt every, single, agonizing minute that ticked away.

I was practically coming out of my skin waiting to see Meg again. I'd decided that I'd tell her tonight about the fact that I hadn't graduated from high school. I wasn't sure how I'd bring it up – it wasn't exactly something that would come up in normal conversation – but I needed her to know. After one night with her I was already in deep. If Meg wasn't able to overlook the fact that I was a high school dropout, I needed to know now. It would suck if she decided to step away from whatever we were building between us, but better she do it now before I got any more invested than I already was.

Fortunately the pub was busy enough to keep me from losing my mind. An added distraction was our newest cook, Grace. She had decent skills and adequate experience, but she was quiet as a mouse and lacked the confidence she needed to not just be a competent member of the kitchen staff, but to excel. I'd hesitated to hire her initially, but when I'd interviewed her, something about her had made me decide to take a chance on her. She had potential and was willing to take feedback and learn, but she had a tendency to hesitate and second-guess herself. Both I and one of our more experienced staff members, Michael, were working with her and she was making progress. The week before she'd suggested we feature gazpacho as our soup of the month. We'd never done a chilled soup before, but Kendrick was featuring a couple of Spanish wines on the bar menu, so the gazpacho made sense. She developed the recipe, I tweaked it a bit to brighten the flavors a little, then we ran with it. I developed an entrée – braised fish with olives and lemons – and Michael created a dessert – flan with caramel sauce – to go along with the theme. Together the items were selling so well we could barely keep up with demand. I'd set aside some of the soup and flan for dinner with Meg that evening. She'd said she wasn't a fan of un-fried seafood so I wasn't going to push it on the fish entrée.

I spent some time working with Grace on her knife skills, which, as I said, were decent, but had room for improvement in efficiency and, most importantly, safety. That helped pass some time and also gave me some one-on-one time with her to reinforce the progress she'd made. I even got a small smile out of her so I counted that as a success.

After what seemed like an eternity, the busiest part of the evening rush was over. I did a last check-in with the staff, texted Meg to let her know I was leaving, and headed out. As I drove the short distance home, I could feel my stomach start to tie itself in knots. By the time Meg arrived a little while later, I'd almost convinced myself not to bring up the topic I dreaded and to just grab one more night with her. I reasoned with myself that I could tell her in the morning when she wasn't trying to relax after a stressful day.

As soon as I opened the door to Meg's knock and saw the spark in her beautiful blue eyes, I knew our conversation couldn't wait until the morning. I needed to come clean before she trusted any more of herself to me.

After a long, deep, scorching hot hello kiss that got both of our heart rates up, we headed into the kitchen and talked about our days as I dished out dinner. As nervous as I was, I still noticed once again how easy it was to be with Meg. There was none of the awkwardness of a new relationship, no uncomfortable pauses or stilted conversations. Somehow Meg and I just fit.

Meg was game to try both the soup and the flan. We gathered them up along with a glass of wine for her and a beer for me and settled on the couch. We'd texted during the day and decided to check out a new documentary series about female serial killers. Weird date material maybe, but we were both into it, so it worked for us. I teed up the first episode and we ate as we watched, making occasional comments about the food – which Meg rated as 'fantastic' – or the show, but mostly just watching in companionable silence. My nerves had settled down earlier when Meg had arrived and I'd felt the connection between us click in. But as we watched the show, thoughts began to creep in again about how to bring up what I needed to tell her. Should I just blurt it out, like "Hey, by the way, just thought you might want to know…" or lighten it up, like "Fun fact, did you know the average serial killer attends at least a few years of college? I never even graduated from high school, so you're safe with me"? Neither option seemed like the way to go. Could I just ease into the conversation somehow?

I thought I was doing a pretty good job keeping my chaotic thoughts to myself until Meg suddenly grabbed the remote and paused the program.

She turned to face me on the couch, her knee bumping my hip and 100% of her attention focused on me.

"Okay, spill it. What the hell is up with you tonight?"

My muscles tensed even more at her abrupt actions and question. I tried to force myself to relax and look Meg in the eyes as I answered, evading her direct question.

"Why do you think something's up?"

Meg couldn't have rolled her eyes any more dramatically. She really was a master at that.

"You're so tense you're practically quivering. I can literally feel your brain spinning. You seemed fine when I got here, but now…"

I dropped my eyes and stared at the floor, running my now-damp palms across my thighs, concentrating on the roughness of the denim to ground myself. I swallowed hard and was about to try to answer Meg when she spoke again.

"Have you changed your mind about this Jamey? About us? You have, haven't you? I'll just go. This was a mistake, it was all just..a mistake and…"

I heard the hurt in Meg's voice just as I felt her start to push away and rise from the couch. Knowing I had to fix my fuck-up fast, I reacted without thinking and grabbed Meg as she started to stand. I heard her squeak of surprise as my hands wrapped around her waist and she lost her balance and ended up sitting on my lap straddling me. One hand secured firmly on her hip, I reached out with my other to tip her chin up until her eyes met mine.

"I haven't changed my mind. Not even close. This wasn't a mistake and I don't want you to go, okay?"

Meg sat still, looking at me as I silently willed her to hear the sincerity in my voice and see it in my eyes. After a few seconds she relaxed a little and let out a breath.

"Okay, I believe you. Tell me why you're freaking out then."

"I'm not freaking out exactly." Okay, that was a lie. I was completely freaking out. The expression on Meg's face said she knew it, but was letting my lie slide.

"I just..I'm not.." Dammit why was this so hard? Just say it already!

Even as I thought that I heard myself say, "I'm not like Aaron, Meg. I'm never gonna be that guy."

Meg frowned and tilted her head like she was curious.

"Which guy is that?"

"The guy who wears a suit that costs more than my rent and drives an expensive car and lives in the penthouse. Who went to the right school and got the right degree and works for the right firm. The guy who makes more money in one year than I make in ten."

Meg's frown intensified, but she didn't make any move to leave her spot on my lap. I kept my hands firm on her hips, needing the contact.

"And that's what you think I want? That guy?"

Hoping I wasn't stepping out onto thin ice, I blew out a breath and pushed on.

"I don't know. When you got back with Aaron, I thought..."

"Wait. Whoa." Meg did shift a little now, holding her hand up in a "stop" motion.

"When I got back with Aaron? I haven't seen or spoken to him since the night I ended up sleeping on this couch. Why would you think I was back with him?"

I was sure my expression mirrored the confusion I saw in Meg's.

"A few weeks ago when you and Dev and Mia were talking about your MBA program, Mia said it was Aaron's idea and you agreed and…" I shrugged and finished, starting to feel like a fool, "…it sounded like you were back together."

Understanding dawned on Meg's face and she tilted her head again, staring off into space, thinking.

"I remember that conversation. Yeah, I guess I can see how it might have sounded that way."

Meg looked back at me again, resting her hands on my arms as she spoke.

"So that's why you said you aren't the right guy for me? Why you didn't want to be around me?"

I couldn't let that second part stand.

"For the record, I always wanted to be around you." *Next to you. On top of you. Inside you.* I shook my head and went on. I still needed to tell her...

"I never even graduated from high school, Meg." There, it was out. "I'm a cook at my friends' pub. I live in a one-bedroom apartment and drive a five-year-old car. That's a pretty big leap to go from Aaron to me. Like Grand Canyon big."

I felt my hands tighten involuntarily on Meg's hips as I waited for her reaction.

She was quiet for a few seconds, the longest fucking seconds of my life.

"You know, you're right. You're not like Aaron at all."

My heart rose into my throat, choking me. My whole body tensed, not sure where this was going. I knew Meg had to feel the death grip I had on her hips, but she didn't show any sign of discomfort.

"Aaron...hmm, how do I put this?" Meg tapped her fingertip against her lips, considering. "Aaron puts himself first. In all things. He's the center of his own universe. In his little world, he makes the decisions. He determines the path and sets the standards and expectations and they're high - very, very high. As long as you fall in line with all of that.." Meg shrugged, "...everything's fine. If not, things get rocky quick."

Shaking her head, she poked me very lightly in my stomach.

"You couldn't be more different than that."

"Is that good?" Shit, I hadn't meant to say that out loud, but it made Meg laugh, so I'd take it.

"Yes, it's good." Meg squeezed my forearms. "Jamey, you treated me better when we were barely speaking than Aaron did at times when we were dating. I don't expect you to be Aaron. I don't want you to be Aaron. Got it?"

"Yeah, got it." I was still a little off-balance, unsure how to process Meg's complete non-reaction to the secret I'd carried for so long. Had she heard me? She'd seemed to hear everything else I'd said.

Meg leaned forward, getting my attention in the nicest way possible – with her mouth on mine. After a kiss that was way too brief, she leaned back slightly and grabbed my ears, making me grin. She held my head in place and stared at me like she was trying to read my mind.

"We okay?"

I moved a hand to her back and tipped her forward for another kiss before letting her sit back.

"We're okay."

She narrowed her eyes and continued to stare at me for a few seconds. Whatever she saw must have satisfied her because she gave a quick nod and sat back a bit more.

"How about we clean up our dishes, get a refill on our drinks, and watch our show?"

I gave Meg's thighs a squeeze, loving the feel of her, and agreed.

"I'm in."

Meg pushed up off my lap and I couldn't resist giving her ass a light smack as she turned away. She laughed and grinned at me over her shoulder as she walked toward the kitchen, her dishes and wine glass in hand, and it struck me again how incredibly beautiful she was. She was wearing jeans and a sweater again tonight, her gorgeous blond hair down, and she took my breath away. I still wasn't sure what to make of the fact that she'd shown no reaction at all to my lack of a high school diploma – the secret that I'd buried for years and agonized over telling her. It left me a little unsettled, like it was still unresolved in some way, but I knew I needed to drop it and move on. If Meg brought it up at some point in the future, we could hash it out then, and if not...well, maybe I'd dodged a bullet and it just genuinely didn't matter to her. But right now, I needed to pull my shit together and get on with my evening with my girl.

Chapter 17

Jamey

I was kissing Meg goodbye at my front door the next morning when I heard the door to Dante and Mia's apartment open. Meg stayed where she was, held securely in my arms, her hands on the back of my neck, her lips on mine. Mia and Dante would know soon enough that Meg and I were together – might already know if Meg had told Mia – so I wasn't concerned about either one seeing me kissing Meg goodbye too early in the morning to have any doubt that she'd spent the night.

After a few seconds, Meg started to draw back, so I shifted my hold to her hips to give her a little room.

"I'll call you when I get settled in tonight, okay? I don't know if I'll have a chance before then."

Meg was headed home to shower, change, and pack, then had a flight to catch for yet another out-of-town client meeting.

"Whatever works for you, sweetheart. Depending on what time it is, I might still be finishing up at the pub, but it's not a problem."

"Okay." Meg lifted on her toes to give me a quick kiss, then turned to look at Dante, who was leaning in his open doorway, arms crossed and smiling, not even trying to act like he wasn't watching us. He returned her "good morning" then we both watched her as she disappeared down the stairs.

As soon as she was out of sight, Dante turned that grin on me.

"Yeah?"

"Yeah," I responded, mirroring Dante's position in my own doorway. "Go ahead and say 'I told you so.'"

"Naw, man, I'm just glad you got your head out of your ass and made your move. Did you tell her?"

Dante's smiled dimmed a bit with his question. I understood what he was asking and knew he realized how much I'd been dreading the conversation with Meg about my lack of a high school diploma.

"Yeah, I told her."

"And?" I should have known Dante wouldn't leave my answer alone.

"And she didn't seem to care. At all." I was still a little leery about her lack of response, but I was sticking with my decision from the night before to let it go. Meg hadn't acted any differently toward me after our conversation last night, and definitely hadn't held back in bed.

Dante's grin returned full force.

"Okay, now I'll say I told you so."

"Asshole," I responded, a matching grin on my face. "Do you have a reason to be out here other than to watch me kiss Meg and give me a load a shit?"

"Yeah, I texted you last night. Now I know why you didn't answer." Dante could grin at me all he wanted. I'd been occupied in the best way possible the night before with all my attention focused on Meg. "Cal's going to be in town for a couple days and we want to try to get the whole group together if we can. I know Meg's got a flight out today, but from what she told Mia she should be back before Cal has to leave."

I told Dante I was in with whatever he got figured out, then headed back into my apartment. I took a quick shower, wishing Meg was there with me to take a much, much longer one. We'd been together for less than 48 hours, and she'd only walked out my door a few minutes before, but I missed her. I was getting in deep fast, but didn't know any way to slow myself down. All I could do was roll with it and hope Meg was right there with me.

⌒

Walking home from the pub that night, I felt my phone buzz in my back pocket. Pulling it out, I saw that it was a text from Meg.

Meg: Thank you, Jamey! Nothing like my favorite wine and beautiful flowers to make my day.

She'd included a selfie showing her with her cheek pressed up against what looked like a huge bouquet of vibrant orange roses, a bottle of wine in her hand. Only problem was, whoever had sent them, it wasn't me. Who the hell was sending flowers to my girl? Instead of texting her back, I called her.

It had barely rung when Meg answered. "Jamey, you're the sweetest."

"I'm glad the wine and flowers made you happy, sweetheart. I'd love to take credit, but they're not from me."

"They're not? Well, that's strange. Who could they be from?"

"I was kind of wondering that myself." Meg sounded truly puzzled and that soothed me a little. I hoped I'd managed to keep most of the irritation I was feeling out of my voice. I didn't want to dim Meg's excitement about the gifts or sound like a jealous ass, but I wasn't exactly thrilled.

I heard rustling on Meg's end of the phone as if she was moving around the room.

"I'm trying to see if there's a card or something...oh, here's one on the flowers. It says..hmm.. well, nothing except my name and room number."

"There's nothing else on the card?"

"No, well, it's not really a card, it's just a delivery slip. They're from the florist in the hotel lobby."

"And someone came in your room and left these things while you were gone?" This all sounded a little off to me. Maybe I was being paranoid, but...

Meg spoke up suddenly. "Oh, wait, I know who they're from! They're from Robert, they have to be."

From the tone of Meg's voice that sounded like a good thing. A thing that she didn't mind sharing with the guy she was currently dating. Or sleeping with. Or whatever the hell we were doing. But still, who was this Robert guy?

"And Robert is?"

"Oh, sorry. Of course, why would you know that? He's the general manager of the hotel. I always see him when I stay here. He spends a lot of time out with the front-line staff instead of sitting behind a desk in an office somewhere. I saw him when I checked in today. He was showing me the latest pictures of his grandkids and we were joking that I stay here so much I should have my own room. Kim at the front desk said that I'm one of their favorite repeat guests, which I thought was really nice. She even got the okay from Robert to upgrade me to the concierge floor since there was a room available. I'm sure they sent the wine and flowers, too, probably as a thank you for staying here so much."

I could feel the tension ease out of my shoulders as Meg talked.

Okay, it sounded like I'd definitely been letting my imagination get away from me a little.

"Yeah, that makes sense, especially the flowers since they're from the hotel florist. But how would they know your favorite wine?"

"I drink it in the lobby bar here and order it with room service all the time. It would be easy enough to look it up. Some of the regular bartenders would probably know it off the top of their head if Robert or someone asked them."

I made a note to take a closer look at the bottle of wine Meg was holding in the photo she'd sent. I'd have to stock up and recommend to Kendrick that we add it to the wine list at the pub.

I reached my apartment building and started up the stairs. Meg and I talked for a few more minutes. I could have talked to her all night, but it was late and I could tell from her voice she was tired. She'd had a long day of travel and meetings and had to be up early to jump right back in the next day. Long before I wanted to we said our good nights and both promised to text the next day when we had a chance. I usually took a quick shower when I got home, then hung out for a while before I felt ready to go to bed. Tonight, though, I headed straight for my bedroom after my shower. As tense as I'd been during the first part of our call, talking with Meg had helped me come down from my hectic day. Talking with Meg, being with Meg, just made me feel good. It was as simple and, at the same time, as complicated, as that.

Chapter 18

Meg

The next couple of weeks passed by in a blur. Jamey and I were together every minute that we could be given our busy schedules, including spending several nights a week with each other. Tonight, unfortunately, wasn't one of those nights. Cal was back in town unexpectedly for a few days, so the guys were having a poker night. I'd hoped to be able to have a girls' night with Mia and Ellie, but Ellie hadn't been able to make it to town and I was currently in my office trying desperately to crank out the last few things I needed to complete for a client report that I absolutely had to send out the next day. My stomach was growling, my head was killing me, and at this rate, I was going to be at the office all night.

Just as I had that thought, my boss, David, appeared at my office door. I'd worked for David since I'd joined the company. He was a great boss and he'd given me every opportunity to excel. He wasn't typically at the office this late, though – it was getting close to 8pm – so I was surprised to see him.

"Hi, Meg. Have a minute?"

"Sure." I mean, not really, but... "You're here late. What's up?"

David settled into one of the chairs in front of my desk with a sigh.

"I just got off a conference call with Connor Meyers and the nomination committee for the Leadership Circle. We ran way past our scheduled time."

Connor Meyers was the President and CEO of our company

and the Leadership Circle was a prestigious leadership development program at our company. It was well-known that Leadership Circle participants were virtually guaranteed a promotion to a management position within a year and many of our most senior leaders were Leadership Circle alumni. You had to be nominated to participate in the program, and even then, not all nominees were ultimately invited to participate. Many people were nominated several times before they finally made the cut and received an invitation. It was a little crazy how competitive it was. I couldn't imagine how contentious the nomination discussion could be, with all of the different directors vying to get their people in the program. No wonder David looked tired.

David didn't continue after his statement, just looked at me as if he expected me to say something. I had no idea how any of what he'd said could be relevant to me. For a second I wondered if my mind had drifted off while he'd been talking, but I was pretty sure I'd heard everything he'd said.

"Well, that sounds like loads of fun. So what did you need to talk with me about?"

David laughed and shook his head.

"Direct as always. Two things. First, I wanted to give you a heads up that you were nominated for the Circle this year."

I sat back in my chair, shocked.

"You nominated me? I didn't think I'd been here long enough."

David sat back in his chair, as well, resting his ankle on his knee.

"No, there's really no requirement about the number of years a person needs to have worked here. It's true that it's usually more tenured employees, but it's not required. And no, I didn't nominate you. I advocated for you, but you were nominated by a client."

I was getting more confused by the minute.

"I was? I didn't know that was allowed."

David shrugged. "To be honest, I've never heard of it. Apparently, it's rare, but it happens." He looked at me with a smile. "Do you want to guess who nominated you?"

"I have absolutely no clue."

"Geoffrey Manning from Manning, Inc."

I jolted a little at the name. Manning, Inc. was the company that Aaron worked for. Geoffrey Manning was the founder. My only direct contact with him during our work with his company had been after we'd completed our organizational assessment and had presented our recommendations to the senior executives and board of directors. Granted our team had worked extensively with Manning, Inc for months – that was how I'd gotten introduced to Aaron – but I hadn't done any work with them recently. Why had he nominated me now?

I didn't even try to hide my confusion from David.

"I have to admit that I don't really get it, but I appreciate it."

David stood and walked toward my door.

"You deserve it, no question. I fully supported your nomination. Whether the committee feels you're ready or not…we'll see. I just wanted to let you in on the fact that you're being considered."

"Well, thanks. I appreciate it."

David stopped in my doorway and turned to face me.

"You're welcome. The other thing I wanted to tell you is that I need you to attend a charity event in my place Thursday night. I'm double-booked. I'd send Anne or Mike but they're both out of town. We're a sponsor, so someone has to go."

Crap. I was supposed to spend Thursday evening with Jamey, but what was I going to do? Tell my boss no?

"Wow, that sounds great, David. Thanks!"

David's laugh told me that he had picked up on my fake enthusiasm, although it would have been hard to miss.

"It's a gallery opening. Go, have a glass of wine, shake a few hands, and you're done."

"Alright, I've got it."

David turned to leave.

"I'll forward the details. See you tomorrow."

"Ok, thanks. See you."

I decided to pack up my stuff and finish the work I needed to do at home. My concentration was completely broken and my mind was spinning with the strange fact that Geoffrey Manning had nominated me for the Circle seemingly out of the blue. Hopefully the drive home would give me some time to re-set my brain and I'd be able to focus on work. Besides, I had food and comfy clothes at home and I was pretty desperate for both at this point.

Once I was in my car, I decided to call Mia. I was still disappointed we hadn't been able to get together. At least I could chat with her for a few minutes.

Twenty minutes later I hung up with Mia as I pulled into my driveway. I was really glad I'd had the chance to talk to her. I hated that I was going to end the day without seeing or talking with Jamey, too, but I didn't want to interrupt the rare time he had with the guys.

Right now I just needed to push through this deadline and I'd have a little room to breathe again. For how long, I didn't know. The long hours I'd been working had gotten even longer lately and the start of my MBA program loomed like a dark cloud in the distance. I wanted to look forward to it, to be excited to take a big step in my plans for my future, but at the moment all I could see was the extra work and stress it was going to bring. And how much less time I was going to have to spend with Jamey. His schedule was crazy, too, and he was completely understanding and supportive about mine, but that didn't create more hours in the day to spend with him. Add in the extra work for the Leadership Circle if I ended up being invited, and it seemed impossible. I knew it would be an honor to be chosen to participate, but I couldn't help but hope that I wasn't. I felt ashamed at the thought – after all, it would be a huge boost to my career – but I didn't know how much more I could handle. At least the amount of travel I'd been doing for work was going to calm down for a while because my two main clients at the moment were local. That fact alone might just save my sanity.

I'd just finished changing when I heard my doorbell ring. I groaned out loud at the sound. Whoever it was, I was tempted to ignore it. I hadn't eaten since breakfast and I was starving. All I wanted to do was find something quick and edible in my kitchen before I hit my laptop for a couple more hours. If I focused I could crank out the rest of what I needed to do on this report and have the day at work tomorrow to work on other things. If I could pull that off I might be able to squeeze in some time with Jamey tomorrow night, even if it meant hanging out at the pub and talking to him a few minutes at a time as he was able to take breaks. And of course, hopefully spending the night with him, even if we were both too tired to do anything but literally sleep together.

As I headed down the stairs, the doorbell rang again followed by a knock. Whoever was out there was being persistent. Resigning myself, I detoured to the front door instead of my kitchen. I opened the door to find Denny, the delivery guy from Jade Garden, the nearby Asian restaurant. Yes, I ordered from them enough to know his name and he knew mine, too.

"Here ya go, Ms. Kennedy." Denny held out a bag with an expectant look on his face. Too bad I hadn't ordered anything.

"Hey, Denny. It's good to see you and I wish that was mine, but sadly it's not. I must be ordering too often if you just automatically come to my door."

I smiled at Denny as I teased him, not wanting him to feel bad about his mistake. It really was too bad that I hadn't ordered the food because it smelled incredible. As hungry as I was it was all I could do not to snatch the bag out of Denny's hand.

I expected Denny to be a little flustered at his mistake and maybe check the delivery slip, but he just shook his head and continued to offer the bag to me.

"No, ma'am. I packed it up myself. It's your usual order, wonton soup and veggie lo mein with no bean sprouts. It's got your name on it and it's paid for, tip and everything."

I frowned, puzzled, but finally reached for the food. Still not sure I should take it, I reiterated, "But I didn't order it."

Denny stepped back with a smile. "Well, then, I guess a secret admirer bought you dinner."

I watched Denny as he walked away, his words stirring a vague unease in me. A secret admirer? That was just...weird, wasn't it? How would anyone know that I'd just gotten home? I looked up and down my street. Was someone watching me?

Then I remembered ending my call with Mia as I'd pulled into my driveway. I'd told her I was starving and that I was probably going to throw something in the microwave for dinner. She and I had ordered food from Jade Garden many times. She knew my favorites and also knew that I hated bean sprouts. She was such a natural caretaker, she'd obviously called the restaurant when we'd hung up and ordered me dinner. I'd have to text her later to say thanks.

I felt my shoulders drop and my muscles relax as I exhaled in relief. I laughed a little at how quickly I'd started to freak out. Obviously, the stress from work was getting to me even more than I'd realized.

Chapter 19

Meg

The invitation for the Leadership Circle program showed up in my inbox the next day. I sat at the bar at the pub later that night thinking about what to do. The same thoughts I'd had the night before swam through my head. The only thing I could think to do was delay starting the MBA program for a year, if that was even possible. If not, that meant I'd have to reapply – I almost groaned out loud at the thought of going through that whole process again – and there was no guarantee that I'd get accepted a second time. I knew the invitation to participate in the Leadership Circle was an honor and privilege, but at the moment it was hard to see it as anything other than an unwanted detour from the path I'd mapped out for myself.

I stared at my glass of wine, turning the base around and around on the bar top, weighing my options. The wine was my favorite – Kendrick had added it to the regular wine inventory for me – but even that wasn't enough to break me out of my funk at the moment.

"That's the face of a woman with a lot on her mind."

I looked up at Kendrick as he stopped and leaned on the bar in front of me. He hadn't been behind the bar when I first sat down, but I knew he'd show up eventually. I hadn't seen Jamey yet either. I'd texted him when I arrived and I knew he would come out and see me when he had a free minute. It wasn't the best way to spend time with him, but sometimes you had to take what you could get. I had an overnight bag in the car, so at least I'd get to spend the night with him, although at this point, I was so exhausted I was pretty sure I was going to fall asleep on him.

I rested my elbow on the bar with my chin in my hand. I knew I probably looked pathetic, but I also knew I didn't have to fake being okay for Kendrick's benefit. He'd see right through it, anyway, so why bother?

"Hey, Kendrick. I'm trying to figure something out and just confusing myself in the process."

Kendrick finished filling a glass of water for himself and took a sip before responding.

"Lucky for you, your friend is bartender. Everybody knows bartenders are great listeners and give the best advice."

Kendrick's comment came with a grin and a teasing look in his gorgeous green eyes, momentarily distracting me.

"Why don't you have a girlfriend, Kendrick?" I hadn't meant for that to pop out of my mouth, but I didn't have much of a filter on a good day, much less when I was so tired mentally and physically I could barely focus.

Kendrick smiled and shook his head at my question.

"Conversations with you are always interesting, Meg. I never have any idea what you'll say next."

Kendrick took another sip of his water before setting the glass down behind the bar. His cheeks had flushed a little and I wondered if I might have embarrassed him a bit. Feeling bad about that, I'd just opened my mouth to tell him to ignore me when he held up his finger in a "hang on a second" motion. He checked with the other bartender, Amy, to make sure she had everything under control, then came around the end of the bar and sat down beside me.

"Don't think I'm gonna forget about the weight of the world you had sitting on your shoulders a minute ago. We're coming back to that. But I'll distract you for a minute with the sad story of my nonexistent love life. And it really will only be a minute because there's not much to say."

I looked at Kendrick, still feeling bad about the blunt question I'd asked out of the blue. Not to mention that it was absolutely none of my business. I mean, sure, he was a friend and all, but the friendship was still new-ish and that question had been pretty rude even for me.

"You don't have to tell me anything, Kendrick, really."

Kendrick squeezed my hand that was resting on top of the bar.

"It's okay. I don't mind." Kendrick reached over and snagged my glass of wine. "I'll get you another one." He took a sip before he went on and I wondered if this was harder for him to talk about than he wanted me to believe. "The short answer is that I'm not interested in investing that kind of time in someone else right now. And god, that makes me sound like a dick." Kendrick huffed a quick laugh and took another sip of wine. "The longer answer is my last relationship ended in a massive train wreck and I'm not up for getting back on that particular ride again just yet. And the long answer..." Another sip of wine, another laugh. "That's not something anyone needs to listen to."

Kendrick glanced at me and I leaned over to give him a friendly bump with my shoulder.

"Well, if you ever feel like talking about it, my ears are yours for the asking. Heaven knows you listen to everybody else's crap."

Kendrick nodded once and finished off the wine.

"I'll keep it in mind, thanks." Although both his words and his tone were gracious, I was certain he'd never take me up on it. Kendrick didn't give much away. I was surprised he'd told me as much as he had.

"And speaking of listening to people's crap, what were you worrying your pretty head about earlier?"

I knew Kendrick asked the question that way on purpose to get me going. Giving him the reaction he was looking for, I rolled my eyes at him, making him grin.

"Well, the short answer.." I said, echoing Kendrick's words... "is I'm trying to figure out what to do with my life."

"Damn, girl, that's the short answer? Sounds like you're screwed."

Kendrick's response sounded so much like something I'd say that it made me laugh as I responded.

"Wow, thanks, Kendrick. Gosh, I wished I'd talked to you sooner. I feel so much better now."

I felt a pair of strong arms come around me from behind and a kiss on the side of my head.

"You feeling bad, sweetheart?" Jamey said in my ear as he tightened his arms around me.

I ran my hands along Jamey's arms and shook my head, leaning to the side a bit to give him a kiss.

"Just stuck in my own head. Kendrick's helping distract me from my crazy."

At my words, Kendrick stood from the bar stool, gripping Jamey's shoulder for a second before stepping back.

"I'll leave you in Jamey's capable hands."

As Kendrick stepped away, I reached out and stopped him with a hand on his arm.

"Thanks, Kendrick. I mean it."

Kendrick gave my hand a squeeze before letting go.

"Anytime, Meg, and thank you, too." He pointed at Jamey. "Let this guy help you figure it out. His advice isn't as good as a bartender's, but..."

Grinning at Jamey's quick response of "bullshit" Kendrick turned and headed down the bar. Jamey sat down on the stool Kendrick had just vacated and turned toward me.

"What are you trying to get figured out?"

"Just some work stuff. I'll tell you later, okay? I know you can only take a couple minutes at a time and it's complicated."

I glanced over as Amy placed a fresh glass of wine in front of me. Sending a silent 'thank you' to Kendrick for remembering, I thanked Amy and took a sip.

"You'll have all my attention later, I promise."

"I know. I understand you need to work. I'm just glad I get to see you tonight."

"Me, too, sweetheart." Jamey leaned over to give me a kiss, studying my face as he leaned back again. He reached out and cupped my cheek in his hand, brushing his thumb lightly along the edge of the dark circles I knew were visible under my eyes. "You look tired."

In the past I probably would have taken offense if a man had said that to me, but with Jamey I knew he wasn't criticizing or pointing out a flaw. He was just concerned about me. I *was* tired and there was no point in acting like it didn't show.

"I know. You, too." I returned his gesture, brushing my thumb along his cheekbone. He didn't have dark circles like I did, but his usually bright eyes looked beat.

"Well, damn. Cancel all the big plans we had for tonight, then. Sounds like we both need to crash."

Since we usually ended up just hanging out when we were together, I knew Jamey was being sarcastic about our "big plans" but I played along.

"Okay, just this once." I sighed loudly as if it was a huge sacrifice. "Next time, though, big plans."

"The biggest." Jamey's grin as he leaned forward to kiss me told me that his dirty mind had jumped to a whole different topic than what we'd been talking about. He stood up from the stool. "I'd better get back."

"You're so bad, Jamey." And I loved it, but I wouldn't be me if I didn't give him crap for it.

"No, sweetheart. So good." I was still shaking my head at him as he gave me another kiss. "I'll be back out when I can."

I watched Jamey as he walked back to the kitchen and noticed several other women at the bar doing the same. I couldn't blame them. Jamey was hot from any angle, but the way he filled out a pair of jeans was something to behold. As long as the other women only touched him with their eyes, we wouldn't have a problem.

Unfortunately, I didn't see much more of Jamey over the next couple hours. The kitchen stayed busy so he was only able to come out to see me once more for a few minutes. He and Kendrick were experimenting with keeping the kitchen open a little later to see if the demand was there and so far, it looked like it was. That was great news for the pub's bottom line, but not such great news for Jamey's workload.

Thinking about Jamey's crazy schedule made me think again about my own. I couldn't help but wonder how the hell we were going to keep this thing between us going when we barely had time to breathe. How long would it be before we just couldn't find time for each other anymore?

Shaking away that depressing thought, I helped Amy dry some glasses as I waited for Jamey to finish shutting down the kitchen for the night. When he was ready to go we said our goodbyes to Kendrick and Amy and walked to my car hand-in-hand. I gave the keys to Jamey and let him drive. I was just too tired to be safe behind the wheel.

As soon as he started the car, Jamey picked up our earlier conversation.

"Okay, tell me what's got your head going in circles."

It was a quick drive to Jamey's apartment, so I gave him a shortened version of the huge maze of thoughts that had been filling my mind. I told him about the Leadership Circle and how it was such a big deal to be invited to participate, but also how it felt impossible to balance it with both my demanding job and the MBA program. I told him I was afraid I would completely burn myself out and fail at everything, and finally, how worried I was about not having time to spend with him.

I finished the last part as we walked into Jamey's apartment.

"You're important to me, Jamey, and I don't want you to get sick of waiting around for me to have time to be with you."

Jamey stepped close, pressing me back against the door.

"I'd wait forever for you, sweetheart. Don't worry about me."

He dipped his head down, brushing his lips over mine, then giving me a soft kiss. He raised his head and stepped back a little, resting his hands on my hips.

"You want to know what I think?"

I reached out and put my hands on Jamey's chest, soaking up his warmth and the feel of his hard body through his shirt.

"Yeah, I really do."

"I think you should do what makes you happy, what fills up your soul. When you think about your options, which one do you really want, just for yourself? Which one makes you want to jump in and get going on it? Gives you energy just thinking about it? Whichever one does, there's your answer. And if neither one does, well, then there's your answer, too."

"You make it sound so easy." I blew out a breath, feeling dejected and overwhelmed.

Jamey gripped my chin lightly and raised my eyes to his. He shook his head.

"No, not easy. Simple, maybe, but easy? Not at all."

I rested my forehead on Jamey's chest and breathed in his scent. Being close to him always felt so good.

"Maybe I'll just flip a coin."

"That's an option, too." Jamey kissed me on the top of my head and stepped back. He picked up my bag from where I'd set it down and held out his hand. "What do you say we sleep on it and talk more in the morning? Everything will be clearer with coffee."

"Best idea ever."

I took Jamey's hand and followed him down the hall to the bedroom. Within a few minutes we were curled up in bed together, already drifting off to sleep.

It was so nice, just being with Jamey like this, warm and safe and so, so happy. This was exactly where I wanted to be. I didn't realize I'd spoken that thought out loud until I heard Jamey respond, his voice just a whisper in my ear.

"Me, too, sweetheart. Nowhere else but with you."

Chapter 20

Meg

I woke the next morning to the sound of the alarm on my phone and the shower running. I rolled over and silenced the alarm, then lay there wishing Jamey was still in bed with me and we had nowhere to be. I heard the shower shut off and groaned, knowing that the reality was I needed to get up and moving. If Jamey was done with the shower, I had no more excuse to lay in bed.

I was just sitting up as Jamey strolled in the room, completely naked, beautiful body on display, still rubbing his hair with a towel.

"It's completely unfair that you're so gorgeous right out of the shower. You know that, right?"

Jamey gave me the cocky grin I loved so much and walked over to sit down next to me on the bed. "No one's more gorgeous than you are, sweetheart." He ran his hair over my hair, which I was sure was a complete mess. "With your wild curls and sleepy eyes and" – he tugged the sheet down, exposing my bare breasts to his gaze – "nipples that look so soft and sweet. It's enough to get me going just looking at you." He moved the towel from where he had dropped it on his lap and I could see that his cock was, in fact, taking quite an interest in the conversation. And unfortunately, I had zero time to do anything about it.

I leaned forward and gave Jamey a kiss, grabbing his hand as I felt him start to reach for me. Knowing him, he was likely going straight for my breast since he seemed to have a hard time resisting them.

"Only you can make a serious case of bedhead sound sexy."

Jamey took the hint and simply held my hand as he gave me another kiss.

"That's because you are, sweetheart." Jamey stood from the bed and I watched him without shame as he walked to his dresser and pulled out a pair of briefs. "Now get your sexy self in the shower while I make you some breakfast."

Jamey stepped into his tiny walk-in closet to finish getting dressed. With the temptation of his naked body gone, I managed to push myself out of bed.

Thirty minutes later I walked into the kitchen, dressed for work, makeup done, and hair pinned up in some semblance of an office-appropriate style. It wasn't exactly my normal look, but it was going to have to be good enough for today.

There was coffee waiting for me – in a travel mug, of course, because Jamey knew I'd be re-filling it and taking it with me – sitting on the counter next to one of "my" breakfasts, a piece of peanut butter cinnamon banana toast. When Jamey had first started trying to get me to eat breakfast, I'd mentioned to him that I couldn't stomach the thought of much food in the morning and didn't have time to make anything anyway. I loved eggs and bacon as much as the next person, but they were 'go out for brunch' food for me, not something I'd ever make at home. After Jamey had persuaded me that breakfast was important, especially since I typically worked out in the morning, he'd set out to create a few simple items that I liked. My favorite was peanut butter with a little bit of cinnamon mixed in spread on a piece of whole wheat toast with half a banana sliced on top. I'd made it a few times for myself and thought it was good, but it always tasted better when Jamey made it for me.

Jamey was leaning back against the counter, dressed in a Brothers Pub t-shirt and jeans, sipping coffee and thumbing through something on his phone. A half-eaten piece of toast – no peanut butter for Jamey – sat on a plate near his hip and a banana peel lay next to it, showing where the other half of the banana had gone. It struck me how domestic the scene would appear to anyone looking in on our world. We could have been any couple anywhere, starting our day together, heading off to work, counting on the fact that we'd see each other that evening, and the next day, and the next. For the first time, I realized I how much I wanted that with Jamey, wanted to know that we were committed to spending our future together. Then Jamey looked up and smiled at me, pulling me back in to the moment.

"Hey, beautiful. I'm flipping through ideas for dinner tomorrow night. Anything you're in the mood for?"

"Oh crap." I'd picked up my coffee mug, but set it back on the counter as I turned to answer Jamey. "I'm so sorry, Jamey. I was so wiped out last night I forgot to tell you. I have to cover for my boss tomorrow night at some charity event that we're a sponsor for. He said I don't have to stay long. It would be too late for dinner but maybe I could still come over after?"

Jamey set his phone down and slipped his fingers in his front pockets, a thoughtful look on his face. "Or maybe I could just come with you, then we could come back here or go to your place."

"Oh no, that's okay. It's a gallery opening and basically sounds like a 'see and be seen' thing. I can't imagine that you'd enjoy it." It didn't sound like Jamey's kind of thing at all and I didn't want him to feel like I expected him to come with me. "Like David told me, I'll have a glass of wine, shake a few hands, and be here as soon as I can. Knowing I get to see you when I'm done will be great motivation to get out there as quickly as humanly possible."

Jamey didn't return my smile, looking away and then down at the floor instead. After a few seconds, he shrugged and looked at me again.

"Yeah, okay. That'll work."

He said it was okay, but the vibe I was getting from him felt anything but.

"Jamey, I'm really sorry. I know you took the night off and this really sucks, but I.."

Jamey pushed away from the counter, dumping the remainder of his toast and the banana peel in the trash.

"It's fine, Meg. I know how demanding your job is. We'll still have time together, right?"

I crossed to Jamey, wrapping my arms around his waist and feeling infinitely better when he wrapped his around me, too. I couldn't fault him for acting a little disappointed. After all, I was disappointed, too. And that was actually good, right? If he didn't care that I couldn't spend the whole evening with him like we'd planned, then maybe that was a sign he didn't like me that much. So the fact that he wasn't really happy about it was a good sign. Mentally shaking my head at my tendency to overthink, I raised up on my toes and gave Jamey a kiss.

"Forgive me?" I was still bothered by the look on Jamey's face. It reminded me a little too much of the days when he'd been avoiding me.

"Of course, nothing to forgive." Jamey gave me a quick squeeze, then let me go, reaching past me to grab my coffee and toast. "You're going to have to take these for the road if you don't want to be late."

Taking a look at the clock, I saw that Jamey was right.

"Shoot, okay. I need to get my bag." I hurried to the bedroom to grab my bag, then met Jamey at the door. He set my purse strap on my shoulder then handed me my coffee and my toast, which he'd folded over and wrapped in a paper towel.

Jamey leaned down to give me a kiss, then opened the door for me.

"Have a good day, sweetheart. I'll try to call you tonight if I can." Wednesdays were trivia night at the pub, which meant they had a full crowd that all stayed late, rather than slowly winding down like a normal weeknight.

"I understand if you can't. I'll see you tomorrow if I don't talk to you before." I headed for the steps and heard Jamey's door close softly behind me. I wished again that I didn't have to leave, especially since things still felt a little off with Jamey. But I had a mountain of work waiting for me at the office and no one else was magically going to get it done for me. I reminded myself that the sooner I got it all done and got the charity event out of the way, the sooner I could see Jamey. That would have to be enough for now.

Jamey wasn't able to take a break to talk with me that night, but he sent a text now and then when he had a chance. Apparently there was some drama between two servers who'd been seeing each other but broken up, and the kitchen staff was taking bets when the two would start throwing food or plates at each other and which one would strike first. At the same time, Kendrick was being pursued hard by a woman who apparently wasn't at all discouraged by any of his usual tactics to keep women at bay. Kendrick kept breaking away from the bar to "check on the kitchen" to escape from her and Jamey was doing his best to give Kendrick a hard time about it. Jamey's comments on the two situations kept me laughing most of the evening.

In the midst of texting with Jamey, my mom started texting me, as well. I hadn't talked with her in a few weeks, which wasn't unusual, but she was on vacation – it looked somewhere tropical from the pictures she sent – and had time to catch up. We texted back and forth, nothing too deep, just filling each other in on the main events in our lives. She knew I was dating Jamey, so I told her things were still great there and that my job was still crazy. She told me about all of her volunteer activities and about a new tennis league she was playing in.

The night flew by and before I knew it, it was past time for me to head to bed if I was going to get a decent amount of sleep. I said good night to both my mom and Jamey and threw my phone on my bed as I got ready. I heard my phone ping with a text just as I finished. Figuring either my mom or Jamey had one last something they wanted to tell me for the night, I grabbed my phone and looked down at it as I turned to get a sleep shirt out of my drawer.

When I saw the name on the screen, I froze in mid-step. The text was from Aaron.

Aaron: It's been awhile. How have you been?

I stood just looking at my phone, not sure what to think. It felt strange to even see Aaron's name on my phone. I hadn't so much as thought about Aaron in weeks until David had mentioned a couple nights before that Aaron's boss had nominated me for the Leadership Circle. And now here he was texting me out of nowhere. It made me think of the saying "Speak of the devil and he shall appear." It kind of felt like I'd conjured Aaron up just by thinking about him. Not that Aaron was evil, he was just a jerk who I wanted nothing to do with. I didn't even want to text him back. I had nothing to say to him and no interest in anything he had to say to me. Mind made up, I deleted the message and resolved to forget about it. Not responding to the text would send a clear message to Aaron without me having to say a word. We were over and done. That was that.

⌒

I woke the next morning to two texts on my phone…one welcome and one not.

I deleted the message from Aaron without even reading it and focused on the message from Jamey.

Jamey: Morning, sweetheart. I hope you have a day as beautiful as you are. I'm looking forward to seeing you tonight.

I knew Jamey wasn't trying to make me feel guilty, but his sweet text reminded me how much it sucked that I was only going to have a few hours with him at most tonight, rather than the whole evening like we'd planned.

Me: I'll be there as soon as I can. I'll text you on my way. Can't wait!

I knew Jamey would have a late night at the pub again tomorrow since Fridays were always busy, but I decided to ask him to spend the night at my place, anyway. I'd even offer to go to the farmers market with him on Saturday morning if he wanted to. I'd have my laptop at home with me so I could always get in a few hours of work after Jamey left for the pub. It wasn't ideal but at the moment I was feeling like Jamey and I needed to squeeze in time together whenever we could.

Chapter 21

Jamey

By about 7 o'clock Thursday night, I realized the mistake I'd made by not just planning to go into work when Meg had told me she had the charity event to go to that night. If things had gone as planned, she'd already be there with me and we'd be getting started making dinner together. As it was, I had a couple of hours to go before she arrived.

I couldn't get my mind off the fact that Meg hadn't wanted me to go to the event with her. She'd gone to several other dinners and events without me, so why was this one bothering me so much? Maybe because this was the first time I had the evening completely free and was actually able to attend? Maybe because I'd offered to go and she'd turned me down? She'd just told me the night before how worried she was about us not having enough time for each other, yet she hadn't hesitated a second to tell me that she didn't want me there at the event with her. She'd said it was a 'see and be seen' kind of thing that I wouldn't enjoy. Was the truth that she didn't want to be with me where we'd 'be seen' together by her professional colleagues? I cleaned up pretty well when I made the effort, but there was no hiding the fact that I didn't fit the corporate mold. I'd met several of Meg's co-workers in passing when they were all at the pub for happy hour, but never as her boyfriend. I wondered now if that wasn't a coincidence.

I was tempted to walk down to the pub just to check-in, but I didn't want the kitchen staff to think I didn't trust them to handle things just fine on their own. They didn't need me looking over their shoulder and

I didn't want to give the impression that I thought they did.

I distracted myself for a while watching a cooking show that featured a chef I admired, making a few notes about ideas that might work for the pub's menu. When my phone rang, I assumed it was Meg calling to let me know she was headed my way and answered it on speaker without looking.

"Hey, sweetheart. You on your way?"

I had to laugh when Michael's voice came through the phone instead of Meg's.

"No, sugar bear, but I'm glad to hear I'm not interrupting you and Meg."

"Yeah, it's a good thing, too. I'd hate to have to kick your scrawny ass tomorrow."

Now it was Michael's turn to laugh. I was in good shape, but Michael was a former college football player who looked like he still played. He was anything but scrawny and the odds of me ever kicking his ass were slim to none.

"Yeah, woo. I'll count myself lucky on that one."

"You definitely should. What's up?"

"It's probably nothing to worry about...well, maybe...but Grace never came back from her break." Although Michael's words said it wasn't anything to worry about, his tone was definitely concerned. I frowned as I considered what he'd said.

"You mean she left the pub for her break and hasn't come back yet? How long has it been?"

"She came in at 3 like normal. She seemed a little jumpy, but you know Grace...she can get that way sometimes. She's scheduled til close so she took her break a little before 7. I didn't even know she'd left the pub, but when she didn't come back from break I checked outside and her car's gone. One of the servers said he saw Grace leave when he was out back taking a smoke break. It's weird enough that she left in the first place, but it's really not like her to not be back on time."

He was right. That wasn't like Grace at all.

"So she should have been back..." I checked the clock "...almost an hour ago. And she hasn't texted or called?" I knew the answer – Michael would have told me already if he'd heard from her – but I felt like I had to ask.

"No, nothing. And she didn't mention to anybody where she was going or even that she was leaving. Maybe I'm making too much of it, but something just feels off. I mean, if it was just car trouble or something she would have called, right? I tried her number, but it goes right to voicemail."

"Maybe her phone died, but yeah, something doesn't feel right."

I checked the clock again. Meg would probably show up soon, but I knew there was no way I'd be able to relax not knowing what was up with one of my staff. Grace was a sweet girl, but it was clear from the way she acted that she had a lot going on in her life. If she were in some kind of trouble, I needed to do whatever I could to help.

"Okay, I'll be there in a few. I'll pull Grace's address from her file and go check things out. If she had car trouble or got sick or something, maybe I'll come across her on the way or find her at her place."

I hung up with Michael, then texted Meg to let her know what was up. Hopefully there was some logical explanation for why Grace hadn't returned from break. I figured I'd find her, we'd get it sorted out, and I'd still have a few hours to spend with Meg.

~

It was close to midnight when I walked back into my apartment, still having found no sign of Grace and still unable to reach her on her phone. Michael had ended up going with me to look for her, but between the two of us we'd come up with nothing. We'd gone to the address she'd listed on her application, which had turned out to be an extended stay motel that had seen better days. There had been no response to our knock on Grace's door, no one in the office – which had been locked and dark – and no sign of Grace's car in the lot. After coming up with nothing there, we'd driven each of the main roads around the pub, trying to cover all possible routes that Grace may have taken when she'd left on her break, looking for either Grace or her car, but saw nothing that gave us any clue where Grace might have gone.

Out of ideas, we'd given up for the night. Grace was scheduled for the lunch shift the next day. Although Michael and I both hoped she'd show up at the pub, reasonable explanation or not, I didn't think either of us believed that would actually happen. Plan B was to go back to her address again during the day and hope to talk to someone in the office who might know something. But for tonight I planned to salvage whatever I could of my time with Meg.

Seeing no sign of Meg, I turned to go down the hall to the bedroom, thinking she may be watching a movie or reading in bed, but then stopped in my tracks when I caught sight of her asleep on the couch. She was curled up on her side, her head resting on the arm of the couch. She was wearing one of my t-shirts, which she loved to steal, and a pair of boy short panties. My mind flashed back to the first night Meg had stayed with me, the night she'd crashed on that same couch after Aaron had driven off and left her. As much as the thought of him doing that still riled me up, I couldn't help but be grateful he'd been such an ass. If he hadn't, who knew if or when Meg and I would have ever gotten together. It wouldn't stop me from telling him what I thought of him if I ever got the chance – or better yet, showing him if it wouldn't get Meg pissed off at me – but yeah, I was definitely grateful.

Hoping not to wake Meg, I scooped her up from the couch and headed down the hall to the bedroom. Meg stirred awake just as I laid her on the bed.

"Mm, Jamey." Meg barely opened her eyes as she ran her hand across my shoulder and down my arm. "I fell asleep."

"I see that, sweetheart." My heart swelled as I looked down at Meg, her face free of makeup, eyes closed and curls mussed. I was almost afraid to put a name to the emotion that flooded me. I could admit that I liked Meg more than any woman I'd ever been with and wanted her to the point it made me crazy, but this….this was more.

Much, much, more.

Eyes still closed, Meg curled into me, pulling me down to nestle against her. "I'm sorry, I tried to stay awake."

I held her close, running my nose along her neck and across her cheek, inhaling her scent that was uniquely Meg.

"It's okay, sweetheart. I know you're running yourself ragged. I'm beat, too. You go back to sleep. I'll join you in just a minute."

With a soft sound that I took for agreement, Meg unwound her arms from around me and settled on her side again. I sat just watching her sleep for a minute before finally rousing myself to get ready to join her in bed. When I slid in next to her a few minutes later, Meg turned toward me in her sleep. With her head on my chest and my arm around her, we clicked right into place like two perfect halves of one whole. Pulling Meg close, I felt myself relax as I started to drift off to sleep. The night hadn't gone anything like I'd planned, but at least I'd still ended it with Meg in my arms.

Chapter 22

Jamey

I pulled into Meg's driveway Friday night, more than ready to spend some waking hours with my girl. With our schedules the way they were, I knew I should be glad I'd gotten to see her at all over the past few days. But as much as I loved starting and ending my day with Meg, sleeping in the same bed with her and seeing her the moment I opened my eyes, I wanted more. I wanted to talk with her and laugh with her. I wanted to hear about her day as I made dinner for us, curl up on the couch with her to watch a game or movie, then take her to bed and make her come again and again. I knew I was being greedy, that I should be happy with what I had, but that didn't change the way I felt.

Grace's disappearance the night before had distracted me from obsessing over why Meg hadn't wanted me to attend the charity event with her. I was still worried about Grace. She hadn't called or shown up for her shift and the front desk clerk at the hotel where she was staying had been either unwilling or unable to give Michael any helpful information when he'd stopped there again to check for her. It was as if Grace had disappeared into thin air. Michael's reaction to her disappearance made me suspect that his interest in Grace went well beyond that of a fellow co-worker. He was taking it hard and I knew it was going to be difficult for him to let it go.

As concerned as I was about Grace, doubts about Meg's motivation for spending the evening before apart when we could have been together had begun to nag at me again throughout the day. I just needed some time with Meg to get my head straight and convince myself not to read more into it than the reasoning she'd given.

I grabbed the bag containing the flatbreads I'd brought for our dinner, locked up my car, and let myself into Meg's condo. As soon as I opened the door I heard one of Meg's favorite playlists blaring from somewhere upstairs, Meg singing along at the top of her lungs. Knowing she wouldn't have heard me come in and not wanting to scare her, I set the food in the kitchen, then yelled up the stairs to let her know I was there.

"Honey, I'm home!" I was joking, true, but the thought of living with Meg appealed to me more and more.

The music shut off abruptly and Meg appeared at the top of the stairs. The smile that lit up her face when she saw me and the way she flew down the stairs went a long way to soothing the doubts that had crept into my mind.

Meg skipped the last two steps, jumping directly into my arms. Her arms came around my shoulders and her legs wrapped around my waist as I caught her and held her against me.

"I'm glad to see you." I felt the worst of my tension fade with Meg's simple statement.

"I'm glad to see you, too." I pressed my lips to Meg's, slipping my tongue along hers when she opened for me. The familiar sense of contentment filled me as we kissed. I never felt more complete than I did with Meg in my arms.

A few minutes later, we were settled on the couch, plates in hand and drinks on the table next to us. We talked as we ate, Meg asking me if there were any updates on Grace and me asking her about work. I shared my frustration at the dead-end Michael and I had hit with trying to find out what had happened to Grace, and Meg shared how overwhelmed her job was making her feel. As much as I hated to add more to Meg's stress, it felt good to be able to lean on her a little, while she leaned on me in return.

As I held Meg and slipped into her tight, wet heat later than night, I felt the rest of my tension melt away. I'd let myself get too far down a dark road, wondering and worrying and second-guessing Meg's reasons for going to the charity event without me. I was getting stressed about it for no reason, "borrowing trouble" as Cal and Kendrick's mom, Mama Reid, would say. It was just one more work event that Meg had needed to get through, just like all the other events she had to attend. There was nothing more to it than that.

Chapter 23

Meg

I woke the next morning alone in the bed, the lovely scents of coffee and bacon telling me where I'd find Jamey.

I walked into the kitchen a few minutes later and found Jamey standing at the counter, cracking eggs one-handed into a bowl. When he saw me, he smiled and held out his free hand to me. Pulling me close, he wrapped his arm around me, kissing me on the temple before dipping his head down to kiss me on my cheek.

"Morning, sweetheart. I didn't mean to wake you."

I leaned up a little and kissed Jamey on the jaw, his stubble prickly against my lips.

"You didn't. The coffee and bacon did. That's a combo I couldn't resist."

Jamey's smile lit up his face again as he squeezed me close for another second, then released me.

"I know better than to get between you and your coffee. It should be ready to go. The bacon is still in the oven, so you'll have to wait a few minutes for that."

So that was why I smelled bacon but didn't see any evidence of Jamey cooking it. I crossed to the cabinet to get coffee mugs and poured a cup for Jamey and for myself.

"You'll have to tell me how to cook the bacon in the oven. I know I shouldn't eat it, but I love it. I hate the mess it makes, though."

Jamey paused from whisking the eggs to give me a kiss as I handed him his coffee.

"No problem, it couldn't be easier. And life is definitely better with bacon."

Jamey reached up to lift a pan off the rack as I pulled plates put of the cabinet. I loved to watch Jamey cook. Seeing his confidence in the kitchen was a huge turn-on. The great food he always made me was a wonderful bonus.

Speaking of food…

"That's good news about the bacon. You know I don't do complicated in the kitchen. I just wish you could make scrambled eggs easy, too."

Jamey stopped in the middle of adding butter to the pan he'd set on the stove and looked at me in disbelief.

"Are you telling me that you don't know how to make scrambled eggs? It doesn't get any more basic than that."

I shrugged and leaned back against the counter as I sipped my coffee.

"I know in theory, but mine always turn out rubbery and just gross."

"Well, this is the perfect day to learn." Jamey held out his hand to me again. "Come here, sweetheart. We'll have you making the world's best eggs in no time."

I had way more confidence in Jamey's ability to teach than I did in my ability to learn. My mom had tried to teach me to cook numerous times, but I just never got the hang of it. Each time she would eventually run out of patience with having to show me every step and banish me from the kitchen while she tried to salvage whatever we'd been making. I didn't want Jamey to get frustrated with me, but I also didn't want to disappoint him by not even trying. Deciding to give it my best shot and hope to not screw things up too badly, I set down my coffee and crossed to Jamey.

Apparently my expression wasn't exactly one of eager excitement. Jamey chuckled as I reached him and leaned down to kiss me.

"It's scrambled eggs, Meg, not a firing squad. I know you can do this."

"You wouldn't be so sure if you'd seen my past attempts."

"That changes today. And hey, if we ruin the eggs, we still have bacon and coffee. Nothing can be too bad if we have bacon and coffee, right?"

This time I allowed Jamey's smile to coax one out of me, as well.

"Very true." I stepped back from Jamey and eyed the pan on the stove. "Okay, what's our first step?"

Jamey had me add butter to the pan, then heat it a bit before pouring in the eggs. Following his directions, I resisted the urge to continually scrape the eggs around, scared that they would burn, and instead, gently pushed the cooked eggs to the middle every few seconds until all the eggs were done. I never would have imagined I'd use the word "beautiful" to describe eggs, but these were. They were creamy and fresh-looking, nothing like the dried-up rubbery shreds I'd always ended up with in the past.

"See, what did I tell you? They're perfect."

Jamey couldn't have sounded prouder. My sense of accomplishment was way out of proportion to the task I'd just completed, but I had to give credit where it was due.

"You're a great teacher, Jamey."

"Nah, you're just a quick learner."

That was typical Jamey, deflecting praise onto everyone but himself. I was about to argue and tell him that my mom would definitely disagree with his assessment of my learning capabilities in the kitchen when the oven timer went off, cutting off my words.

"Perfect timing, too. You plate the eggs, I'll grab the bacon."

I was tempted to press the point and make Jamey take credit for his skills, but I knew that the moment for doing so without making a big deal of it had passed. Promising myself I'd circle back to it with him later, I grabbed the plates full of the best eggs I'd likely ever make and sat down to my favorite breakfast with my favorite man.

~

For the first time I could remember, I'd turned my ringer and notifications off and ignored my phone for a whole weekend while I was with Jamey. I was risking missing an urgent text from work or from a client, but I knew if I saw that I had a text from Aaron, my face would give me away. Jamey could read me much too easily and would know that something was wrong. If Jamey knew Aaron was contacting me, he wouldn't be happy about it. The last thing Jamey needed, especially now that he was worried about Grace, was something more to add to his stress. I just needed to continue to ignore Aaron. He'd eventually get the message and go away.

Chapter 24

Meg

*O*ver the next week it became obvious that Aaron was not, in fact, getting the message. He continued to text me, day after day, at all hours.

Aaron: I probably deserved the silent treatment. I should have contacted you weeks ago. Is that better?

Aaron: Are you really still that pissed at me? Come on, Meg. Text me.

Aaron: You're being childish, Meg. I just want to talk to you.

Aaron: This has gone on long enough. You've made your point. Text or call me TODAY.

Aaron: Do you really think you can just ignore me?

I ignored all of them, and all the ones that followed.

Then the voicemail messages started. I was driving home from work, listening to my messages in the car, when Aaron's voice came through my speakers and I almost drove off the road.

"Megan, why are you acting like this? I know you were mad, but you've had weeks to get over it. Let's talk so we can get past this."

"You know I'm not a patient man, Meg. I've been far more than patient with you. Don't push me, Meg."

Just like the text messages, I ignored them all.

Every day, I got more stressed, to the point where I was almost afraid to look at my phone or check my messages. I was never sure when a message from Aaron would pop up. My voicemail box filled up and I left it that way, knowing that the messages were likely from

Aaron. When Jamey noticed how on edge I was, I bent the truth and told him that a client was being overly demanding, bothering me constantly and basically driving me crazy. I soothed my conscience by telling myself that it wasn't really a lie. Aaron was a *former* client, after all, and he was definitely stressing me to the breaking point. The deadline for responding to participate in the Leadership Circle was fast approaching, too. I hadn't decided what to do about it and it was weighing heavy on my mind, so that was a legitimate excuse for part of my stress, as well.

Finally it occurred to me to block Aaron's number. Why it hadn't occurred to me before then, I had no idea. I'd been so overwhelmed by the barrage of messages that I'd been completely off balance.

I decided to send one response to Aaron before blocking him. I hoped that maybe, just maybe, one clear message after all my silence would finally convince Aaron that he was wasting his time.

Sitting in my office at work, I brought up a new text message to Aaron.

Me: *Stop contacting me, Aaron. I have no desire to talk to you.*

There. I couldn't be clearer than that. I hit send, then quickly blocked his number, hoping with everything in me that was the last contact I would ever have with Aaron.

I turned my thoughts to the get-together Dante and Mia were hosting that night. Ellie was in town and Jamey and Kendrick were both taking the night off from the pub. Dev would be there, too. I couldn't wait to relax with my friends and spend some time with Jamey.

I managed to focus on work enough to get done what I absolutely had to before leaving that evening. As much as I tried to put Aaron out of my mind, I was still on edge. Though I'd felt hopeful earlier in the day that he would finally go away, my gut told me that one message wasn't going to accomplish what days of silence hadn't. I couldn't help wondering what his reaction had been to that message, how he'd reacted to being told to stop. He wasn't a man who responded well to being told no and that was essentially what I'd done. Not knowing what he was thinking, what he might be doing, was almost worse than the constant messages. I wished I knew one of his friends, someone who might be able to help me to persuade him to leave me alone, but in all the time we'd dated, I'd never been introduced to anyone Aaron called a friend. I wasn't sure he even had any. He had guys he golfed with and guys he played tennis with, but they seemed more like a group of guys he competed against than real friends. Even if I knew one of them, I doubted it would help me. Aaron only saw things one way – his way. No one, even a friend, was going to get him to do something he didn't want to do.

Thoughts swirling and brain on autopilot, I reached my car in the parking garage, threw my bags inside, then climbed in. I was backing out of my spot when I suddenly got a whiff of Aaron's cologne. I slammed on my brakes and for some reason checked my rear-view mirror as if he might be standing behind me. Realizing what I'd done, I leaned my head back on my head rest and closed my eyes.

"I've officially lost my mind. Completely, absolutely lost it." I was smelling cologne that couldn't be there and imaging Aaron in places that he wouldn't be.

Taking a deep breath, I rolled down the windows to fill my car with fresh air and eased out of my parking spot. I was going to focus on the evening ahead with my friends and put Aaron out of my mind. I'd given him too much of my time already, much more than he deserved, and I wasn't going to give him any more.

I voice-texted Jamey as I pulled into the parking lot of the apartment building, letting him know I was there. By the time I climbed out of my car, Jamey was jogging across the lot toward me. I'd really been looking forward to seeing him. From the expression on his face, he was just as eager to see me.

"Hey, you," I said as he reached me.

Without a word, Jamey stepped into my body, pushing me against my car. Framing my face in his hands, he bent his head and kissed me, running his tongue along the seam of my lips until I opened for him, then sliding his hands into my hair and diving deeper into the kiss. The kiss went on as I ran my hands over Jamey's back and gave him what he needed, taking what I needed in return. Jamey finally slowed things down, kissing me softly on the lips and cheek and finally the tip of my nose. He drew back a little, sliding his hands down to rest on my hips.

"Hi."

Jamey's simple greeting after that scorching hot kiss made me smile.

"That's all you have to say after a 'hello' kiss like that?"

"Yeah." Jamey shrugged, as a smile stretched across his face, as well. "I figured the kiss said the rest."

He had a fair point.

"That it did. Thanks for coming out to meet me."

I reached back into the car for my work bag and overnight bag, which Jamey took from me and settled on his shoulder with an exaggerated grunt as we started across the parking lot.

"What do you have in here, woman? Did you bring your entire closet?"

I knew he was teasing. With the huge crates of food and cases of alcohol he was always toting around at the pub, there was no way my bags were too heavy for him.

"Oh, please, you know those bags aren't heavy. It's just the normal stuff – a change of clothes for tonight and my workout clothes and work clothes and makeup and stuff, and then my computer and all that."

"Hmm, well…maybe you should consider leaving more things here so you don't have to carry it all back and forth all the time. I mean, you already have your body wash and hair stuff taking up all the space in the shower…"

Out of the corner of my eye, I saw Jamey glance over at me, then look down, that sexy smirk of his firmly in place.

I stopped a few steps away from the stairs up to Jamey's apartment.

"So I'm taking up all the bathroom space, am I?"

"Well, you're a girl and all, so…" Jamey shrugged as if that said it all, then chuckled as I poked him in his hard stomach in retaliation for his sexist remark.

I wasn't sure exactly what to think. I knew Jamey was teasing about how much stuff I had in his tiny bathroom, but was he serious about me leaving clothes and other things at his apartment, kind of…moving some of my things in?

Jamey reached out and grabbed my hand, focusing on it and playing with my fingers as he went on. "You've staked your claim on the bathroom, you might as well take up some space in the other rooms, too."

Jamey's tone was still light and teasing, but the fact that he wasn't meeting my eyes told me this wasn't a casual suggestion.

"Maybe I'll do that. Maybe I like the idea of my things all mixed up with yours."

Jamey's eyes met mine then, their clear blue color telling me how happy my answer had made him.

"Yeah?" I nodded in response to Jamey's question as he pulled me in for a kiss, then tugged me toward the stairs. "Maybe I like that idea, too."

When we reached Jamey's floor and our gathering of friends, I ducked quickly into Jamey's apartment to change. Since Jamey seemed serious, I decided that I would take him up on keeping some clothes and other things at his apartment. I spent so much time and so many nights here that it just made good sense. And good sense or not, I really did like the thought of my things sharing Jamey's space, like maybe, hopefully, Jamey and I would, ourselves, in the not too distant future.

I grabbed a drink out of the fridge and joined the group mid-conversation. Dev seemed to be answering a question Mia had asked him about something, or actually, someone.

"It's only been a week, but I haven't scared her off so far." Dev was leaned back in his seat, beer in hand, the perfect picture of a relaxed alpha male, but I swore I heard a hint of something else in his voice.

"Wait, what's this?" I asked as I took a seat in the empty chair next to Jamey. Kendrick sat on the other side of him and Mia and Ellie sat across our little circle next to Dev. Dante sat a bit outside our circle watching over a small grill with who knew what on it. He and Jamey were always coming up with new things to grill, though I suspected it was more to satisfy their desire to cook over fire than anything else.

"Mia is very sweetly prying into Dev's love life," Ellie filled me in then laughed as Mia huffed in protest.

"I'm not prying, I'm just...asking. I like Holly and of course I like Dev.." Mia smiled over at Dev and shrugged... "so I'm interested."

"And you know if I minded, I'd tell you to mind your own business, only probably not that politely," Dev responded.

That was true. I knew I could be blunt sometimes, but Dev had me beat hands-down. Since he seemed okay with the prying..um, *asking*...I did some of my own.

"Sorry if you already said all of this, but who's Holly? It sounds like Mia's met her?"

Dev nodded and finished off his beer before responding.

"Yeah, Dante has, too. Her brother, TJ, is in our youth program. We crossed paths when she picked him up one day and..." Dev shrugged as if the rest was self-explanatory.

"She seems like a really sweet girl. And TJ and his friend, Tyler, are a hoot," Mia shared.

Dante spoke up while he turned whatever was on the grill. "TJ and Tyler are definitely a handful. They're both good kids, though. I haven't really interacted with Holly, but TJ seems to be all about her."

"He stays with her a lot so they're pretty tight." Dev stood and tossed his empty can in the recycling bin, then bent to grab another from the cooler that sat beside it. "She has him tonight or I would have asked her if she wanted to come hang out. Anyway, I agree that she's great, but she's also really young, so...I don't know."

No one said anything for a moment, then Kendrick spoke for the first time since I'd sat down.

"Okay, somebody has to say it. How young is she?"

Dev sat down and popped open his fresh beer. "She's 23."

I didn't think that sounded that young. Only 2 years younger than me. But considering Dev was 34...

Kendrick winced a little at Dev's response. "That's a pretty big gap, man. Not saying you shouldn't date her, but..."

Dev nodded and sat back in his chair, an expression on his face that I couldn't decipher.

Jamey elbowed Kendrick.

"So you're saying if some sweet 21 year old hit you up, you wouldn't consider it?"

Kendrick gave Jamey a push, bumping Jamey into me since we were sitting so close.

"Hell, no. What the hell do I have in common with a 21-year-old?"

"You never know, Kendrick," I told him. "Besides, there's a big difference between 21 and 23." Both Mia and Ellie nodded in agreement, helping me make my case. "And anyway, I hang out with this old guy," I looked over at Jamey with a smile, "and he manages to keep up with me just fine." Granted the age difference between me and Jamey was only 7 years, not 11 like Dev and Holly, but still.

"Old guy? What?" Jamey yelped at my comment and leaned back in his chair in an exaggerated "who, me?" motion. He reached over to scoop me onto his lap as the others laughed. "Keep up with you? I can run circles around your ass."

He wrapped his arms around me and squeezed me until I squeaked, then nuzzled his face into my hair and continued for my ears only, "and do a lot of other things to it, too." I couldn't quite control the small thrill that shivered through me at his comment, but my only response was to raise my eyebrows as if to say "oh yeah?". Jamey's response, whatever it would have been, was interrupted by Dante.

"Jamey, quit mauling your girlfriend and come give me your professional opinion on these wings."

That solved the mystery of what was on the grill this time. After a kiss from Jamey, I switched back to my own seat and bent to pick up my drink where I'd set it next to the chair. Jamey made his way over to Dante's side and I shook my head as they conferred over the wings with a level of seriousness that seemed a little over the top for grilled meat.

Turning my attention back to the rest of the group, I was really glad to see Kendrick and Ellie talking together without any apparent awkwardness. I knew there had been some tension between them, but it looked like they'd worked their way through it.

I said as much to Jamey as we lay in bed that night, my head on his shoulder, both of us relaxed and mellow after a round of intense, toe-curling sex.

Jamey played with my hair as he responded, curling his fingers through it gently.

"Yeah, it seems like they're doing better. For a while it seemed like they'd never be okay again. I don't know if they'll ever be like they were but yeah…it's better."

I rested my hand over Jamey's heart, feeling its steady beat under my hand. "That had to be hard on Dante, having one of his best friends and his sister at odds."

"It was," Jamey agreed. "It was hard on all of us, even Dante's parents since they see all of us as their kids in a way. But yeah, it was hardest on Dante. He would have done anything to fix it, but sometimes there's nothing you can do."

"Can I ask what happened?"

"It's really Kendrick and Ellie's story to tell, but what it came down to was Ellie broke Kendrick's trust and it tore him apart. It's taken him awhile to trust her again and I can't say I blame him."

I tensed up a little thinking about everything I was keeping from Jamey. I wasn't exactly *lying* to him, but I also wasn't being 100% honest. Would he still feel like he could trust me after I told him? Would he understand? Would things be the same between us once he knew?

Jamey must have felt my tension because he rolled toward me, pushing me gently to my back and raising up on his elbow. He brushed my hair back from my face and looked down at me with concerned eyes.

"You okay, sweetheart?"

For a second, I considered telling him about Aaron contacting me. Telling him about the texts, the calls, and Aaron's relentless insistence on talking with me. But in the next second I knew I wouldn't, at least not yet. Like Dante, he'd want to fix it, and I knew he couldn't. I'd tell him after it was all resolved and just an annoying memory.

"I'm okay." I ran my hands over the smooth, warm skin on Jamey's back as I reassured him. "My brain just gets going."

Jamey nodded slowly, still looking in my eyes. He kissed me softly on the mouth, then bent his head to brush his lips down my neck and across my collarbone, making my breath hitch from the soft caress.

"Well, I know a guaranteed way to take care of that."

Yes, he did. All night long.

Chapter 25

Meg

"*Megan, this is Aaron. Please return my call.*"

I sat in my office and stared at my desk phone as if Aaron might rise up out of it along with his voice. So much for hoping he would leave me alone. He must have realized that I'd blocked him and had taken a guaranteed route to contact me – my work number. There was no way I could block him and no way to get him to stop contacting me unless I asked to have my work number changed, which would require an explanation I wasn't ready to give. And he'd worded his message so politely, there was nothing I could claim was inappropriate, again, without a much longer explanation.

What the hell was I going to do? Whatever happened, I wasn't returning his call right away. Aaron knew how crazy my schedule was. It was completely plausible that I wouldn't hear the message until late in the day. Hopefully that would hold Aaron off at least until the next day, which was all I could really hope for. I had no idea what to do next and no idea why Aaron was being so damn persistent, but it was starting to piss me off. It was more than obvious that Aaron wasn't going to go away. I suppose I'd known all along that that was wishful thinking. It had been worth a try, but it seemed that it may have backfired. I'd hoped that Aaron would take my silence as evidence that I wasn't worth his time. Instead it seemed it had made him more determined to get me to respond.

I wished that I could talk to Mia or Jamey and strategize what to do next, but I didn't want to drag either of them into it at this point. I'd created the mess by letting it get this far; now I needed to clean it up. I was a smart woman. Surely I could figure this out on my own.

⌒

I still didn't have an answer when I walked back into the office the next morning. All through my workout that morning I'd thought about it. That was usually when I came up with my best ideas, but it had failed me this time. After hearing Aaron's voicemail the day before, I'd let all of my other calls go directly to voicemail throughout the day. I knew I couldn't continue to do that - I was all but guaranteed to miss an important call from someone other than Aaron if I did. The only thing I could think to do was talk with him, which of course was also the very last thing I wanted to do.

I heard someone call my name just as I reached the door to my office and turned around to see Jenny, my boss, David's, executive assistant, walking toward me. Jenny and I weren't friends, but we were friendly.

"Good morning." I greeted Jenny as she reached me. "What's up?" I assumed there was a reason Jenny had sought me out in person. Like I said, we were friendly, but usually she'd just send an email or text if she needed something from me.

"Why don't we go in your office?" Jenny's tone and expression were pleasant, so anyone who saw or overheard us wouldn't think anything of the exchange, but there was something in Jenny's manner that had warning bells going off in my head. Whatever she had to tell me, I wasn't going to like it.

"Sure, let's do that." I turned and led the way into my office. I set my purse and bag on the floor, then turned and rested on the edge of my desk. Jenny followed me in and shut my office door, raising my concern a little more. Was something going on with David? Jenny didn't seem upset, though, just concerned. I was about to ask her again what was going on when Jenny spoke up.

"I thought you should know that Aaron Wellmann left a message regarding you on David's voicemail this morning." As David's executive assistant, Jenny screened all his calls and voicemails, even those that went to his direct line. So I knew it was possible, but still her words floored me. Aaron had called my boss? What the hell was he thinking?

"Okay, from the look on your face I can see that I was right to tell you." Jenny sounded relieved. I could only imagine that I looked as horrified as I felt. I hurried to reassure her.

"Yes, you definitely were. Did David hear it?" I mentally crossed my fingers and hoped the answer was no. I didn't know what the hell Aaron was up to, but I'd definitely have to come up with some sort of explanation for David if he'd heard the message.

My breath rushed out of me in relief as Jenny shook her head.

"No, I almost always get to David's messages before he does. When I heard this one, well, as I said, I thought you should know."

"What did it say?" I was almost afraid to hear the answer, but knew I needed to.

"Mr. Wellmann said that he's been trying to get in contact with you, but you haven't returned his calls."

I stared at Jenny in disbelief as a buzzing in my ears all but drowned out her next few words. I'd known Aaron could be an arrogant asshole, but to stoop to this? The situation between us had nothing at all to do with my job or his, yet like a child, he'd run to my boss and told on me for not contacting him. What the hell was wrong with him?

"You know how serious David is about always returning calls within one business day and Mr. Wellmann did sound concerned, but.." Jenny shook her head again and regarded me with worried eyes. "I also know you two had a personal relationship at one point and it's just not like you to ignore a client, so…"

"I owe you big time, Jenny." I didn't really want anybody at work knowing my personal business, but I figured I owed Jenny at least some kind of explanation. "Aaron and I haven't been together for months. He started contacting me again out of the blue, but I want nothing to do with him. At first I ignored him, then I finally told him to leave me alone, but he doesn't seem to want to listen."

"I wondered if it was something like that. It sounds like something my ex would have done if he'd been smart enough to think of it." Jenny moved to the door, turning back to me as she put her hand on the doorknob. "I have a folder where I save voicemails I think I might need later. You let me know if you need a copy of Mr. Wellmann's message or if you need someone to vouch for the fact that the jerk is harassing you at work. I'm happy to back you up."

I thanked Jenny again as she left my office, then walked around my desk and sank into my chair. I was going to have to talk to Aaron. I no longer saw any alternative. I still couldn't believe he'd actually had the balls to contact my boss. I had no idea how he might escalate things next if I continued to ignore him.

I also couldn't believe that he still wanted to talk to me after I'd made it clear I had no interest. Whatever his reasoning, I knew I was going to have to give in.

I pulled my phone out of my purse and unblocked Aaron's number. Still hoping for minimum contact, I sent him a text rather than calling him.

Me: You obviously have something you feel you need to say to me. So say it.

Aaron started a text back to me almost immediately. I could just picture the smug look on his face knowing that his latest move had worked. What I wouldn't give to punch him right in that smug smile.

Aaron: Now that you've finally decided to be reasonable I want to see you in person. I'll even let you pick the time and place.

I was tempted to tell him to meet me at the local strip club at midnight just to piss him off, but thought better of it. If I had to see Aaron, I wanted it to be during the day, somewhere familiar with lots of people around.

Me: Café on Elm 2pm tomorrow.

Aaron: Not tomorrow, I'm busy.

No way was I letting Aaron call the shots on this. I wanted it over as soon as possible. If he wanted to see me so badly, he could rearrange his schedule to make it happen.

Me: Tomorrow. Take it or leave it.

After a short delay, Aaron's return text popped up.

Aaron: Fine then. Tomorrow.

I could almost feel Aaron wanting to push back, but his text gave no indication. I wondered how much it had hurt him to give in and agree to meet tomorrow. Call me a bitch but with all the trouble he was causing me, I hoped it hurt like hell.

Chapter 26

Meg

I got to the café early so I could be sure to grab a table on the patio. Aaron hated scenes. The patio was always crowded and had maximum exposure, with people passing by on foot and in cars in addition to the surrounding tables full of customers. I knew Aaron wasn't going to be happy with what I had to say, so I was hoping that all the people around us would keep his temper in check. I would have loved to have arrived late, knowing it would drive Aaron crazy, but the assurance of getting a table on the patio was more important.

Although it was a little past lunch time, there were still a lot of people seated on the patio, including several that I recognized as colleagues or employees of past clients. I knew Aaron would recognize several of them, as well. I nodded at them with a smile but didn't join any of them for a chat. Once Aaron arrived I wanted to get this over as quickly as possible, not prolong it chatting with others.

I sipped the iced green tea I'd picked up on my way through the café and checked my messages quickly. I was just putting my phone away when Aaron stepped out on the patio. As I had done earlier, he nodded and raised a hand in greeting to a couple of people he knew but didn't stop to chat. When he reached the table, he stopped next to my chair and started to bend toward me like he intended to kiss my cheek. I put up a hand, causing him to stop mid-motion. He sighed, but straightened up and took the chair across from me.

He smiled and settled back in his seat, a confident man secure in the belief that everything was going his way. He was in for a rude surprise.

"It's good to see you, Meg."

"I can't say the same. What the hell are you doing, Aaron?"

Aaron chuckled, shaking his head.

"Blunt as always. I've warned you that mouth of yours is going to get you into trouble someday."

"Is that some kind of threat, Aaron?"

Aaron sighed again, his way of letting me know that I was already wearing on his patience.

"If you'll stop being dramatic, we can have a conversation like adults." He leaned forward, arms resting on the table, and lowered his voice a little.

"Look, I should have contacted you after our disagreement. I let my anger get in the way and I regret it. I've regretted it for a while. I shouldn't have reacted that way and I'd like to rectify that now and start over."

Aaron sat back a bit like he'd said all he needed to say. I was sure my disbelief was clear on my face.

"You're kidding, right? After the way you acted you think you can just say 'I regret that but oh well, I'm back now'? And I'm supposed to just run right back to you, so grateful that you want to be with me again? Is that how you pictured this going?"

Aaron frowned and sat forward again.

"Keep your voice down. And no, I didn't think it would be that easy because nothing is with you. Obviously, you're still angry."

"Oh, you can tell?" My sarcasm could not have been more obvious.

Aaron's frown intensified, his irritation showing.

"If you'd quit acting like a bratty teenager and listen..."

"You listen." I cut Aaron off mid-sentence, knowing and not caring that it would piss him off even more. "If you insult me again this conversation is over."

Aaron closed his eyes for a second, his jaw clenched. He took a deep breath, opened his eyes, and gave me a slight smile.

"I didn't mean to insult you. You know your attitude sets me off. Listen..." he shifted in his seat as if he was settling in to confide something. "What I wanted to say is that I miss you. I miss being with you. You know that's not easy for me to admit. We're a great couple, Meg. The perfect team. Don't throw that away over what amounts to a misunderstanding."

A misunderstanding? Really? Did he really believe he'd done

nothing wrong that night?

Cutting to the chase, I asked, "Do you realize that you never apologized to me for that night?"

Aaron straightened a bit, visibly taken aback by my comment.

"What exactly do you think I have to apologize for?"

Could he really be that oblivious? Or was it just arrogance?

"Seriously? You left me stranded, not to mention that you drove while you were intoxicated!"

Aaron glanced at the nearby tables, seeming nervous that someone might overhear.

"You're exaggerating. I was fine to drive. Yes, I left you, but I warned you I would. Maybe I should have told you again, but you know I don't like to repeat myself. And you have to accept your share of the responsibility for your own behavior that night. If you hadn't pushed me and been so stubborn, it never would have happened."

I stared at Aaron, still not able to believe what I was hearing. *My* behavior that night? I'd own the fact that I'd had too much to drink, but the only other thing I regretted was trusting Aaron to get me home safely.

Sitting there, I suddenly realized that none of this mattered. Aaron was never going to apologize for his behavior, let alone change it. Most importantly, though, I didn't care. I didn't care how Aaron acted because he was completely irrelevant to my life. All I wanted was for him to leave me alone. That was my goal in agreeing to meet with him. I needed to focus on that and just ignore my irritation at his self-importance. Time to say my piece and get out of there.

"This discussion is pointless. It doesn't matter what you think about that night or about anything really." I rested my forearms on the table and leaned toward Aaron, wanting to be sure that he heard me loud and clear. "You need to leave me alone, Aaron. Whatever we may have had, it's over. I've moved on. You should do the same."

Prepared to pick up my bag and leave, I stopped in shock as Aaron completely changed tactics, grabbing my hand and kissing it, then holding it securely between both of his.

"I know you're with Jamey now. I've seen you together." That stopped me in my tracks just as I was about to yank my hand away from Aaron's. Jamey and I had barely been out in public together. Because of our crazy schedules, almost all our time together was spent either at my condo or at Jamey's apartment, hanging out, either just the two of us or gathering with the whole gang. Had Aaron been *watching* one of those times? Had he been following me? Suddenly his behavior seemed a lot more sinister than just being a pain in the ass.

Aaron apparently took my lack of response as an invitation to continue.

"I know what you're going to say. Jamey's a good guy. And I'm sure that's true. I only met him that one time at that pub when we met your friends, but he seemed like a decent person. But he's not on your level, Meg. You have to know that. He's not and he never will be. He can't give you what I can."

Against my better judgement, I voiced the question that sprang to mind.

"And what exactly do you think you can give me that Jamey can't?"

Aaron's arrogant laugh set my teeth on edge.

"Everything? Really, Meg, be serious. There's nothing we can't have together. Who do you think got you nominated for your company's Leadership Circle?"

Okay, well, that settled that. That invitation was getting a 'decline' response as soon as I got back to the office.

Aaron sat back in his seat, finally releasing my hand and spreading his hands wide, smug smile firmly in place on his face again.

"We're the ultimate power couple, Meg. You belong with me, not Jamey. You and me - we think alike, we want all the same things. We're a perfect fit."

The fact that he thought that could be true – the possibility that I'd *acted* like that could be true – made me physically ill.

Out of nowhere, the strange incidents of the past few weeks filled my mind. The wine and roses at the hotel. The delivery of dinner just after I'd gotten home much later than usual. The scent of Aaron's cologne in my car. With a shock, I realized they'd all happened just as Aaron had suddenly contacted me after months of silence. He *had* been watching me, tracking me. He'd known that I was seeing Jamey. He'd known when and where I was traveling out of town for work and when I got home at night. He'd been in my car. For what reason, I had no idea. Had he done something to it so he could monitor where I was? Had he been in my condo? My blood ran cold at the thought.

"It's all been you, hasn't it?" My voice was barely above a whisper, my sudden realization all but choking me. "The wine, the flowers, the dinner…that was all you."

Aaron avoided my eyes, glancing down at his phone, deliberately casual.

"You're being overly dramatic as usual."

Incredibly grateful that I'd demanded to meet Aaron in a public place in broad daylight, I fought to keep my expression calm. Inside I was reeling. I'd never thought of Aaron as a physical threat, but after all this? I had no idea what he might be capable of. I needed to end this right now and make sure Aaron knew I was serious.

I straightened in my seat and looked Aaron directly in the eye, ready to be done with this.

"What you said – that we're the perfect couple? That couldn't be further from the truth. We don't fit at all. I want nothing from you, Aaron, except for you to leave me alone. Do not contact me in any way for any reason. If you contact me again or do anything that impacts me or anyone connected to me, I'll be sure to inform both the police and your employer that you've been stalking me."

Aaron laughed again, this time in disbelief.

"What? Stalking you? You've lost your mind. Who would believe that?"

"Anyone who sees your text messages or listens to your voicemail messages. You contacted me repeatedly, way beyond what was reasonable. Not just on my personal number, but at work. And you kept it up after I told you very clearly to stop."

"If you hadn't been so stubborn, I wouldn't have had to! And sending you gifts? Oh yeah, sounds really threatening." Aaron shook his head as if he couldn't believe how ridiculous I was being.

"It is when it means that you've obviously either been watching me or having me watched. From what you said today, that's exactly what you've been doing. I know you somehow got in my car. And made me question my sanity along the way. Add that all together? Sounds like stalking to me."

Aaron's eyes narrowed as he glared at me.

"And yet you agreed to meet me today. And all these people can confirm it." He looked briefly around the patio, making his point, then back at me. "How do you explain that?"

"You forced my hand. You completely crossed the line when you called my boss and you know it. You know it, I know it, and guess who else knows it? Jenny, David's assistant. She's the one who intercepted your message and told me about it. You know why? Because she knew as well as I did exactly what you were trying to do. And she's willing to back me up if I need her to. Do you want all your colleagues to know about this? Because they will. Just think about it, Aaron. Is that what you want? Do not push me. I promise you, I'll do it."

Aaron's hands clenched and unclenched on his thighs, like he was picturing them around my neck. Aaron hated to lose, rabidly, passionately, hated it. That was how he'd see this. He wanted something, I'd told him no. I won, he lost.

"You fucking bitch."

I dipped my chin in agreement, but maintained eye contact.

"You better believe it. And you'll want to remember that if you decide to ignore what I've said and contact me again. Or try to mess with me in any way. Just walk away, Aaron. Forget we ever knew each other."

"I wouldn't want you now if you begged to come back to me." I could feel Aaron's rage from across the table. His face was starting to get red and his glare was intense. It was past time for me to go.

"Good, then, we're in agreement." I picked up my bag and settled it on my shoulder as I stood. "Goodbye, Aaron."

Not waiting for a response, I turned and walked away. It was against every instinct I had to turn my back on Aaron, but I had to trust that the presence of the other customers would keep me safe, at least for the moment. I could only hope that Aaron's obsessive need to maintain his image would keep me safe from him retaliating later. I'd just have to be careful. If something happened, I would deal with it, but for now, I'd done what I could. The next thing I needed to do was tell Jamey what had been going on. He wasn't going to be happy that I'd kept it from him. Okay, that was a massive understatement. He was going to be furious with me, but I'd just have to make him understand.

Chapter 27

Jamey

*O*n my way out of downtown I stopped by the café near Meg's office to pick up a couple of her favorite orange scones. She was spending most nights at my apartment and I liked having them for her when she was there. It was a small thing that made her happy, and I loved seeing my girl smile.

I found a parking spot across the street just past the café. As I waited next to my car for a break in traffic, my eyes wandered over the customers at the tables on the café's patio. I started to smile when I saw a familiar blonde sitting at one of the patio tables, then froze as I realized that Meg was sitting across from a man, one who unfortunately looked familiar, too. What the hell was Meg doing with Aaron? Why would she be meeting him? She hadn't so much as mentioned his name in the weeks we'd been together, much less said anything about being in contact with him. Had she been seeing him the whole time? I couldn't believe that could be true. Meg was too straightforward to go behind someone's back and cheat. Besides, we'd been with each other almost constantly when we were both free. *But what about all those nights when you're working?*, my mind whispered to me. *What about her work events or when she's out of town?* Aaron moved in those same business circles and traveled for work, too. Could she have been meeting up with him? Could I have been that blind and stupid?

Fighting to stay calm, I crossed to the passenger side of my car so I was out of the street, then stood and watched them. Maybe I was wrong. Maybe I should trust Meg and just leave and ask her about it later. But I couldn't make myself look away. If my world was going to fall apart, I needed to watch it happen. I watched as Meg & Aaron sat and talked. I tried to read the expression on Meg's face, but with her sunglasses on, it was hard to do. She wasn't smiling. That had to be good, right? I'd almost convinced myself that whatever was going on, things between me and Meg were going to somehow be okay, when Meg leaned in toward Aaron across the small table. My breath stuttered and stopped as Aaron took Meg's hand, raised it to his lips for a kiss, then continued to hold it between both of his. I stared at their joined hands, willing Meg to pull her hand from his, to stand up and walk away, to do anything to indicate that she didn't welcome his touch and his kiss. As she just sat there, her hand in Aaron's, still talking, I felt my world begin to collapse around me.

Meg was with Aaron.

She'd chosen him over me.

When had this happened? I'd thought Meg and I were happy. Yet she'd apparently walked away from me and I hadn't even seen it coming. Sure, she'd seemed a little distracted lately, but she'd said it was just the stress of her job. Had she lied to me? Finally realized I wasn't good enough for her? I'd had no clue things had changed between us, no time to brace myself for the blow that was nearly bringing me to my knees.

Reeling from the impact, I got back in my car and drove, no direction in mind. I found myself sitting in the parking lot of my apartment building, with no recollection of how I got there and no idea how long I'd sat there, staring through the windshield.

She's gone. Meg's gone.

The thought circled again and again on an endless loop in my brain. All the hopes I'd never told her about, never shared with her, all gone.

I pushed myself out of the car and walked slowly toward my apartment, not knowing what I would do once I got there. I was unlocking my door when I heard Dante's door open behind me.

"Hey, Jamey. What's up?"

I stood where I was, head down, hand on my doorknob, no idea how to respond. My brain felt like it was buried in sludge. I couldn't think, didn't want to think.

She's gone.

When I didn't respond, I felt Dante behind me, then his hand gripping my shoulder.

"Jamey, man. Are you okay?"

Knowing I couldn't lie to him, I turned around to face him. His hand fell from my shoulder as I turned. When he saw my expression,

Dante took a deep breath, his eyes full of concern.

"What is it, Jamey? You look like somebody died. What the hell happened?"

I swallowed hard and looked away. I didn't know if I could say the words. Saying the words would make it real.

Dante's hand landed on my shoulder again.

"Jamey, talk to me. You're freaking me out. Tell me what happened."

I took a breath and forced the words out.

"Meg, she..."

My throat closed up. I swallowed again and shook my head, my eyes fixed on nothing.

Dante grabbed my other shoulder and shook me lightly, forcing my eyes back to his.

"Meg, what? Is she hurt, Jamey? Did something happen? Jesus, Jamey, what the hell is going on?"

I could hear the rising worry in Dante's voice. I knew I had to pull it together.

"No. No, she's okay. Meg's okay. She just..." I forced myself to go on. "She's with Aaron. I saw her with Aaron. She doesn't..."

Want me. Love me. I shook my head again, trying without success to dislodge those words from my head.

"She's with Aaron. She's gone."

There it was. I'd said the words out loud.

Dante shifted, but kept one hand on my shoulder. He frowned as he took in my words.

"Did she say that? Did she tell you she wanted Aaron? When did this all of this happen?"

I leaned back against my door, dislodging Dante's hand, suddenly almost too exhausted to stand.

"I saw them. Just now downtown, sitting at the cafe, holding hands."

Dante shook his head like he couldn't believe what I was saying.

"Maybe there's something else going on, some explanation..."

I felt my anger rise, breaking through the numbness I'd felt since I realized the dream I'd been dreaming for the past few weeks was over. I straightened and shoved Dante back, my rage spilling over onto him.

"Didn't you hear me? I *saw* them. I fucking saw them. They were right in front of me. He kissed her fucking hand, Dante. He kissed her hand. And she didn't pull away. Didn't get up and leave. She stayed right there, with her hand in his. Does that sound like I have it wrong?"

My hands clenched into fists. The urge to hit something welled up inside me. I wanted to punch and hit and kick something until the physical pain equaled the pain inside me. I hadn't lost control like that in a long time, but now I was teetering on the edge, ready to explode.

Dante wisely stayed where he was, hands raised in surrender.

"Fuck. Okay, that sounds bad." Dante kept his voice low and even. I knew he was trying to talk me down. "But Jamey, there has to be an explanation. Something's not right. Meg loves you. I know she does. Everyone can see that."

Dante's words were a knife cutting right through my chest. I felt my breath hitch at the slash of pain. Meg didn't love me. She couldn't. Why would she?

As suddenly as the rage had filled me, it disappeared, exhaustion and numbness returning in its place. I leaned back against my door again, resting my head on it as I responded.

"She's never said it, Dante. Never hinted at it."

Dante's look turned challenging.

"Have you told her, Jamey? Have you told Meg that you love her? I know you do."

I hadn't. I'd known for weeks that what I felt for Meg was love, but I'd never said the words. I'd held back, waiting. For what, I didn't know. Some kind of sign, maybe? Well, I sure as fuck had gotten one.

I straightened away from my door and met Dante's eyes. I was too tired to talk anymore.

"It doesn't matter. Whatever I thought I felt, it's over."

I turned away from Dante and opened my door. He didn't say a word as I stepped inside and closed it behind me. He knew I was right. There was nothing left to say.

⌒

I stood looking around my apartment and knew that I had to get out. I saw Meg everywhere - sitting at the breakfast bar wearing my t-shirt and drinking coffee; curled up on the couch, ready to watch a movie; standing by my side in the kitchen, a little frown of concentration on her face as I taught her how to cook one of her favorite things. Walking down the hall, the scent of Meg's body wash permeated the bathroom and her toothbrush sat next to mine in the holder on the sink. But the worst room by far was my bedroom. All the nights and mornings we'd spent in my bed, tangled up together, completely focused on each other's pleasure or just lying there together, talking about anything and everything, played in my head. I knew the scent of Meg's skin, the feel of her hands on my body, the sound of her voice saying my name as she came, would never leave my mind.

Feeling the walls closing in, I threw a few things in a bag and grabbed my old camping sleeping bag from the back of my closet. I'd crash at the apartment over the pub. I'd left a few things behind when I moved out. Between those and the things I was taking I could buy a few days to figure out what to do next. Drowning some of the pain in whatever liquor I could get my hands on was first on the agenda. After that, who knew?

On the way to the pub, I texted Kendrick that to let him know that I would be crashing at the apartment and that I wouldn't be in to work that night. It was a dick move to leave the kitchen short-handed with almost no notice, but it wasn't one of our busiest nights of the week and I knew the staff could handle it. Even if they couldn't, I knew I wasn't capable of doing anything else right then. I heard my phone ping with Kendrick's return text asking if everything was okay, but I didn't respond. I knew he'd come looking for me sooner or later and would probably hear most of it from Dante before then, anyway.

I pulled in behind the pub and took the exterior steps up to the apartment. I let myself in and set my bag and sleeping bag on the futon Kendrick kept there in case he needed to crash after a late night, then turned and headed down the inside set of stairs that led to the back hallway of the pub. Luckily the door to the stairs opened right next to the storeroom where we kept most of the bar inventory. I grabbed a couple bottles of bourbon off the shelf, mentally writing Kendrick and Cal an IOU, then climbed the stairs back up to the apartment. I'd planned to hole up there and drink until I passed out, but the silence pressed in on me. I left one bottle on the table of the 2-seater kitchen set that still sat along one wall, took the other bottle outside, and settled in the shade at the top of the steps. I braced my back against the wall and listened to the traffic and the birds and the voices of people coming from the street and businesses nearby. I drank steadily and did my best to keep my mind blank. When thoughts and images of Meg rose up, I shoved them back down.

I had no idea how much time had passed when I heard the back door of the pub open and saw Kendrick walking toward me carrying a bottle. He rounded the bottom of the stairs and saw me sitting there, bottle already in hand.

"I took a chance you'd be sitting out here. I should have known you'd hit the storeroom first."

I rested my head against the building and watched as he climbed the stairs toward me.

"Yeah, got another one inside. I'll pay you back."

Kendrick frowned as he stopped and stood several steps below me, setting down the bottle he held.

"You know this place belongs to you as much as it does me and Cal. But I won't let that comment piss me off because I know you've got a lot on your mind right now."

I shook my head and took a drink.

"Not me, man. Nothin' on my mind but drinking some good bourbon and listening to the birds."

Kendrick nodded, his expression telling me he knew better than that.

"Yeah, Dante texted me, so I know most of what's going on. Or at least what you *think* is going on. Jamey, are you sure about what you saw?"

I looked at Kendrick, not even trying to hide my confusion and pain. Kendrick was the quiet, steady one of our group. Of all of us, he was the one who saw people most clearly, the one who could keep a level head and reason his way through almost anything. But I didn't think even Kendrick could help me reason my way through this destruction.

I forced out a response, my throat tight as the images of Meg and Aaron raced through my mind again.

"I'm sure, Kendrick." I had to stop and swallow, my next words tearing a hole in my chest as I forced myself to say them. "I don't know the when or how, but I know she's gone, and I know why. That's all that matters. I can't…" I couldn't say anything else, my questions about how I'd been so stupid as to think Meg might want me for the long-term piling up in my throat and choking me. I swallowed more bourbon to try to wash them away.

"Okay. I know I didn't see whatever you saw. It just doesn't seem like something Meg would do."

I had no response for that. The fact that the other guys were as blindsided as I was didn't really help. Whatever any of us had thought, I knew what I'd seen.

When Kendrick spoke again his tone had changed. The tension in his words drew my eyes to his face.

"I know you're hurting, Jamey, but I need you to promise me something. I need you promise me that when Meg comes to talk with you, because you know she will, that you'll listen to her. Really, really listen Jamey, with both your head and your heart as corny as that sounds."

He went on, shadows of remembered pain clouding his eyes.

"You know what happened with me and Julia. She swore I was cheating on her and refused to listen to me no matter how I tried to explain. It was complete bullshit, but she just refused to hear me. I lost the girl I thought I was in love with and damn near lost Ellie in the process, too. Ellie and I still haven't made it back all the way."

I remembered Kendrick's devastation during the weeks and months following his break-up with his girlfriend, Julia, who also happened to be the best friend of Ellie, Dante's younger sister. Julia had always had a bit of a tendency to overreact to things, but the explosion when she'd thought that Kendrick was cheating on her had been epic, scarring everyone in its wake. She'd confronted Kendrick in public, tearing him apart and nearly ruining the career of the supposed "other woman." Kendrick had been completely innocent, but Julia had flat out refused to listen. Worse yet, Ellie had sided with Julia. She'd turned her back on Kendrick, had believed the worst about him when he needed her most. She'd eventually realized she was wrong and asked Kendrick to forgive her, but like I'd told Meg, their relationship still hadn't fully recovered and maybe never would.

"I know you went through hell, Kendrick, but this isn't the same. I'm not some crazy bitch adding two and two and coming up with fifteen. I saw what I saw."

"I know. And it can seem so clear. But things aren't always what they seem. I'm not saying you're wrong, Jamey, although I hope you are. I'm just asking you to listen to whatever Meg needs to tell you."

I let out a breath and rubbed my hand over my face. I rested my head against the building again and closed my eyes. The bourbon was starting to catch up to me.

"If she wants to talk to me, I'll listen. I don't know what good it will do, but I'll listen."

Listen to her tell me why I hadn't been enough for her, not that I had any doubt about the reason. Meg was direct, but she wasn't a bitch. She'd try to slice me open and cut my heart out as gently as she could. It never would have worked out between me and Meg, anyway. I'd known that from the beginning.

I didn't realize I'd said those words out loud until Kendrick responded, his frustration with me clear.

"I know why you think that, Jamey, and you're wrong. Meg doesn't care that you never graduated from high school or that you have no desire to move on from the pub to something "bigger and better" whatever the hell that is. You're happy, Jamey. You're doing something you love. That's what she cares about. That's what we all care about. No one thinks less of you. Any thoughts about that are all in your own head."

Kendrick's words rolled around in my mind. I tried to sort out the truth, but I was too tired to make any sense of it.

I opened my eyes and met Kendrick's.

"I don't know. You might be right. I'm too tired and drunk to sort it out."

I made my way to my feet, using the wall for support, Kendrick tensed and ready to catch me if I took a nosedive down the stairs. I held the bourbon bottle up to eye level and squinted at the contents. It wasn't enough, but I had another bottle inside. I moved toward the door to the apartment.

"I'm gonna finish this inside. I appreciate you checking on me."

I could tell there was more Kendrick wanted to say, but thankfully he held back. He picked up the bottle he'd brought with him and eyed me for another second.

"You know I'm gonna check on your drunk ass again before I leave tonight, so for the love of God keep your pants on and don't puke all over yourself."

I saluted Kendrick with the bottle in my hand, then pushed through the door into the apartment. I leaned back against it and raised the bottle for long drink. The sooner I passed out, the sooner I could forget.

Chapter 28

Meg

By the time I got back to the office I had myself back under control. I'd kept my game face on during the confrontation with Aaron, but as soon as I'd stepped out of the café I'd started to shake. I'd known Aaron would be angry, but the intensity of his rage had taken me by surprise. My main concern was whether Aaron would let it go now, let *me* go.

As I tried to work, thoughts about how angry Aaron had been and how vindictive he could be kept circling my mind. What if he went to the pub to confront Jamey? I knew Jamey had the day off, but what if Aaron tried to start trouble with Kendrick or the other staff? I thought about calling Jamey but didn't want to go into the whole mess over the phone. Time and again, I dragged my attention back to the work in front of me, only to find myself staring into space again a few minutes later, thoughts in a tangle. After struggling for a couple of hours, I was ready to give up and head to Jamey's.

I had just started to get my things together when I heard my phone ping with a text, then another, and another. Wondering what was going on, I dug it out of my bag and saw three texts from Mia.

Mia: Meg, where are you?

Mia: Are you with Aaron? What's going on?

Mia: Call me as soon as you see this.

What the hell? How did Mia know that I'd seen Aaron? If he'd found her number and called her or worse, gone to the gym…

Huffing in frustration, I got up and shut my office door, dialing Mia as I returned to my seat. Mia answered, sounding out of breath.

"Meg, thank God. What is going on?"

She sounded panicked and given how tense I was already it made me start to panic, too.

"Did Aaron contact you, Mia? Did he threaten you? I swear if he tried to scare you..."

Mia spoke, cutting me off.

"So you did see him today? Are you still with him?"

Now I was confused.

"Yes, I saw him and no, I'm not still with him. How…?"

"Jamey saw you, Meg. He saw you and Aaron together."

My heart stopped. Oh no. This could be really, really bad. Not bothering to ask how Mia knew all this I got straight to the point.

"How pissed is he?"

"Oh, Meg." The concern I heard in Mia's voice told me that whatever she was about to say, the situation was way more than just bad. "Honey, he's not just mad. Dante saw him a while ago. He said Jamey looked devastated, Meg. Completely destroyed. He thinks that you've gone back to Aaron, that you've left him."

I was so shocked, I could hardly even process what Mia was telling me.

"What?! Why would he think that? I met with Aaron to tell him to leave me the hell alone. I was with him for all of 20 minutes! I was going to tell Jamey about it tonight. I figured he'd be mad, but…"

"He told Dante you were holding hands. That you were sitting at a table holding hands."

Oh fuck. Oh no. This was worse than I could have imagined. It was just my luck that Jamey happened to be downtown and pass by the café at the exact moment that Aaron grabbed my hand. My brain raced. How did I fix this? What the hell did I do now?

I realized I hadn't answered Mia when she spoke again.

"Is Jamey right, Meg? Are you back with Aaron?"

"No!" Wasn't she listening to me? "I told you I met him to tell him to leave me alone! He's been texting and calling and…dammit, we weren't holding hands! *He* was holding *my* hand. I know it probably looked bad to Jamey, but…"

Hearing myself say that out loud, I completely ran out of steam. There was no "probably" about it. I knew how I'd have taken it if I'd seen Jamey holding some other woman's hand, especially a former girlfriend's. He'd have been lucky if I didn't kick his ass on the spot. Why wouldn't he think I was getting back with Aaron? Defeated, I concentrated on the only thing I could.

"Where is he, Mia? Is Dante with him?"

"No, Dante said Jamey left. Kendrick called a little bit ago and said that Jamey's crashing at his old apartment above the pub."

"Okay." I looked at my desk, seeing all the work that waiting on me and knowing there was no way I could focus on doing it tonight. Anything I did manage to work on would probably have to be redone anyway. I didn't care about anything in front of me. All I could think of was Jamey. I took a deep breath and started shutting things down. "I'll head that way as soon as I can get out of here."

"That might not be the best idea. Kendrick said Jamey was drinking, so by the time you get there, well, it probably won't be the best time to talk. Meet me at your condo instead. We'll figure out a plan and you can go see Jamey in the morning."

Bless Mia. She had to be wondering why the hell I hadn't told her what was going on with Aaron, why I hadn't confided in her and let her help me. That was what was expected when you'd been best friends with someone forever, right? But even though she had every right to be hurt and confused and all kinds of pissed at me, here she was talking me through my mess and helping me.

Even though Mia's plan made sense, the need to see Jamey, to talk to him and make him understand, was almost overwhelming. I wanted to ignore Mia's suggestion, to rush over to the pub and demand that Jamey talk to me. But I knew that Mia was right. Forcing a drunk, angry Jamey to talk to me sounded like a recipe for disaster. I reluctantly agreed to meet Mia at my condo and headed out of the office, not even stopping to tell anyone I was leaving. I didn't want to get into explanations or answer any questions. If anyone from work contacted me, I'd just tell them I'd gotten sick suddenly. I was certainly feeling nauseated at the thought of what Jamey had seen. I had to figure out how to get him to forgive me. Whatever plan Mia and I can up with, it had to work. I couldn't bear to even consider the alternative.

Chapter 29

Meg

The next morning, I held off showing up at Jamey's place as long as I could. It was still pretty early when I arrived, but I couldn't stand it anymore. I wasn't sure if Jamey would be ready to see me yet, or even awake for that matter, but I was prepared to shove my way into the apartment if I had to. I wasn't sure what I'd do if Jamey refused to even open the door. I just hoped it didn't come to that.

I'd talked with Kendrick the night before for an update on how Jamey was doing. He'd said that Jamey didn't seem angry. Instead he used the same word Dante had yesterday – he said that Jamey seemed devastated. I just couldn't understand why Jamey would so easily believe that I'd leave him for Aaron. I'd said as much to Kendrick and he'd gone silent on me. It had felt like he was weighing his words carefully, deciding what to say and how much to reveal. Finally, he simply said that Jamey didn't think he was enough.

Thinking about those words as I'd tried to sleep, my mind had gone back to the night that Jamey and I had talked about how much he wasn't like Aaron. I'd agreed that he wasn't and he'd asked if that was good. I'd laughed and told him it was, but I realized now that I'd pretty much just brushed right past it and gone on like everything was fine. I'd barely even acknowledged the things that Jamey had said to me. It was so obvious to me how amazing Jamey was that I'd missed how important the conversation was to him and how much he'd needed to hear that yes, it was perfect and wonderful that he wasn't like Aaron. I should have paid more attention and been more clear.

If Jamey would give me another chance, he'd never again have reason to doubt that he was the only man I would ever want. Now I just had to get him to listen to me.

I climbed the outside stairs to the apartment armed with two cups of coffee from our favorite place, The Coffee Spot. I wasn't sure that bribery in the form of the world's best coffee would help, but I didn't think it would hurt.

I reached the door and knocked quickly, not wanting to let my nerves get the best of me. I heard movement inside the apartment and suddenly all the butterflies that had been flapping around in my stomach swarmed up into my throat. Then Jamey opened the door and my breath froze in my lungs.

God, he's beautiful filled my mind as we stood looking at each other, neither of us saying a word. Jamey's hair was going all directions and stubble covered his jaw. He was wearing a sleeveless navy blue t-shirt that showcased his stunning arms and body, and his favorite gray sweatpants, his feet bare, as usual. He'd never looked better to me than he did in that moment. Just being able to see him settled something in me.

But then I looked in his eyes. His eyes, when they met mine, spoke volumes. I've read that the eyes are the windows to the soul. If that was true, Jamey was allowing me to see into the very center of his. His eyes were full of pain and doubt and uncertainty. But above all that was longing. Longing so deep and desperate and strong that I felt it reach into my own soul and wrap around my heart. If I hadn't already been in love with Jamey, I'd have fallen in that moment. He was hiding nothing from me, wasn't protecting himself at all. He was laying it all out there without a single word and leaving the rest up to me.

Realizing I was still standing in the doorway, I took a deep breath. Time to put back together what I'd so carelessly let be torn apart.

Holding Jamey's gaze, I jumped in.

"I know what you saw, Jamey. I know what you think, and why. But you're wrong."

I didn't know what I'd expected Jamey to say, but I'd definitely expected him to say *something*. Instead he stood looking at me wordlessly, one hand still on the door, one hand at his side, expression unchanged.

Okay, then. Taking another breath, I started again.

"Can I come in?"

Still without a word, he simply turned and walked away, leaving me to step inside the apartment. It was a small space with a two-seater table against one wall, a futon with an open sleeping bag thrown across it against the other, and a tiny kitchen. A short hallway led past the kitchen to two closed doors, which I assumed were the bathroom and the inside stairs down into the pub. The kitchen was where Jamey stood now, leaned back against the counter, arms crossed. I set one cup of coffee down on the table, then walked toward him, holding out the other in offering. Nodding at my unspoken question, he stepped forward and took it from my hand with a quiet "thanks", then settled back against the counter. Unsure what to do with myself, I crossed back over to the table and sat down. Jamey was avoiding my eyes now, sipping his coffee and looking anywhere but at me.

"I wasn't sure you'd be awake yet." Not a brilliant start, but Jamey's continued silence was making me nervous.

He ran his hand through his hair and down his face.

"I've been up for a while."

It wasn't much, but at least he'd spoken. And he'd let me in the apartment. That was good, right? At this point, I'd take whatever hopeful signs I could get.

"I'm glad I didn't wake you up. Jamey, what I said a minute ago is true. I know you saw me and Aaron together yesterday. I'm not with him, Jamey. I'm not leaving you."

Jamey set his coffee down on the counter, gripped the counter's edge, and finally met my eyes again.

"I know what I saw, Meg. You don't sit and hold hands with a guy you're saying no to."

For some reason, even though both Dante and Kendrick had said that Jamey didn't seem mad, I'd expected anger from him. I knew he'd never hurt me, but I'd expected raised voices and heated accusations at the very least. I hadn't expected to face a Jamey who sounded tired and defeated.

I had the urge to jump in and defend myself, but I was afraid that would just make Jamey shut down.

So instead, I asked "Can I start at the beginning? It's a bit of a story, but I think you need to hear it all to really understand."

Jamey hesitated a second, as if he wasn't sure he wanted to hear it, but then nodded, giving me the okay to spill it all.

I started with the wine and roses I'd received at the hotel, which Jamey already knew about, and told him the connection to Aaron. I walked through the other incidents that I was now convinced were all due to Aaron, whether he admitted it or not. Then I told him about the dozens of texts and calls, and finally the call to my boss that had made me realize Aaron wasn't going to stop until I confronted him. I told Jamey my plan to meet Aaron in a public place in a setting where I knew mutual colleagues would be present in order to take advantage of Aaron's dislike of scenes. And finally, I told him how Aaron came to be holding my hand and that I'd promised to report him to both the police and his employer for stalking if he ever again contacted me in any way.

The longer I talked, the more tense Jamey became. He was practically quivering by the time I finished, his knuckles white from gripping the counter so tightly. When his eyes met mine this time, I saw the anger I'd expected earlier, and I knew it was directed solely at Aaron.

"Are you in danger, Meg? Will he come after you?"

The anger I'd seen in Jamey's eyes was echoed in his words, his voice low and filled with tension.

"No." I responded quickly, hoping I was right about that and that I sounded more confident than I felt. I was definitely concerned about the possibility given the rage I'd seen on Aaron's face. But I knew with absolute certainty that if Jamey believed I was in physical danger, he and Dante, and heck, probably Dev and Kendrick, too, would find Aaron and send a clear message that he should stay far, far away from me. Aaron was just the type to try to have them arrested if they even threatened him, much less if they took it farther than that. That could be disastrous for any of them and I wasn't about to let it happen.

"No, I don't think so. If he does anything, he'll probably start a rumor about me or try to discredit me in some way to ruin my career. If that happens, I'll just have to handle it."

Jamey exhaled roughly and shook his head, shoving his hand through his hair again.

"Why didn't you tell me about all of this before?"

"I didn't connect the dots on a lot of it until I was talking to Aaron yesterday. I had no idea it was all connected to him. And the calls and texts" – this was the hard part, because I knew I really should have told Jamey about them – "I hoped if I ignored him, he would go away."

I shrugged and couldn't stop the sigh that left me. "It was dumb, I realize that now. Aaron is way too arrogant to put up with being ignored. And it was dumb not to tell you. I just didn't want to upset you and I really thought he'd stop."

Jamey shook his head again and stared silently at the floor.

"Are you mad at me? I know I should have told you."

"No, I'm not mad."

When Jamey didn't go on, I pushed for more. It was obvious we weren't in the clear yet.

"And you believe me? You know I didn't cheat on you and go back to Aaron?"

"I do, but..."

Uh oh. I did not like the sound of that.

"But what? You believe me, but...?"

Jamey leaned back against the counter again and crossed his arms. This time, I saw it for the defensive position that it was.

"I'm not sure it really changes anything. This thing between us...it would have ended eventually. You're way out of my league. We ignored that for a while, but that doesn't mean it isn't true. At some point you're going to want a guy more like you. I'll always care about you, but maybe it's better this way. Maybe it's for the best."

My heart clenched at Jamey's words and I wondered if he was trying to convince me or himself. Either way, I didn't believe for one second that he really meant what he was saying. I couldn't, because if he really believed it was better for us to be apart, my only two options were to live the rest of my life in misery without him or beat some sense into him, and I really didn't like the sound of either one. If he thought I was giving him up without a fight, he was in for a surprise.

"That's bullshit, Jamey, and you know it." Jamey's head snapped up and his eyes narrowed as he looked at me. "My life is far better with you than it could ever be without you, and you damn well know I make yours better, too. I know you think you'll never measure up because you don't have a bunch of letters behind your name and you don't have a fancy job with a fancy title. I know I brushed past those things when we talked about them before and I'm sorry for that. They're important to you and I acted like they weren't. I should have told you loud and clear that those things don't make me think less of you. They don't mean anything about the person you are. You're an amazing man in so many ways. I wish you could see yourself in my eyes. Then you'd see how very wrong you are."

I knew Jamey wasn't buying it even before he spoke.

"You may say that now, you may even believe that now, but what about in a few years when you're a Global VP of whatever, flying all around the world, and I'm still not fitting in at your events, still holding you back."

Okay, apparently not asking him to attend those events with me had left a mark, one that I'd have to fix later. For now, I was sticking to making Jamey understand how incredible he was to me.

"Remember when you told me that I sell myself too short? Do you remember that conversation?" Seeing Jamey's cautious nod, I forged on. "Well, we're a pair, because you do the exact same thing. You have unbelievable talent, whether you admit it or not. And the fact that so much of it is self-taught is even more impressive, even if you do just brush it off as 'playing around'. But even if you cooked like me, God forbid, you'd still be amazing, Jamey. You're funny and generous and caring. And you're one of the smartest people I know. I don't care what school you did or didn't graduate from. You know so much and you're a great teacher. You've had to be to get me to the point of cooking things that actually resemble edible food. You're patient and encouraging and make people believe they can do it. The kitchen staff loves you, Jamey, and the rest of the pub staff, too. There's a reason for that. You build people up...."

Jamey stood, still looking at the floor, shaking his head.

"And you completely suck at accepting compliments of your own."

Jamey made a noise that just might have been a laugh.

"Don't worry, though. We'll work on that."

It was time to cut to the chase and say what I had really come to say. "Jamey, please look at me."

Jamey cleared his throat and hesitated a second, then took a breath like he was gathering his courage. I knew the feeling. I was about the take the biggest risk of my life and there was no net to catch me if I fell.

Jamey finally raised his eyes to mine and I saw nervousness that echoed mine. He was still, waiting, not sure what I was going to do next, but trusting me enough to show me what he was feeling. It gave me the courage to jump.

"You told me to decide for myself what I want. To focus on what makes me happy, what makes me whole. Remember?"

Jamey dipped his chin slightly, which I took as a 'yes'.

"Well, I'm doing that starting right now." My hands were shaking and my heart was about to jump out of my chest. "I want you, Jamey. Only you." I saw Jamey's eyes widen with shock, but I pushed on. I had to get the rest out.

"*You* make me happy. *You* make me whole. You're everything I want, Jamey. I love you."

Jamey held himself completely still, his eyes burning into mine. I wasn't even sure if he was breathing.

"Say that again." His words were quiet, almost a whisper, his voice tight and rough.

"I love you, Jamey."

At my words, Jamey exploded into motion. He was on me before I could blink, scooping me up off my chair and wrapping his arms around me so tightly I could barely breathe. He didn't say a word, just crushed me to him and held me, his head bent next to mine, his breath harsh in my ear. I held on, giving him time, letting the moment wash over me.

Finally, he loosened his hold on me just a fraction and kissed me on the side of my head.

"Say it one more time," he said softly, his breath tickling my ear.

"I love you."

Jamey took a deep breath and let it out, then loosened his hold a bit more. His lips brushed across mine several times, then he settled in for a long, slow, deep kiss. Finally pulling back, he rested his forehead against mine.

"I'm going to need to hear that from you a lot. Like every hour on the hour for a while. Or maybe every half hour."

I ran my hands up and down his sides and nodded as much as I could with his forehead still resting on mine.

"I can do that. But it sure would be nice to hear it back first."

Jamey smiled for the first time since I'd walked into the apartment.

"I've thought it so many times, I can't believe I haven't said it out loud before now. I love you, Meg. More than I have words to tell you. I think I fell for you the first time I ever met you."

I pulled back a little now so I could really look at Jamey.

"What, you mean when I was criticizing your food before I'd ever tried it?"

Jamey shook his head as he reached up to push a few strands of my hair behind my ear. He left his hand where it was, cupping the side of my neck, as he answered.

"Uh-uh. Later when you came over to *apologize* for criticizing my food before you'd ever tried it."

Jamey looked off over my shoulder like he was remembering the night we first met.

"When I heard you call my name and turned around to see you walking toward me, I had no idea what you wanted. I didn't know if you were coming over to complain some more or what."

I pinched Jamey on his side for that comment, and he smiled as he squirmed away from my hand. Then he settled back in my hold and looked down at me.

"All I did know was that I would stand there all night and wait for you. Whatever you wanted, whatever you had to say, the chance to be close to you and have your attention was too good to pass up."

I sighed and leaned up to give Jamey a soft kiss.

"I should have dumped Aaron on the spot."

"Yeah, but you're stubborn like that."

I wanted to argue, and I knew Jamey was half-teasing, but the truth was I *was* stubborn. If someone had told me the night I'd first met Jamey that I'd end up falling in love with him a few short weeks later, I'd have told them that they'd lost their mind. He hadn't been part of my plan, hadn't fit in the blueprint I'd created for my life, yet somehow he'd become the best part of it. Every single day was better with Jamey in it.

"You're right, I admit it. You know me so well."

I rested my head on Jamey's chest as his arms came around me.

"I do know you. And I love everything about you." Jamey shifted a little, resting his head on mine.

"I thought you were gone, Meg." Jamey's voice was quiet and rough, full of the pain he'd lived over the past few hours. "I thought I'd lost you and I didn't…" Jamey swallowed hard and drew back a little, raising his hands to cup my face. The desolation in his eyes made me catch my breath.

"I didn't know how I'd keep breathing without you."

I tucked my head under Jamey's chin and wrapped my arms around him, holding him as tight as I could. He folded me into his body, curling around me and pulling me into him.

"I'm so sorry, Jamey. So sorry I hurt you that way. I was so scared that you wouldn't listen to me, wouldn't believe me. I swear I'll never hurt you again."

"Shh, I know." Still holding me tight, Jamey ran his hand over my hair and pressed a kiss to the top of my head. "It's not your fault. I should have waited and talked to you. I just wasn't thinking straight. But we're okay. It's all okay now."

I tipped my head back and sighed as Jamey brushed his lips over mine. As Jamey pulled me into his body and deepened the kiss, I let myself begin to believe. I hadn't damaged us beyond repair. We truly were okay.

Chapter 30

Jamey

The second Meg opened for me it was like setting fire to kindling. The flame between Meg and I caught and flashed into an inferno in seconds. I turned and boosted her up on the kitchen counter and felt her wrap her legs around my waist. I leaned into her, loving the feel of her breasts pressed against my chest, rocking my hardening cock against the softness and heat between her legs.

Meg pulled at my shirt and I eased back for a second to allow her to pull it over my head. I fused my mouth to hers again and felt my cock swell even more as she scraped her fingernails lightly across my shoulders.

Releasing Meg's mouth, I ran my teeth down her neck, biting down lightly on the spot where her neck met her shoulder. Meg's breath hitched and she pressed hard against me.

"I need you inside me, Jamey. Right now." Though her words were demanding, Meg's tone bordered on desperate, as if she somehow thought I might deny her. There was no way that was happening.

Pushing away from the counter, I took Meg's mouth again as I carried her to the futon. I lowered Meg until she could stand, then pulled her shirt off over her head, revealing her pale yellow lace bra. As pretty as it was, I wanted it off. As I reached around her back to remove it, Meg's hands were busy pushing at my sweatpants and briefs. I dropped Meg's bra to the floor, feasting my eyes on her beautiful breasts as I pushed the jeans she was wearing off her hips and down her legs, taking her panties with them so that she stood in front of me naked.

Meg got my sweats and briefs over my hips, but then paused as I cupped her breasts in my hands and rolled her nipples between my fingertips. Her eyes closed and her hands clutched at my hips.

"Jamey, that's not fair. I can't think when you do that."

I loved how responsive Meg was, how she always showed me what she was feeling, what I was doing to her. My cock strained against the fabric still confining it, trying desperately to get closer to Meg's heat.

I brought my mouth to Meg's neck again, sucking lightly against her skin and loving the feel of her pulse racing against my lips.

"I don't want you to think. I want you to feel."

Meg whimpered as I ran the tip of my tongue back and forth across one of her nipples before sucking it into my mouth. She slid her hands into my hair, holding my head against her as she strained to get closer.

Unable to wait another second, I pulled away from Meg. I pushed my sweats and briefs off and my cock sprung back against my stomach, hard and ready to slip inside Meg's heat. I was reaching for Meg again when I stopped with a groan, realizing I didn't have any condoms with me. Grabbing some hadn't exactly been top-of-mind when I'd left my apartment in a daze the day before. Meg watched me, a puzzled look on her face as I reached for the drawer of the side table next to the futon, hoping with everything in me that I'd find a condom still tucked away in one of my old spots from when this had been my place.

"Fuck, yes." I said a silent thanks to the universe when I saw several condoms laying in the drawer.

I grabbed one and handed it to Meg, then sat on the futon and leaned back.

"All yours, sweetheart. Take what you want."

The heat in Meg's eyes flared even hotter as she took the condom from my hand. She moved closer, resting one knee then the other on the futon as she straddled me. Holding my eyes with hers, she tore open the condom. She moved her gaze to my swollen cock, licking her lips and sending me so close to the edge I had to close my eyes for a second to regain control. Eyes still closed, I jerked as I felt Meg's hands on me, then gritted my teeth and again fought for control as she slowly rolled the condom down my length. I knew it had only been two days since I'd been inside Meg, but at that moment it felt like forever. Feeling her soft little hands on me had me close to desperate. I'd told her to take what she wanted. I hoped like hell that she wanted all of me hard and fast.

Fitting the head of my cock against her entrance, Meg lowered herself a little at a time until I filled her completely. Bracing her hands on my shoulders, she began to rock against me. I filled my hands with her beautiful ass but let her control the pace. She quickly found her rhythm, swiveling her hips against me in a way that seemed designed to drive me crazy.

As Meg began to rock harder, the futon frame suddenly shrieked in protest, startling both of us. Meg and I stayed motionless for a second, looking at each other with wide eyes, then Meg cautiously began to rock again. The futon frame remained silent at first, but as Meg picked up her pace again the futon frame began to shriek with every thrust. Meg and I froze again, afraid of what might happen if we moved. Picturing what we must look like - both of us completely naked, frozen in place with me still inside Meg as she straddled me, looks of guilty horror on our faces – I started to laugh. The absurdity of the situation hit me and I couldn't help it. Meg looked at me for a second, then her smile grew and soon she was laughing, too. We held on to each other, laughter rolling through us. We'd start to calm down, then one of us would get started again and set the other one off, too. After a few moments, we finally wound down. Meg leaned back a little, pushing her hair back, a smile still on her face.

"I don't think I've every laughed like that in the middle of sex before."

I had to agree.

"That's a new one for me, too. As much as I liked it, my goal here was to make you scream, not the futon."

As Meg laughed again, I lifted her off me and stood. "I think we're going to need to move this party to the floor."

I dragged the futon mattress and the sleeping bag I'd spread out over it off the frame onto the floor. Laying down on my back, I reached my hand out for Meg and drew her closer until she once again straddled me.

"Now, where were we?"

Meg lowered herself on my still rock-hard cock until she rested fully against me again. I groaned at how incredibly good she felt, swept right back up into the heat between us.

"Yeah, sweetheart. Right there."

Meg began to move again, picking up her rhythm from before. The sight of her above me had me on the edge in no time. I reached up and palmed Meg's breasts, rolling her nipples between my fingertips as I had earlier. Meg's head fell back on her shoulders and her pace picked up even more as I gripped her hips to help her.

"Jamey, oh please." Meg's voice was strained and pleading. I lifted my head as Meg leaned forward over me, capturing her nipple in my mouth and sucking hard. I heard Meg gasp, then seconds later her core began to pulse around me. I felt my cock swell even more and my balls drew up as Meg's core tightened around me again and again, and every muscle in my body clenched as I fought not to come yet. As soon as I felt Meg begin to come down, I grabbed her around the waist and flipped us so that Meg was on her back with me stretched over her. She gripped my biceps as I slammed into her. She felt so insanely good that I knew I wouldn't last much longer. The pressure built inside me until suddenly I was coming, my muscles shaking as I filled the condom. A few seconds later I all but collapsed on top of Meg, knowing I was probably crushing her. We lay there for a few moments, both of us getting our breath back. Finally, knowing I needed to take care of the condom, I pushed myself off her, giving Meg a kiss as I rose.

When I came back in the room, I thought for a second about asking Meg if she wanted me to move the futon mattress back on the frame. But the sight of her curled up like a kitten, naked and beautiful, and the thought of a possible round 2 sometime very soon made me decide to stay where we were. I lay down behind her and pulled her into me little spoon style. She settled against me, running her hand across my forearm and tangling her fingers with mine as my hand rested on her stomach.

"That futon has to be the worst piece of furniture in the history of the world."

Meg's assessment made me laugh.

"At least it didn't collapse. Just imagine the entire kitchen staff hearing the racket and running up here to see what the hell was going on."

"Okay, fine. It gets half a star for not collapsing," Meg conceded.

Meg was completely relaxed in my arms and her voice was soft and low, as if she were seconds from drifting off to sleep. There was so much I wanted to say to her, so many plans I wanted to make. But I was sure she'd gotten as little sleep as I had the night before and I knew that we had all the time in the world to make whatever plans we wanted. So I said the only thing that really mattered in that moment, the one thing I wanted to say to Meg every day for the rest of our lives. Kissing her gently on her shoulder, I whispered, "I love you, Meg," and heard her soft "I love you, Jamey" in reply.

⌒

I woke a few hours later, bright sun shining directly in my eyes through the cracks in the blinds. It took a second to get my bearings, then the events of the past 24 hours came rushing back. It had been a roller coaster for both Meg and me, all caused by my doubts about myself and whether I was good enough for Meg. I'd put her through hell – put *both* of us through hell – all because I hadn't believed that Meg could possibly want me for the long term. She'd told me and she'd showed me that she did, and I'd still continued to doubt both her and myself.

Laying there, holding Meg in my arms, I knew it was time to let those doubts go. If I didn't, they would slowly chip away at us until we collapsed the way we'd thought the futon was going to hours before. No one was judging me but me. In reality, no one I cared about ever had except my father and he was long gone from my life. I'd almost let the best thing in my life slip away because I wouldn't let myself believe. Fortunately, I had a kickass woman, and she hadn't let me get away with it. She'd believed enough for both of us, known we were meant to be together. It was way past time I believed it, too.

Chapter 31

Meg

A month later

I stood next to Jamey in the middle of the huge hotel ballroom, surrounded by lots of people I knew and many more people that I didn't. We were at the Chamber of Commerce's annual gala, an event that always drew several hundred businesspeople from across our region. It was a dressy affair and the first time I'd seen Jamey in anything other than casual clothes or nothing at all. His navy blue suit, pale blue shirt and dark tie made his eyes a vibrant blue. His blond hair was tamed, but still just the tiniest bit messy and his jaw was covered with its usual dark blond scruff. He looked confident, at ease, and oh so hot. He'd drawn a lot appreciative looks from the females at the event. I couldn't blame them. When he'd walked out of the bedroom earlier looking like he'd just stepped off a magazine cover, the temptation to skip the gala had been strong.

Seeing how confident Jamey was in this setting I wished I could go back in time a few months and ask him to go with me to all those work events and dinners I'd attended solo, thinking he wouldn't have time or he'd hate them or be uncomfortable. Jamey took full responsibility for our near breakup the month before, blaming his own self-doubt for the way he'd reacted to seeing me with Aaron. But I knew I shared some of the responsibility. I'd sown the seeds of at least some of

Jamey's doubt by keeping him separate from my work, not wanting to bother him or add to his already crazy schedule. Even if he hadn't ended up attending the events with me, if I'd invited him at least he would have known that I wanted him there, that I wasn't hesitant about being with him or trying to hide him from my colleagues. As it was I'd left the door open for him to wonder, and it had almost cost us everything. I wondered, too, if Aaron had been more persistent about his pursuit of me because Jamey and I hadn't been very public about our relationship. Although one or two colleagues may have seen Jamey and me together at the pub, I'd never spoken to anyone at work about him. If Aaron had asked around, likely everyone would have told him that I was on my own. Granted, he'd known about me and Jamey, but still I wondered. I hadn't heard anything from Aaron since our confrontation at the café. Jamey and I both thought it was possible Aaron was laying low for a while, watching for an opportunity to harm me in some way. What I hoped, though, was that he'd taken me seriously and known that I wasn't bluffing when I said I'd report him. I'd still do it if it came to that, but hopefully he'd stay far, far away.

At the moment, Jamey and I were talking with someone Jamey knew from the local food and beverage community. Jamey had actually seen several people he knew since we'd arrived, but Vaughn was the only one we'd stopped to talk to so far. Vaughn and his business partners owned a brewery that was about 30 minutes away from the pub. We talked about general things for a few minutes and Jamey and I promised to stop by the brewery soon to try it out. When Jamey and Vaughn started comparing notes on the business trends they were seeing, I excused myself to go to the ladies' room.

As I exited the ladies' room, I saw Marty Mason, the founder and owner of a local management consulting company, standing nearby. While her company was technically a competitor of my employer, they tended to focus on mid-size local or regional companies, while we worked almost exclusively with large companies located across the country and, increasingly, around the world. Though I knew Marty's company had a great reputation and was growing, there had never been much, if any, true competition between the companies. I knew Marty well and liked her, so I didn't hesitate to head her way when she waved me over.

I walked away from Marty a few minutes later, my head buzzing with our conversation. Jamey saw me coming from across the room and I saw him shake Vaughn's hand before starting toward me. Just as Jamey and I reached each other, the band started playing the first slow song of the evening and couples began moving toward the dance floor. Jamey glanced toward the dance floor, then back at me, offering his hand.

"Dance with me?"

I put my hand in Jamey's and let him lead me to the dance floor, slipping into his arms when we reached it. I knew my surprise showed on my face as Jamey began to move us slowly and smoothly around the floor.

"What, you didn't think I knew how to dance?" How I loved the sexy little smile he always got when he was teasing me.

"I don't think *most* men know how to dance, at least not any under the age of about 70. Where did you learn?"

"Gym class, 8ᵗʰ grade. We learned to square dance and waltz and a couple other things. Most of the boys hated it. The girls, though – they seemed to love it and a little bell went off in my head. I was already getting interested in girls at that point so if they liked, yeah, I was paying attention. I picked up a few things and have just never forgotten them."

Before I could respond, Jamey rotated us slightly to avoid another couple and said, "Enough about my dance skills. What had you looking so thoughtful a minute ago?"

During my conversation with Marty, she had shocked me with an offer to join her company. She'd said the company was growing, which I knew, and that she wanted me for a new regional senior director position that would play a pivotal role in the company's future. I knew Marty well enough to know that we'd work well together. She had started her company on her own and had built it from the ground up. She had ambitious plans and she was giving me a chance to join her and work alongside her to get there; to not just take direction on what should be done, but to set that direction. She told me she was 100% confident that I was the one she wanted for the job. I was simultaneously thrilled and terrified by the offer.

I told Jamey all of this as he held me close, his head bent slightly to rest against mine, listening intently. He'd moved us away from the other couples on the dance floor, essentially swaying us in place in our own little corner. When I finished speaking, Jamey brushed his lips across my cheek and drew back slightly.

"It sounds like you have a decision to make."

"I guess I do."

As soon as I said it, as soon as I opened my mind even the tiniest bit to the possibility of joining Marty's company, I knew my answer.

Excitement flooded through me. I knew it may mean a cut in my salary and bonuses and my MBA program would need to go on the back burner, too. But it would also mean little to no travel since all the clients were local or in the surrounding area. The chance to have a hand in creating the future of a company while also spending much less time away from Jamey was too good to pass up. I promised myself I'd map it all out later, write down the pros and cons and whys and why nots, and do everything a planner like me needed to do, but already, in my heart, I knew.

Looking in my eyes, Jamey nodded as if he knew, too.

We moved off the dance floor as the band started into an up tempo song, and spent the next hour talking with people Jamey or I knew and being introduced to a few others. I introduced Jamey to my boss, David, and his wife, Lisa, who I'd met at previous events, and they spent a few minutes talking about their shared love of bourbon.

Finally, we called it a night and headed to the parking garage for the car. As we stepped out of the elevator into the garage, Jamey surprised me by scooping me up in his arms.

Jamey answered my question without me even asking it.

"You wear some hot-as-hell heels, but the car is all the way at the other end of this floor and those shoes are not made for walking."

This guy. How did I get so lucky?

When I voiced that question to Jamey, he shrugged like it was no big deal.

"I told you if you were mine, taking care of you would be my top priority. Those weren't just words to me, sweetheart. I meant every one, even if I never dreamt at that moment that I'd ever have an opportunity to make them true."

I ran my fingers over the lapel of Jamey's jacket.

"You know, as good as you look in this suit, I think my favorite is when you're in the kitchen, wearing just your sweatpants or jeans, making breakfast with your hair going all directions."

Jamey grinned in response to my comment.

"Yeah? Trying to keep me barefoot and shirtless in the kitchen?"

It was my turn to shrug and smile at Jamey as he lowered me to my feet next to the car, then leaned into me.

"That's where you're happiest, so yeah, why not?"

Jamey shook his head.

"Uh uh. With you, sweetheart. That's where I'm happiest."

As if he hadn't already melted my heart with his words, Jamey wound his fingers in my hair and tipped my face up to his, kissing me softly.

"And someday I hope you'll make me even happier and agree to be mine forever."

Opening my eyes wide, the picture of innocence, I teased Jamey.

"Why Mr. MacGregor, is that a proposal?"

"No, it's not, Ms. Kennedy. Not just yet." Jamey smiled and tugged lightly on one of my curls. "I'll surprise you one of these days. And I promise you'll have no doubt what I'm asking you when I do."

"Just don't wait too long, Mr. MacGregor. Or I might just surprise *you* one of these days and be the one to do the asking."

"Well, you know I can never say no to you, so…" Jamey replied, his eyes shining with love and happiness.

I nodded solemnly. "I do know. It's all part of my plan," I responded, fighting to keep a smile off my face.

Jamey laughed and pulled me close, folding me into his arms.

"Gotta love a woman with a plan."

The End

Don't miss Dev and Holly's story in
Count on Me *(Brothers Pub Book 3)!*

Author bio

Kristyn DeMaster is a contemporary romance author. She writes everyday heroes and heroines who are finding their way to once-in-a-lifetime love through all of life's up and downs. She's a true believer in happily-ever-after and is living hers with her very own romance hero and their fur babies in the American Midwest.

www.ingramcontent.com/pod-product-compliance
Lightning Source LLC
Chambersburg PA
CBHW070027120726
47909CB00003B/1087